NOT A HUSBAND IN SIGHT

NANCY SMITH GIBSON

Enjoy!

Nancy Smith Gibson

SOUL MATE PUBLISHING

New York

NOT A HUSBAND IN SIGHT

NANCY SMITH GIBSON

Cover Design by Melody A. Pond

Published in the United States of America by
Soul Mate Publishing
P.O. Box 24
Macedon, New York, 14502

ISBN: 978-1-68291-657-5

ebook ISBN: 978-1-68291-646-9

www.SoulMatePublishing.com

Acknowledgments

My thanks go to Diane K Bodemann, MD, not only for keeping me healthy, but also for being available for consultations on the medical conditions of the characters in my novels. Thank you, Doctor Diane!

Chapter 1

Uma paused in the doorway and scanned the desktop, the walls, and the bookshelves, checking for anything she had brought to the job and didn't want to leave behind. Everything she had carried in she was carrying out in the same worn tote with the University of Texas logo printed on the side—everything except the framed oil painting of a field of wildflowers that went with her to each new job. The picture was wrapped securely in newspaper to prevent any damage and held tightly under her left arm.

Most of the contents of the tote could be easily replaced. Hand lotion, tissues, the can of air freshener, the jar of peppermints and the sack of chocolate drops, a tube of lip gloss—in case of chapped lips—and emery boards. Uma didn't have the time or the money to worry about her appearance beyond what was necessary, hence the mini-brush to tame her honey-blond hair that was fashioned into a bun suitable for her position as an editorial assistant. *Only the essentials, thank you very much*. The candy and the lotion were reminders of what she had done without but could now afford.

Not so effortlessly substituted—and necessary if Uma was to do her job to her own satisfaction—were two books. One was a reference book about the use of footnotes, citations, bibliographies, and other such minutia as would be required based on the institution, subject, or country of publication. The other book was a practical volume laying out ways to organize information and—possibly even more importantly—sharing methods of establishing a filing system which would make the sources of information readily accessible to the researcher upon a moment's notice, no matter the age or obscurity of the source. This volume, like the other, was well-worn and filled with highlighted passages, underlined sentences, and slips of paper marking important spots. Both books went with her to each job, carried in the canvas bag, despite the fact she thought she probably had them memorized at that point in her career.

Although Uma didn't think of it that way, her reputation had been built on those two books, along with her skill in organizing and rearranging the written thoughts of her employers, and in her expertise of making them think they were the mastermind behind the theme and flow of the words attributed to them in the published volume. The words were theirs, but Uma was the one who arranged them on the page. It was she who helped them present their best to the world of readers and scholars.

Uma had gained valuable practice and know-how as a child with the necessity of presenting evidences to the people around her that they ought to take her advice in order to gain their desired outcome. She would never call it manipulating, although others might. To Uma, it had been a way to survive the dysfunction in her home life. After she escaped to college by way of work and scholarships, she seldom glanced back.

She took one final look around the office, switched off the light, and exited the room.

"Uma." The tall gray-headed professor who had been walking down the hall stopped her by putting his hands on her shoulders before she stepped into his path. "I thought you were already gone."

Uma steadied herself before speaking. "Dr. Carter. I'm out of here. I just came by to get my personal items."

"I heard you did a wonderful job on Abernathy's manuscript—and working with him."

She smiled. Compliments made her happy. They were signs her life was in order. "I don't know about a wonderful job, but we got the book finished and off to the publisher," Uma said as they walked together.

"He's been trying to get his work published for years. He ran through so many assistants that the word was out about how difficult he is, and nobody would work with him. Until you, that is. How did you do it?"

"Dr. Abernathy is an old teddy bear. Don't let anyone tell you differently. He's just disorganized, that's all, and he was concerned about his notes getting misplaced or lost." She boosted the picture higher under her arm. "And he was worried that his words would be misinterpreted. It was difficult to get his exact meaning down on paper." That was putting it mildly, but she refused to talk about her recent boss's shortcomings. The assignment was finished and over with. She was beyond thankful. She had been paid for the job and was eager to move on to what she hoped were bigger and better projects.

"Disorganized but he wouldn't let anybody touch his notes to help. If anyone lost anything, it was Abernathy himself. He couldn't find what he wrote an hour before," Carter said.

When they reached the stairs, Carter moved to toward them. He paused a moment to say, "Good luck to you, Uma. I'm sure you'll find a new job quickly, as experienced as you are." He bounded up the steps to the next floor.

Uma punched the elevator button and waited for its arrival. She wanted to be as optimistic as the professor was, but as usual, doubt nibbled at the edge of her thoughts. She had some savings. She always put money away for the next time her job ended—and they always did—but her

Volkswagen Beetle would need some repairs before long, and she had no idea how long it would be before she was employed again . . . or where. She once again weighed her choices as she punched the button for the first floor.

When the elevator doors opened on the ground floor, a slim woman in a black suit was waiting for it. "Uma!" She smiled as she held the door open with the hand that was not holding a notebook and pen. "I was just thinking about you!"

"Hello, Professor Granby," Uma said as she slid past.

"Everyone is talking about what a good job you did with Abernathy."

"Yes . . . well," Uma said, not wanting to get into another conversation about how hard Abernathy was to work with and how many assistants he had fired or had quit before she had arrived.

"I wish the university had the funds to hire you full time," the older woman said. "But we don't. That was a special grant that paid your salary this time."

"I know. I wish I could stay, too," Uma said. *That may not be entirely true.* She enjoyed moving to new jobs in new cities to organize and facilitate the publishing of books or project papers in various subjects that had once been unknown to her. Although the time period in between finishing one job and being hired for the next was always nerve-wracking, the thrill of a new city and a new subject always excited her.

"I tell you what," Professor Granby said. "I'm having a cocktail party at my place this evening at six. You come and mingle. That's where I always hear about the upcoming studies that haven't even been announced to the public yet. Networking is how you get a new job in academia, and I imagine that is true for you as well." Holding the elevator door open with her shoulder, she opened her notebook, wrote a bit, and tore it off. "Here's my address," she said as she handed it to Uma. "Do try to be there. Maybe you'll hear about something interesting."

As she stepped into the elevator and released the door, she called out, "I'll introduce you to everyone there and give you a good recommendation."

Chapter 2

Uma took a deep breath before ringing the doorbell. She stared at her index finger. *Why did I choose bright pink? Is it too gaudy? Too flashy? What will they think?* She had been to numerous faculty gatherings, even though she could not by any stretch of the imagination be considered a member of that august group. Each venue of education, sometimes each department on the campus, had its own dress code. Usually, this had little meaning to Uma, who had never had the time nor money to spend on her appearance. Her willowy frame could wear anything well, even when she didn't give any thought to it. Her clear skin didn't need the addition of powder or blush, and her eyes shown brighter than if they were accented with shadow or eyeliner.

Clothing, however, was a bit different. Through her attire, she demonstrated her suitability for a job. She needed to present herself as a serious professional, ready to take on a new project in the academic world. She couldn't be too frilly and definitely not provocative in any way, even if it was a cocktail party. Moving to a new city at least once a year had whittled her wardrobe considerably. The black dress she wore, topped with a black-on-black embroidered jacket, would probably fit the situation no matter if the attendees were dressed formally or casually. It had the advantage of being dual-purpose: top the dress with a blazer and it became work garb. She had applied the loud color on her fingertips in an attempt to boost her optimism and increase her positivity with the idea the soiree would lead to an opportunity. She looked down at her nails. *Too late! That's what it is. Too late to quibble over nail polish.* She rang the bell.

"You came!" Anita Granby said when she opened the door. "I'm so glad you did. Come let me introduce you to everyone."

As they went around the room, Uma found she knew most everyone there. In the year she had been Dr. Abernathy's editorial assistant, she had met most of his colleagues on campus. As Professor Granby guided her from group to group, several people leaned toward her and expressed in a quiet voice that it ought to be Uma getting the credit rather than Abernathy.

"I don't know how you did it," one person said. "Abernathy's a smart man, but nobody could work with him."

"It was my pleasure," Uma said, time and again, biting her tongue to keep from expressing her joy at being finished, at last, with a project that had seemed to go on forever. In the corner, the man himself was going on about the flora and fauna of the Pacific Northwest and its importance to America in the past and future. He took no notice of his editorial assistant's arrival and gave her no credit as he blathered on about the upcoming publication of his work.

"Here, let's get you a drink," Anita Granby said as they reached the bar set up in the far corner.

"A Virgin Bloody Mary," Uma requested of the bartender.

"You mean you worked a whole year with that man now expounding on his brilliance and aren't drinking hard liquor yet?" asked a tall, handsome stranger with a glass in his hand.

"Oh, Alex." Professor Granby laughed as she placed her hand on his arm. "He's not as bad as all that."

Oh yes he is! Uma could have said, but she didn't.

"You couldn't prove that by me." His eyes stayed on Uma as he stirred his drink with a mini-straw. "To hear him tell it, he discovered the secrets of . . . well, I don't know what he discovered. His sentences don't really make for much comprehension of what he is explaining. I can only hope his writing is better."

Uma didn't comment, but Anita said, "It does after Uma got through with it. She got it all straightened out to where anyone can understand what he thinks is so important. I've read some of it. She succeeded where others have failed."

"That's what I understand. Everyone here is singing your praises." He extended his hand. "Alex Keillor," he said.

"Uma Thornton," she said as his large hand swallowed hers.

"Alex is from Chicago," Anita said. "He's only here for a few days. He's on his way to Alaska."

"Alaska!" Uma's imagination fluttered.

"Yes, Alaska. I'm working on a publishing project." His eyes sparkled as he said it. "Isn't everyone?"

Uma laughed. "Sometimes it seems like it, especially in university circles. What is it about?"

"Now that Alaska has become the forty-ninth state, my publisher says the public is calling for reading material. I'm aiming for a book that tells about Alaskan folklore and how it compares to our American tales."

"That sounds interesting, like something anyone would enjoy reading, not just academics," Uma answered.

"I hope so. That would mean better sales."

"If you'll excuse me, I have to go greet the new arrivals," Anita Granby said and walked toward the couple coming through the front door.

Keillor faced Uma and took a step closer to her. "Tell me your secret. How did you handle Professor Abernathy when so many others had failed?"

"It's *Doctor* Abernathy, thank you very much, and the answer is organization. It's my specialty."

Keillor raised his eyebrows, gazing intently into her face. "And how did you become so good at organization?"

"When I was in college, I couldn't settle on a specific area to major in, but I found that I could rearrange, make card files, categorize by various subgroups, and so forth, and make an organized overview of most anything, and I learned about the subject along the way. So, you could say I majored in organizational methods. Too bad there isn't a specific degree for that." What Uma didn't say was that even before graduating from high school being organized was the only way she had been able to fight her way out of a tumultuous, undisciplined household and into college without being buried in the detritus of a non-functioning family.

"But it has paid off for you. Right?"

"You could say that. Right out of college—"

"And which college was that?" Keillor asked.

"The University of Texas. Right after graduation, one of the professors hired me to help organize a project he was working on."

"Your name was already known around the campus for what you do." Keillor understood, even if Uma hadn't said so.

"Yes. One of my instructors had recommended me to him. After that job, he passed my name along to someone at the University of New Mexico, and I moved to Albuquerque for a year."

"You aren't that old, so you must have come to Seattle from Albuquerque," he said, smiling.

"I'm not that young. I'm twenty-five," Uma answered.

"Wow! That old, huh?"

"Yes, that old," she said and moved to set her glass on a nearby table.

"I didn't mean to offend you," Keillor said, placing his hand on her arm. "All this interests me more than you know. Would you allow me to take you to dinner? I would like to discuss my Alaskan job with you. I think perhaps fate brought us together this evening."

Chapter 3

A week later Uma boarded a plane bound for Fairbanks, Alaska.

The conversation the night she and Alex met had lasted until the restaurant closed. He wanted advice as to what method to use to preserve the folk stories that had been handed down among the various Alaskan native groups through the generations. Uma's question about whether the tales not only had any similarity to American Indian legends, but if Russian myths had any influence set the professor's mind twirling in a new direction.

"Whatever you do," Uma said, "you need to keep good records of every legend you hear. Even when they are similar, the slight differences may be telling."

"I carry a tape recorder everywhere I go. I'm diligent at getting everything on tape. Then, when I have it translated, if it wasn't in English originally, I have the translation on tape as well."

"That's good, but I also would advise transcribing the tapes to print as soon as possible," Uma advised. "If they are in English, that ought to be within days, if not hours. Of course, if you have to have them translated, it might be longer."

"Why is that? I had planned to take it all back home and have it typed then."

"Because if you have a question, if something doesn't fit, or if there are contradictions, you'll be back in Chicago and the person who told you the story will be thousands of miles away in Alaska. Even if you return a year later, you may never find the person who related the legend."

"I had never thought of it that way," the professor said. "That's good advice. It will change the way I do things."

When the evening ended, Keillor had a long list of supplies Uma had suggested he take with him. He walked her to her car, standing at her side as she unlocked it. Taking her hand in his, he said, "I can't thank you enough for your help. I have a feeling I would have kicked myself leaving for Alaska unprepared to do the job properly." He lifted her hand to his lips and kissed it.

"If you have any more questions, just call me. I'm glad to help."

"I have your number right here," he said, patting his jacket pocket.

The next day when her phone rang Uma thought it might be Alex. Not many people called her, especially since Dr. Abernathy's project was already at the publisher.

"I've thought of the answer to all my problems," Keillor said. "You come to Alaska and work for me. You'll keep me straight. Not let me goof up."

"Alaska? You want me to come to Alaska?"

"That's right. I'll pay your salary and furnish everything you need, both for the job and your living arrangements. I'd rather pay you from the onset and have everything correct from the beginning than to pay someone to type my notes and recordings back in Chicago only to find that I had omitted something important. How about it?" He named a salary that was below what she had been making in Seattle, but with no rent, utilities, phone bill, or food to consider, it would come out to her advantage. Practically everything she made could go into the bank.

"Where is this located? Where in Alaska, I mean?" she asked.

"A little village a short plane ride northwest of Fairbanks. Why? Does that enter into your decision?"

"Yes, in fact, it does."

"Why?"

"Because I was raised in Freeport, Texas. That's an oil hub on the Gulf of Mexico. All my memories are of a dirty, smelly, poverty-stricken oil town. Only the oil companies made money. The citizens didn't, or if they did, they spent their paychecks on booze. The stench of oil permeated everything—houses, clothes—everything.

"I wouldn't accept the job if it were in or near Valdez or any of the oil ports. The atmosphere would bring back memories I'd just as soon leave far behind."

"I could argue with you about the financial conditions in and around Valdez or any other oil hub, but if that is your mindset, I won't bother. We won't be anywhere near such a location. This is strictly small-town, back country but near to essentials."

They met for lunch, and Uma demanded more details. "My friend, Fred, is loaning me his cabin from now through the summer," Alex explained. "He's a professor at the University of Alaska at Fairbanks. He keeps an apartment close to the school and has this cabin he uses on weekends and holidays. He is on sabbatical and studying in Europe for the duration. He has shown me photographs, and it looks nice. Two bedrooms, one bathroom—and yes, it's inside—a big room with a fireplace and a modern kitchen. He says there is plenty of room to set up an office either in the second bedroom or in the living area. I had planned to use the bedroom as an office, but it dawned on me last night after I left you that you could use it and the office could be in the living room."

"And this in the middle of nowhere? Or is there a town nearby?"

"It's at the edge of a small town—a village really. A couple of hundred residents. Plenty of access to food and supplies, and a doctor should we need one. Anything they don't have we can have flown in. There are a dozen or so businesses, a couple of bars, and at least one café, but no movies, no library, no entertainment." He looked down at the spoon he was fumbling with. "If you find the thought of sharing a house with me objectionable, there are a few rooms to let in town—over the café, I think, or maybe in somebody's home. But I couldn't pay your expenses in that case. That would have to come out of your salary." He paused. "I based my budget, and your salary, on the fact we would share the cabin. I don't have money for anything else."

I'd have to think that over. So far, he's been a perfect gentleman, and with a separate bedroom, it ought to be OK for a few months. If it didn't work out, I could move into town. Maybe I could rent a room for not much money.

"How do we get there?" *That sounds like I've decided to take the job,* Uma thought. *And maybe I have. It is interesting. I'll probably never have another opportunity to live for free in Alaska* and *get paid for it. And the work sounds fascinating as well.*

He looked up at her, a relieved look on his face. "From here we take a commercial airline into Fairbanks. From there, it's a short ride on a smaller plane. At the cabin, we'll have use of a four-wheel-drive vehicle and a motor sled."

"Motor sled? What's that?"

"It's sort of like a sled with a seat on it—big enough for two people to ride, or to haul groceries. It runs and steers kind of like a car. Goes slow, but it is handy for going to the store. Some people call it a snow buggy."

"Can I think about it? Sleep on it?"

"Sure, but not much more than that." He scribbled the name of the hotel where he was staying and his room number on a napkin and shoved it toward her. "Call me as soon as you make your decision. I'm planning on leaving in a couple of days."

A boyish grin appeared on his face. "I sure hope you'll agree to do the job. The more I think about it, the better I like the idea. I would get a tremendous amount of work done with you there. While I'm out in the field, interviewing people, you could be back at the cabin, typing up previous work, or making your cards, or filing, or whatever it is you do. Then, when I get back, you can say, "Alex, you didn't ask . . . this or that . . . and I can correct it, or go back to the same person." His enthusiasm bubbled over. "This would be ideal . . . really perfect."

"I'll think about it. I really will," Uma agreed. She refused to admit even to herself that her mind was already made up. She was too practical to decide so quickly.

Later that evening she called his hotel room. "I'll do it!" She saw the advantages much as he had. *The work will progress at a much faster rate than it would if he brought his notes and recordings back to the States. Oh, yeah, Alaska is a state now.* The difference Uma could make to his finished project simply by being there as it was put in tangible form was enormous. It could shorten the timeline for producing a publishable work by a year or more, and by shortening the timeline, it was saving Alex money. It would cost him less in the long run, even paying her salary and expenses. And she would have a job that might never come along again.

Surely I can set some ground rules about hours and duties. Uma considered herself an editorial assistant, not a run-of-the-mill assistant who ran every errand her boss needed. *If we're going to live in the same house, I'll have to have suitable quarters—private ones. I'll make that clear at the beginning. And I won't do housework. I'm not a maid.*

Now, high above the clouds that covered her view below, Uma thought back over the arrangement she and Alex—he insisted "Dr. Keillor" was too formal since they would be living and working together—had agreed on. Not more than eight hours of work a day, with frequent breaks for stretching her legs, and not more than five and a half days a week. A private room with a comfortable bed and heat.

The food was adequate, and they shared cooking and cleanup duties. Alex would see to having someone come in once a week to clean the place. Access to town. Use of the vehicle and the snowmobile. Her pay deposited in her Seattle bank account twice monthly.

They did not address Alex's behavior in any way, but Uma trusted him when he said, "I'll be a gentleman while we're living together. You don't need to worry about that." Uma believed him.

Tired of looking at nothing but clouds, Uma pulled down the shade to block the view, reclined her seat, and closed her eyes. Her mind drifted back to the conversation she had with her high school counselor, Mrs. Evans, when getting out of Freeport and away from her family was the most important thing on her mind.

"You can do anything you put your mind to, Uma. You are smart. Really smart. Both you and your brother are poised to do whatever you set your minds toward. He'll be getting a scholarship to Texas A&M for next year, and in two years, it will be your turn. I have no doubt you can earn your way into whatever school you set your sights on. Courage and faith, Uma. That's what it will take. Courage and faith."

Uma always remembered Mrs. Evans' guidance and mantras: courage and faith. They had produced a trouble-free life on her own. Here she was, on her way to Alaska—a destination that would have seemed impossible only a few years ago.

When the plane touched down, Uma saw Alex was waiting. He stood taller than the rest of the crowd, his blond hair shining among the small gathering of dark-haired people and knit caps. His smile lit up when he saw her, and it made

Uma feel good to have that grin welcoming her. She thought he was going to hug her when they met, but he pulled back at the last minute. Their relationship wasn't that casual.

"You're here! I was worried you would change your mind at the last minute and not come," he said.

"Never." She frowned. "I don't back down. Once I say I'll do something, I do it." *If I were a quitter, I'd never have left Freeport.*

"Let's go get your luggage and catch the plane home," Alex said.

Home! Uma wondered if Alaska would feel like home. She'd never had one that did.

Chapter 4

"Is this really the correct spelling?" Uma pushed the notebook toward Alex. "Q-a-l-u-p-a-l-i-k?"

He stopped putting things in his backpack and glanced at the unusual word.

"Yep. Qalupalik. It's a sea creature that snatches children who don't obey their parents."

"I got the idea. It's just strange to type a Q without a U." Uma went back to typing.

"I'll be back before dark tomorrow night," Alex said as he slung the pack to his back. "You can manage the snow buggy okay?"

"Yes. I've used it several times now with no problem. I oughtn't to have any trouble." She stood up and, taking her cup, walked to the range to fill it once again.

"Then I'm out of here." Alex pulled on his heavy gloves. Uma opened the front door to save him from the chore of turning the knob after he had donned the sometimes-slippery coverings. "Thanks," he said and grinned. Suddenly, his head dipped toward her, and he kissed her lips—a kiss that started as a peck, then deepened into something else. Not a full-blown romantic kiss, but still—more than a peck. He looked stunned, then quickly went out the door.

Uma was stunned as well. Although they had gotten along well over the past few weeks, the restrictions of being boss and employee put a lid on any romantic thoughts that happened to buzz through her brain. That was something that just did not, could not, take place. Of course, all her previous employers had been older, married college professors. Not ugly, but not handsome, like Alex. If her feelings drifted toward distracting ideas of being wrapped in his arms or what it would be like to kiss him, Uma pulled them back to the present, the real world of Eskimo, Inuit, and Aleut.

Alex had just blown that world to bits.

Did that kiss affect him as it did me? Or was it just an automatic gesture? That's what it must have been. I shouldn't make more of it than it was.

She sat back in front of the typewriter, put on the earphones, and turned the tape player on. She needed to get the tapes from his last trip to the remote village transcribed before he returned with more stories.

It was useless.

Her mind wandered, and she found herself missing whole sections of narration as she relived the kiss.

Uma finally gave up. She would put on her warm gear and drive the snowmobile the short distance into town. There she would pick up the mail, gather the few groceries on their list, and make a long-distance phone call to their office supply store in Seattle, who would ship the same day whatever they needed. Uma thought to double the amount of tapes she had planned to order. They were using them much more quickly than they originally had thought they would. She hoped all that would divert her from the distraction of the kiss.

It was a beautiful day for the short trip. Sunshine sparkling on the pristine snow looked as if someone had thrown glittering crystals over the landscape. It would be another month before the temperatures rose above freezing even for short periods, insuring the ground would stay snow-covered for some time. Over small rises and around towering evergreen trees, it took all Uma's attention to guide the vehicle to the small settlement of houses and businesses that comprised the town. She maneuvered the sled to a parking spot in front of the general store, and when she entered, she was met by the distinctive odors of wooden floors and walls, barrels of potatoes, cabbage, onions, and apples. One side of the room was taken by tables stacked with denim, gloves, socks, and other clothing practical for the Alaskan climate. The other side was filled with shelves chockfull of canned goods. She was greeted by the round-faced Inuit woman behind the counter.

"Hi there, Uma. How are you doing?"

"Just fine, Shelly. I need to make a phone call to Seattle."

"Go on back to the office. You know how to fill out the call log, don't you?"

"Yes. I've done it before." Uma entered the room at the back of the store. There was a battered notebook on the desk, where the caller put their name, date, time of call, and destination. When the bill came in, Shelly collected the money.

There were only a handful of telephones in the village, and Shelly's was the only one available for general use. The town physician had one, but he wouldn't let anyone else use it; the residents believed a doctor, of all people, should make his phone available to the public. The police department had one, but they refused to let anyone but officers use it, saying they might need it to call the doctor or to call Fairbanks in case of emergency. And Joe Bellows had a phone at his house. However, as chief of the volunteer fire department, he needed to be able to get quick word if a blaze raged out of control, although summoning the volunteers had to be done by ringing a bell hanging on his front porch. When the volunteer living closest to him heard the clangor, that person rang the bell on their porch. On and on this spread, until the whole town knew there was a fire.

Everything Uma purchased in town was put on a tab, including long-distance phone calls, and Alex settled up once a month with a check to cover all costs. Uma kept cash of her own to pay for her personal items, and the general store would cash a check for her any time she needed it. The whole small-town system worked well for her, but it was a change from what she was used to in Albuquerque and Seattle.

When Uma emerged from the office, the smells in the store set her taste buds to clamoring, and she realized it was past lunchtime. "Shelly, I think I'm going down to Milt's Café and eat lunch before I buy anything. I'll be back."

When she entered the eating spot down the block, there were still a few diners at the scattering of tables. Everyone stared as she took a seat. As one of the few non-Alaskan Indian women in the town, she received more than her share of intent looks. As it happened, the only other blond woman in town was in the café as well. Angie and Milt, an older Anglo man, moved up from San Francisco a few years before, to escape the rat race, they said, but some of the townspeople thought they had escaped the law or else Angie's irate husband instead. Angie was a couple of decades younger than Milt.

"Hey, Uma," the sprightly young woman said as she approached Uma's table, her pony-tail bouncing.

"Hey, Angie," Uma answered as the waitress plunked down silverware wrapped in a paper napkin. "Alex joining you?"

"No. He left earlier for another visit to the settlement where he is collecting stories."

"He probably could collect stories around here," Angie said. "There's always lots of them floating around."

"That's not the kind he collects," Uma said. "He wants the kind that are passed down from generation to generation."

"Oh." Angie obviously wasn't interested in the subject. "What can I get you? Milt's made some really good chili today."

"That sounds great. A bowl of that, please. Do you happen to have cornbread to go with it?"

"Sure do. What do you want to drink? Coffee?"

"No. A Coke." As Angie walked away, she thought to add, "Over ice, please." She knew that was a big splurge. Cokes were expensive in Alaska, but she wanted her favorite drink. It had been weeks since she had had one.

"Sure thing," Angie called back.

When Uma returned to the general store, she gathered the few items they needed and put them in the burlap bags she had brought with her from the cabin. Paper bags weren't practical to carry items on the snowmobile, since flying snow often dampened the paper and caused them to fall apart.

"I need to pick up our mail, too, Shelly," she requested.

The clerk checked the items in the bank of cubbies on the back wall. "I can give you the mail addressed to the Alaskan Folklore Project and the mail addressed to you, but I can't give you anything addressed to Dr. Keillor," she said.

"Yes, you explained that to me last time," Uma said. When Alaska became a state, all post offices had been cautioned to adhere to the postal regulations, and one of those was not giving someone's mail to a person to whom it was not addressed. The change in what had been a common custom was causing havoc in the community.

"Lots of people are mad about it," Shelly said. "I'm glad you are OK. Mr. Begay got his mail the other day, but I couldn't give him his wife's mail. She had to come in herself to get it. They were mad that they had to make a second trip. They live a couple of miles away, and he had to turn around and bring her back to town. Mrs. Begay was looking forward to her magazines."

"There ought to be a solution that everyone could live with," Uma said. "All our mail, Dr. Keillor, mine, the project's, just come to general delivery. Does anyone in town have an address or post office box number?"

"No. Everyone's mail just comes here to general delivery."

"If everyone had a post office box number, and somebody came in and asked to pick up mail from that box, you could give them everything for that number?"

Shelly thought a minute. "Yes. That would be right."

"Then assign every household a box number. Mr. and Mrs. Begay would have the same box number, so they could pick up everything from that box."

"Oh, what a good idea!" Shelley said. "That ought to solve the problem."

"Well, you'd have to be sure everyone knows their box number and uses it. That might not be easy."

Shelley frowned. "Maybe not, but it would be better than what's going on now. The only people who are happy are the ones who live by themselves. How did you figure that out?"

"That's my job," Uma replied. "Organizing things so they work better."

Chapter 5

When she returned to the cabin, Uma threw herself back into her work. It was easy enough, after the break, to settle her mind on finishing the tape of the old woman telling the tale of the Qalupalik—the long-haired, green-skinned people who stole children and carried them under the sea.

When she finished transcribing that tape, she put on one about the Adlet, the half-man, half-dog people. As she typed, she wondered if the legends of werewolves had evolved from those stories. It grew dusky dark, and she went about the cabin turning on the electric lamps that were placed strategically about the living area. There was a generator to use if the power went out, but Uma didn't know if she could get that started if it became necessary. There were oil lamps to use in place of electric ones, and the logs in the fireplace were kept burning low at all times, ready to be poked into a blaze. Alex kept a pile of logs on the front porch, snow-free, easily accessible, and Uma enjoyed the warmth of the fire more than the electric heaters. She thought since Alex wasn't there she would sleep on the couch instead of in her bedroom.

She soon grew tired of the transcription task and set it aside for the next day. She opened a can of chicken noodle soup and added a can of water. Setting it to heat on the range, she turned on the radio, tuning it to a music station that came clearly through the night air. After eating and washing the pan and bowl, she spent a few minutes making index cards for the story she had finished typing earlier. One went into the folder for stories from that particular village; another went into a set for Qalupalik tales. Still another would be filed by name of the storyteller. Each of these cards would have a code number and the date when the story was collected, but Uma wondered if she ought to make yet another heading for everything collected on the trip.

As she drifted off to sleep, wrapped in blankets and cozy on the plush sofa, the fire softly popping, the kiss came to mind. She thought she was free of it but felt the touch of his lips on hers—her memory refused to let go.

Chapter 6

Alex returned by late morning the next day. Uma was determined that everything would be as usual. Not by anything she did or said would she reveal she had given any significance to that kiss. When he came in the front door, she was busy typing the dialogue from a tape recorded the previous time he made a trip into what she thought of as the wilderness.

A pot of pinto beans was bubbling on the stove. If anyone had told Uma five years ago she would voluntarily be cooking beans, she would have said they were wrong—very wrong. Memories of her childhood, when there was nothing in the house to eat except cans of cheap pork and beans, came flooding back. If she thought about it too long, she felt sick. Those days just before payday, when her mother was out of money and her tips at the local café weren't quite enough to pay the utilities and food, their meals were slim. If there was a mite more money, they would have wieners in their beans, or maybe canned ones, called Vienna Sausages, though that didn't improve the taste.

It wasn't until she was living in Albuquerque that a friend introduced her to home-cooked beans, seasoned and simmered and served with hot cornbread and some specialty salsa or hot relish as a side dish. Now Uma was a devotee of slow-simmered pinto beans. They would be ready when Alex returned.

She didn't hear his truck as it pulled into the garage, but a gust of cold air accompanied him in the front door. Uma switched off the tape she had been listening to and pulled off the headset. "Hey," she said. "Have a good trip?"

He didn't speak, but let the backpack slide from his hand to the floor. He pulled off his gloves and cap and threw them onto the sofa, now bare of the signs Uma had slept there. The puffy down coat came off next.

Alex walked to her and placed his hands on her shoulders. Looking into her eyes, he said, "I couldn't get it out of my mind. I know I said I'd be a gentleman, and I will, I promise. But if you don't want me to kiss you, say so right now. I'll back off. Otherwise . . ." He stared at her, studying her face for an answer. When she didn't speak, but only looked into his gaze, he gathered her close and kissed her . . . long and deep and hard. When he stopped, he pulled back, looked at her face, and then kissed her again, more gently this time. He gathered her against him and rocked back and forth. A sigh escaped him.

That was the beginning, Uma thought later, before everything fell apart. Her whole life changed when she and Alex made love. Everything—all her days—had led to this. She moved into his bedroom and into his bed.

They tried to work, but it was easy to get distracted. One heated glance, a touch of their hands, and the project was forgotten for hours.

A few days later, Alex asked, "Are you on the pill?"

"The pill?"

"The birth control pill."

"Ah . . . no. No, I'm not. I didn't expect I'd need it."

"I'll take care of it then." Alex headed to town later that day and returned with a box of condoms, among other supplies. *I wonder if he charged them to the project expenses,* Uma thought and chuckled to herself.

As the newness of their affair wore off, they devoted less time to making love and more to the project they had traveled to the remote location to work on. Their efforts became more in sync. It was as if they could read each other's minds; they finished the other's sentences, brought up possibilities, or connected themes that formed the potential for new directions of study.

"I wonder what the chances of studying in Russia to connect the folktales of that continent with those of Alaska might be?" Alex mused.

"How far into Canada were these stories also told over campfires and in Eskimo homes? Were they the same as the ones in Alaska?" Uma wondered. "Should we go there as well?" *When did I start calling us "we"? I guess we are a team, though, in more ways than one.*

"I ought to make one more expedition," Alex said. "There is another village, about half a day farther away. I need to visit there—interview the natives in that location."

But he didn't go. On a trip to town, Shelley told him about an old woman who had heard about what he was doing, and she wanted to tell him about the stories of her childhood, legends she no longer heard anyone share. So, he went to the old woman's home and was glad he did.

The word spread among the villagers. Until that point, they hadn't understood what Alex and Uma were doing, but after old Mrs. Tsosie bragged about "putting my voice on the machine so people can hear me tell the old stories long after I'm dead," suddenly other elderly people came forth, wanting to share the tales of their youth, of the Tizherak, Keelut, and Adlet.

Alex left each morning to meet with the citizens of advanced years who were not only willing, but anxious to tell of terrifying encounters with sea creatures and dog-men. As he kissed Uma goodbye, he said, "See what you have brought me? If not for you, for not wanting to go off and leave you for a few days, I wouldn't have found all these people."

"So, I'm good luck, huh?"

"We're a perfect team," he said. "My work has never been better."

Uma agreed. They were a perfect pair, and the manuscript grew substantially better for it. She wondered whether or not she would go with Alex when he returned to Chicago to prepare for the classes he would be teaching during the fall semester. He hadn't mentioned it. Of course, the assumption had been that they would spend their time in Alaska gathering the stories only and that Alex would organize them into chapters and sections and add commentary and comparisons later when he returned home. They were working rapidly, however, and had already begun forming the shape of the book—the "'what comes first and then what next'" conversations. It wouldn't take much more to pull it together. A lot depended on whether Alex was serious about a trip to Russia or the northern reaches of Canada or another spot in Alaska. They had enough to publish a substantial tome already, and more might be too much. An additional volume, researched and published at a later date, might be better.

Alex returned that afternoon with several tapes full of stories gained from the group of men who sat around the pot-bellied stove at the hardware store. He spent several days joining the assemblage of old-timers who had forsaken hunting and fishing and now lived the life of comparative luxury in the homes of their sons or daughters, where they endured or enjoyed, depending on the person, "town life" and talking about the old days. Alex had decided to catch the whole thing on tape, whether he could swing the conversation toward the folktales or not. "I can see another book in the old stories," he told Uma. "A way of life is dying. There is a saying, 'When an old man dies, the library burns,' and I see that happening here. My job is keeping the library alive through my books."

Uma filed separately the stories about how it was in the old days.

Finally tired of spending his days in town, Alex returned to his original premise. He and Uma spent their days talking about the books, revising and planning the structure and sequence of the chapters, which were now written but not arranged in order.

One day, Alex said, "I think one more trip is called for. I have a few more answers I need. As we worked on the chapters, a few things started buzzing around in my brain— questions the reader is going to ask. It will be spring soon, and the resulting mud will make traveling a mess. I need to go now while the ground is still frozen solid."

"Spring? The flowers are already blooming in Seattle and Chicago, and in Texas it is hot by now."

Alex laughed. "They can have snow as late as May here." He started stuffing his backpack. "I'm planning to be gone two days," he told her. "But don't be worried if it is three. If it turns warm, there is a possibility I might get stuck in the mud and need to be pulled out." He carried his bag to the door, where he placed it on the floor, ready to grab on his way out. "Or, I might find more people to talk to. I intend this to be my last visit there."

They made love that night before he left, and Uma never knew when he slipped out of bed. The sun was up when she awoke, the not-quite-dark Alaskan night gone. She stretched, smiled, and pulled the covers back. Putting her hands over her abdomen, she wished she had told him her secret before he left. But she didn't want to be the reason why he might ignore the mission that was so important to him. *I'll plan a special dinner and tell him then. We'll be making plans to leave this place before long, and we need to plan for this as well. For sure I'll go with him now. I can find a job in Chicago, if not with Alex at Northwestern, then at one of the other universities. He'll know where to apply.*

Uma spent the next day typing the last of the sessions Alex spent with the "hardware store gang," as he called them. Everything was indexed on cards and filed. The cards were in neat rows in the cardboard boxes assigned to them. The typed interviews were in well-ordered folders in their own boxes, and the tapes that corresponded to them had a code number so they could be easily matched to the files and the cards. Uma had never been so organized. The next day, when she could do no more, she began preparations for a special dinner.

Checking the supplies in the kitchen, Uma made a list of food she needed from the store in town. *I need to make this perfect,* Uma thought. *Candles. I need candles—something to show it's not an ordinary dinner. A candlelight dinner would be special.* She bundled up, and as she went out to get on the snow buggy, she noticed the snow starting to fall. Light flakes floated to the ground, which was still covered with the winter's accumulation.

"Hey, Shelly," Uma called out as she entered the general store.

"Hi, Uma. I don't think you have any mail today. Alex picked it up a couple of days ago, and there hasn't been any more."

"That's OK. Alex is in back country getting more interviews. I'm just here to get a couple of things."

"I hope he doesn't have any trouble getting home. It looks like the snow is really coming down."

Uma was puzzled. "He's been traveling over the snow for months now. Why would he have trouble this time?"

"Spring snow is bad. It doesn't stay put. Avalanches come." Shelly shook her head as she thought about it.

Uma pushed aside any worry. Finding where the candles were stocked, she picked out half a dozen and took them to the register.

"You not have lamp oil, Uma?" the Inuit woman asked. "It gives more light than candles, if your power goes out."

"Yes, I have plenty of lamp oil, but I like to have candles sometimes." Uma took her billfold out of her coat pocket. She wouldn't charge the candles to the project account. This was for her, but she wouldn't explain to Shelly the importance of this dinner and the atmosphere candles would give to it.

From there, she went to Milt's Café. "Hey, Angie," she said as she slid onto a stool at the counter. "What's the special today?"

"We have beef stew, and Milt made an excellent meatloaf. You want lunch?"

"No. I want something to take home for dinner tonight. I'm not much of a cook, and to tell the truth, I'm sick of my own cuisine."

She hadn't had much of an appetite lately. Everything made her a bit queasy. She'd be glad to get back to the States and start eating vegetables with her meals. For a couple of weeks, Uma had thought it was her own cooking that was putting her off food, until the other possibility had dawned on her.

"I gotcha," Angie said. "We can take care of that."

"Do I dare ask what the meatloaf is made of?"

"Well, it's moose, but you can't tell it's not from a cow. Milt has it seasoned just right." Angie was originally from the "lower forty-eight," so she knew that newcomers to Alaska didn't always take to moose meat like the natives did. "Want me to package you up some to take home?" She glanced out the front window. "You probably need to get going. It's really coming down out there."

Uma could barely see the track in the snow as she maneuvered the snow buggy back to the cabin and into the garage. *Surely Alex won't try to make it home in this blizzard.* It would be a day or two before she'd see him, at least. Maybe longer if the weather didn't improve.

The snow stopped during the night, and next day the sun shone brightly on the new fall. But there was no sign of Alex. *He decided to be safe and stay another night,* Uma thought. *Or he found more stories than expected. I'm glad he took plenty of tapes.*

But he didn't come the next day, either. And when afternoon of the following day came and he still wasn't there, Uma bundled up and went into town. She went directly to the police station.

"Officer Bear, I'm getting worried about Alex—Dr. Keillor. He went up to the Inuit village to get more stories for his book. He was supposed to be home two days ago."

The young Eskimo man had been leaning back in his office chair, reading a Louis L'Amour western. He turned down a corner of the page and placed the book on his desk. In one of the two cells beyond the office, a drunk snored loudly.

"I'll take a look along the trail, ma'am, and see if I can find him. Chances are he had trouble with that old truck he's using and he's waiting for someone to come along and rescue him. He take plenty of food and water with him? And a blanket or two?"

"Yes, he has supplies, and he knows not to get out into the cold—just wait for somebody to come along," Uma answered.

Back at the house, just as the day was turning to that dusky time that was called night in the far north, she answered the knock that sounded on the door. Joe Bear was standing there with his hat held over his heart, and she knew the news was bad—very bad.

Chapter 7

Coiled into the fetal position, Uma dozed, then woke with a start. She had had the most terrible dream. She dreamed that Chief Joe Bear had come to the door and told her Alex was dead—killed when the snow clinging to the side of an embankment came tumbling down and pushed his truck off the road. Over and over it went, gathered in a mighty snowball, until it hit the creek bed at the foot of the slope. Chief Bear couldn't tell her if Alex had been killed when the vehicle plummeted downward and struck the boulders at the bottom, or if he had frozen to death as he lay there, injured, in below-zero temperatures. The doctor could say later, possibly.

It's a dream, Uma thought. *It has to be a dream. It isn't possible for Alex to be dead. We've worked so hard on the folklore project, and it's about complete. It isn't fair! God can't take him away now! Not when the thing that means so much to him, his vision, is almost finished. And I've just found him—found the man I'm meant to be with. I've gone through all those years alone until he appeared in my life.* Then her secret floated back into her brain. The thing Alex didn't know. The thing she hadn't talked with him about. *Maybe if I had just . . ."*

She drifted back to sleep, only to toss restlessly and wake a couple of hours later to the memory of a bad dream. A terrible dream.

Chief Bear came again the next morning. He had called Chicago, he said. He had notified someone about the tragedy.

"You knew who to contact?" Uma said. Worries had begun to permeate her consciousness. *Who should I call? Who will get all his precious research? Will I have to make arrangements for his burial? Surely there are relatives who need to be notified.*

"Yes," the composed young man said. "I had phone numbers from when Dr. Keillor was making preparations to live in Dr. Grant's cabin while he was away."

"It is good that you did that. I was wondering what to do."

"There will be someone here tomorrow. They will fly into Fairbanks late today. We'll clear the landing strip first thing in the morning, and they'll be here by noon." He turned his hat around and around as he sat dangling it between his knees. "Sh— they said I should be sure to secure all his work." Joe Bear looked embarrassed to be saying it. "They said it was valuable and they didn't want it stolen." His dark Eskimo skin reddened a bit.

"I keep it in those boxes," Uma said, motioning toward the stacks on and beside the large worktable she and Alex had set up when they arrived. "It's all there."

"I guess I'd better take it with me." To justify what he was going to do, he said, "They asked me to do it." Another pause. "So it would be safe." He rubbed his forehead. "Not that you would take it or anything."

Uma stared at him. Of course he had to do his job— secure Alex's months of labor. And he didn't know her. The people in Alex's office in Chicago didn't know her. His publisher didn't know her. Joe Bear was only doing what was necessary and right.

"Of course," she said. "I'll help you gather it, to be sure you don't miss anything."

And within minutes, the results of Alex's months of labor, and hers, was loaded into the truck parked by the front door, and then it was gone. Joe said if she needed anything she could come get him, but Uma hadn't needed the lawman before now, and she could survive on her own. She always had, and she could once more.

Uma sat on the sofa in front of the fire she had boosted with additional logs and jabs with the iron poker until the flames shot up the flue. Even with the additional warmth, she was cold. The blanket wrapped around her body didn't help. The icy feeling extended from her physical being into her soul. It froze any tears that might have fallen. She leaned her head back and closed her eyes. Tears did no good. She had learned that twenty years ago, when her precious Papa died. She had cried then. Cried and screamed and kicked her feet and pounded the walls with her fists. "That does no good," Mama said. "It won't bring him back. Nothing will bring him back. It just clutters your mind and keeps you from doing what you have to do." But it didn't stop Mama from taking to her bed and crying.

So now Uma didn't cry. She couldn't have a cluttered mind. She had to think of what to do next.

Finally, she removed the clothes she had worn the previous day and slept in—what bits and pieces of sleep came to her between reliving the nightmare of Joe Bear's visit. She showered and washed her hair—that glorious tangle of honey-gold locks that Alex had insisted she stop pulling into a tight bun. Dressed in fresh clothes, she went to work. With no typing or transcribing or any sort of legitimate labor to accomplish, it was obvious she would be leaving.

One of her suitcases had never been unpacked. It was full of the kind of clothing she would be wearing when she returned to her usual life, whatever that might be. Opening the other piece of luggage onto the bed in what originally had been her bedroom, she carefully folded and packed the clothing she had bought to wear in the arctic environment: long underwear, sweaters, long-sleeved shirts to layer underneath. Trousers and jeans. Socks, lots of heavy socks that would go beneath the boots that sat beside the bed. The high-topped moccasins she wore around the house, the ones she had admired and finally purchased at the general store, would go in at the last minute. She would be wearing the muffler and gloves, and she stuck the extras of each into the bag. She went into the bathroom and gathered her toiletries, putting them into a small zippered bag. She was ready to go . . . somewhere.

Uma thought about the answer to that problem as she went about the cabin, straightening, putting things in their proper place, doing what she always did: organize. *If everything around me is in good shape, maybe my life will be as well. Is that why I learned to put everything just so—just where it needs to be—so my life would be in order as well?*

She put a kettle of water on the range to heat. For weeks she had been unable to stomach coffee. Even the smell of it had started to nauseate her, so she made herself a cup of tea. Memories came flooding back of her mother giving her the brew to drink when as a small girl she had an upset stomach. *Dammit, I don't want to remember that time of my life. Not now, of all times.* Realizing she was hungry, Uma made some toast. It was the only thing that sounded good to her. It had been a long time since she had eaten. *I don't think I've eaten since lunch yesterday, before I went in town,* she thought. *No wonder my stomach is protesting.*

Uma cleaned all day. When the semi-dusk of nighttime fell, she changed into a pair of flannel pajamas. *Now that Alex is gone, it'll be too cold to sleep naked.* She hadn't worn clothing at night since she moved into Alex's bed. Two bodies snuggled up together, skin to skin, create enough heat to keep warm all night.

Having not slept much the night before, Uma fell into a deep, dreamless state, not waking until the dusky night lightened into normal daylight. She donned a cashmere sweater and trousers, aware that whoever would come to make arrangements might be a person who could hire her to oversee the completion of Alex's beloved manuscript. *Courage and faith, Uma. Courage and faith.* She repeated the words over and over to herself.

For the first time in days, she was legitimately hungry. Alex had always been diligent about keeping plenty of food in the house, and she put a precious, expensive egg on to boil as she sliced strips from the hunk of bacon and laid them in the frying pan. *No sense leaving food to waste.* She wondered what they would do with the contents of the refrigerator. The canned goods could be left for Fred Grant—for when he returned from his travels. The pantry would be well-stocked for his weekend visits.

When the dishes were washed and put away, Uma poked the fire a bit, then settled herself to wait in the over-stuffed chair that was perfect for reading.

Before long, there was a rap on the front door, followed quickly by its opening, and Uma heard the voice. "Why knock? It's my house. My money, at least, that paid for this excursion."

Uma saw a tiny woman enter. She was not much over five feet tall. Bright red curls escaped from beneath a multi-colored knit cap, and bright blue eyes looked around the room. When they lit on Uma, still sitting in the comfortable chair, an explosion ensued. "I ought to have known my husband would have a woman installed. So, you are Alex's latest whore, are you? He always has one, you know, so if you think you are his only one, you're wrong. You're just the latest in a long string of undergrads he has seduced. You aren't the first, and if my now-deceased husband hadn't fallen off the side of a mountain and killed himself, you wouldn't be the last. And by the way, you won't be getting an A in whatever class you were planning to take from him in the fall semester."

The angry tirade stopped momentarily as the woman walked around the room. Then she turned toward Uma. "You have twenty-four hours to be packed and out of here. Be sure you are on that puddle-jumper on your way to Fairbanks no later than in the morning. I never want to see you again. Understand?"

Chapter 8

Uma sat in the car for a long while, studying the front of the house. Finally, she gathered her thoughts, exited the vehicle, and made her way up the front walk, skirting broken toys and food wrappers littering the path.

She raised her hand to knock on the rickety screen door but pulled back at the last second. *Courage,* she said to herself. *Courage and faith.* She raised her hand again and rapped quickly, before she could change her mind. She knew someone was home, because the wooden door beyond the screen stood open, and a television blared for all the neighborhood to hear.

When nobody came, Uma made a fist and knocked again, loud enough to be heard over the cartoon music. Footsteps sounded, and a woman's raised voice said, "Turn down that TV, for pity's sake. You can hear it clear to the next block."

The woman who appeared in the doorway looked years older than the age Uma knew her to be. "Yes?" she said. Then her mouth dropped open. "My God!" she said and pushed open the screen. "Uma! My God!" She reached out and flung her arms around Uma, who tensed for several seconds, then tentatively gathered the older woman in her embrace. "My baby! My baby!" the woman repeated like a broken record. "My baby."

"Mama," Uma said. She felt tears prickling at her eyes, but she refused to let them fall.

"Let me look at you," her mother said, and set her away, holding to Uma's shoulders as she studied her daughter. "You're grown up! You're all grown up!"

Uma smiled. *Of course I am.* She had been grown up since she was six and trying to help Corine with the new baby, with the housework, and with life itself. She might be taller now; she might look like a woman instead of a child, but there was still a little girl inside that called out for her *mother* to grow up and be an adult.

She took Uma by the hand and led her inside. "Turn that off and go outside to play," Uma's mother said to the child sitting with eyes glued to the jumping rabbit on the screen. "You hear me?" she yelled.

A whiney voice said, "Can I have a Popsicle?"

"If I give you a Popsicle, will you go outside and not bother me?"

A dirty face indicated it wouldn't be the first sugary treat of the day. The boy's chest and tan shorts showed tracks of Popsicle juice all the way down to his legs. He looked back at Uma as he followed the woman through the door to the kitchen.

When they returned, he had a red object in his hand and was peeling the covering from it, throwing it on the floor as he went. "Here now! Haven't I told you not to do that?" the woman yelled as she picked up the bits of paper behind him.

"Whose is he?" Uma asked.

"That's Danny."

"I mean, who does he belong to? Whose child is he?"

"He's Cindy's."

"Cindy has a child?" Uma had to think about that a minute. Her half-sister was only a kid herself. *Let's see . . . nineteen or so, must be.*

"Lord yes! She . . ." Corine fizzled to a stop, unable to think of what to say about her youngest child.

"Is she married?" The minute the words were out of her mouth, Uma knew better.

Corine snorted. "Yes. To a bum."

The screen door squeaked as a young woman, obviously pregnant, with a toddler on her hip, entered the house. "Well, look who's back," she said, and the smile she threw at Uma could only be called a smirk. "Come home to roost, huh?"

"Hello, Cindy," Uma said. She couldn't think of another word. *If I start talking, who knows what will come out of my mouth. Something entirely inappropriate, for sure. Something like, "I can find someplace better than this to roost, thank you very much." Or "Three children before you're twenty? What are you thinking?" Something that would be especially inappropriate coming from me, of all people. At least Cindy has a husband, even if Mama doesn't think much of him.*

"Where've you been all these years?" Cindy asked.

"All around. Albuquerque, then Seattle. I just got back from Alaska."

"My stars!" Corine said. "What were you doing in all those places?"

"Working. I'm an editorial assistant."

"What does that mean?" Cindy took a seat in the beat-up recliner and eased the toddler to stand on the floor. "What's an editorial assistant?"

"I help authors and researchers get their manuscripts ready to publish. I type and organize and file. Stuff like that."

"Does it pay good?" Cindy asked. "I took typing in school. Maybe I could get a job like that."

Uma refrained from making a comment on the quality of any work Cindy was capable of doing. "It takes training," she said, "and it's a lot of work. I move around to where the job is."

"And you've been in all those places. I bet that was interesting," Corine commented.

"Yes, it was," Uma said to her mother. "Very interesting."

"You wouldn't loan me some money, would you?" Cindy asked. "I'm all out of cigarettes."

"Where's your husband? Can't he give you money?"

Cindy put a pissy look on her face and didn't answer. Uma looked at Corine and raised her eyebrows.

"He's in jail," Corine answered for Cindy. "Still has a month to serve." Uma didn't want to know what he was in for.

She took a deep breath before answering Cindy. "No. No, I can't. I'm between jobs right now, and I have to watch what I spend. I don't know where my next job will be."

"Bummer," Cindy said. "So, what are you doing back here? We can't give you any money. We're broke. You thinkin' you can find a job like that here in Freeport?"

"I just wanted to see how you were doing." Uma turned toward Corine as she said it. She couldn't care less how Cindy was doing, but her heart still hurt for her mother sometimes. "Is Grady still around?"

Her mother drew an imaginary circle on the cloth over her knee and said nothing.

"It's all in how you look at it," Cindy answered for her mother. "His clothes are here, and he is too, every once in a while." She looked disgusted. "When he thinks he can get some money out of Mama. Money to buy booze. He's been gone now about . . ." She looked off into the air. "He's been gone about two weeks. No tellin' where he is."

"Oh, Mama," Uma said, looking at her mother. "I'm so sorry. I thought he was doing good. When I left for college . . ." Not that good meant good. It was just that her stepfather had cut back to a couple or three beers a day and held down a job that paid the utilities and put food on the table. He was still mean and cantankerous, but Corine held to him like a lifeline. "Are you still waiting tables at that seafood place?"

"Yes, when I can. It's hard work. I'm getting old." Corine looked down, not meeting Uma's gaze.

"Old? Mama! You are but . . . what? Forty-five? That's not old!"

"I'll be forty-six in a couple of months. But I've had a hard life. It's taken a lot out of me." Tears came to her eyes.

Uma reached over and rubbed her mother's arm. She had had a hard life, but much of it was her own doing, her own choices that put her in situations that caused problems. Like Grady Miller. It was for Uma to imagine what her mother had looked like when she was Uma's age. The blond hair must have been bright and shining then, not lank and lifeless and streaked with gray. And her skin was once clear and unlined, before the years of worry and cigarettes had worked their toll.

Uma still remembered her papa and how things were before he was killed. She wasn't but five, and Tommy was seven, and they were happy. Her parents bought the house Corine was still living in and made payments on it every month, and it was all painted pretty colors. Mama kept it clean, too, and there were always meals on the table. She remembered when Papa came home every evening after work and picked her up and carried her around, singing along with the radio, dancing with Uma. After dinner, he'd go out in the yard and play catch with Tommy until it was too dark to see. And when they went to bed, he'd read Uma a story from the big fairytale book he brought home one time.

Everyone was happy. Everything was perfect. Until the accident. Papa worked on the equipment that transferred oil from one place to another—Uma didn't understand exactly what he did or what happened—but one morning two men came from the plant and told Mama that Thomas Thornton had fallen to his death. And in that instance, Uma's happy life was over, and she had to try to be the adult in the family. She and Tommy, that is. They had to take care of their mother, and fix their own meals, and remember on their own to brush their teeth and take a bath.

Corine fell apart. Even after the tears stopped, she took to her bed, lying in the dark. The one silver lining was that

Thomas had special insurance at the bank to pay off the mortgage if he died; so the house was theirs, and nobody could take it away from them, if only Corine managed to pay the taxes when they came due every year.

The next-door neighbor, Betty, was Corine's best friend, and she kept prodding. "You can't just go to bed and stay. Thomas wouldn't want you to do that. He was all about life, you know that. He would want you to be happy." She finally persuaded Corine to get dressed up and go to the bar with her. "Just listen to the music and have one beer. It'll make you feel better." So, she did. And went again. And again. That's where she met Grady Miller. He made her laugh, she said. He made her forget she was sad.

It wasn't long before Cindy was on the way, and Grady, knowing about the money the company paid for Thomas's death, said that the only right thing to do was for them to get married. That was the end of the laughter and the beginning of the sadness.

Soon it was the end of the money as well, and Corine had to go to work waiting tables. Life was never good again.

"So where is Tommy?" Uma asked. "Do you ever hear from him?"

"He don't want nothin' to do with us," Cindy said. "Like you."

"Cindy," Corine cautioned. "People got to go where they can make a living." She turned to Uma. "We get a letter from time to time, but he don't say where he is, exactly."

Uma knew how that went. She sent letters as well. Every few months she wrote her mother, telling her what city she was in and how interesting her job was, and how pretty the town. But she never included a return address. She was always torn between guilt over leaving the family behind and not wanting to hear anything about what was going on back in Freeport.

Uma had still been in college in Austin when her brother graduated from Texas A&M. It took every penny she could scrape together just to stay in school, and she hadn't been able to travel to College Station to attend the ceremony to see Tom get the diploma he had worked so hard to attain. She had nothing on her mind except completing her degree. It was the only way she knew to escape Freeport and her family. Uma didn't go home for holidays. She found a job instead. Summer was taken up by classes and work. There was nothing at home for her, not without her brother being there.

"Last I remember," Corine said, "he was working on some ranch."

"Ranch? Tom?" Uma was surprised. Tom had attended Texas Agricultural and Mechanical College for the mechanical part, not the agricultural. He had majored in business, especially as it pertained to the oil industry.

"His friend owns a ranch. The Big B. I don't know where it is. Nowhere around here, that's for sure," Corine said.

Cindy spoke up. "Not that far from where he went to school, I don't think. He and his friend used to go there on the weekends. Up toward Waco, maybe."

Uma didn't stay much longer. Their lives were just too different, and there wasn't anything more to say. She encouraged her mother to walk with her to the rental car and slipped her a twenty-dollar bill. It helped her conscience a bit for being a success and leaving Corine behind.

As she wound her way through town on her way back to the highway, she drove by the ever-growing industrial area, with the tanks and stacks and pipes which moved oil and sulfur along the canals that ran beside the Brazos to where the mighty river poured into the Gulf of Mexico. From there, ships would carry it to the rest of the world.

She put her hand on her belly as she paused to take in the scene. *Little one, you'll grow up in a better place than this. I'll see to it.* But the thought occurred to her that both she and Cindy were repeating a pattern, the pattern her mother had started years ago . . . a baby on the way and no husband in sight.

Chapter 9

When Uma left Freeport, she drove toward Houston until heat, fatigue, and an overload of emotion forced her to find a motel room. Once in her room, she immediately stripped off all her clothing and left it in a disorganized pile in the corner of the room. Switching the air conditioning to the coldest setting, she turned on a hot shower and scrubbed her skin and hair, trying to eliminate the slightest possibility of the scent of petroleum or sulfur that might cling to her body. As she bathed, Uma realized she was trying to wash away the memories of the past as well as the scent of it. After she dried off, by rubbing roughly with the coarse motel towel, she pulled a pair of flannel pajamas from the suitcase—a pair bought to keep her warm in the Arctic cold of Alaska—and put them on.

Burrowed under the blanket on the bed and another she found on the shelf over the clothes rack, she imagined herself in the familiar cold of Alaska and soon fell asleep. The whole ordeal had exhausted her. Seeing her mother again, seeing herself as she might have turned out if she had not run, and seeing what she feared she might yet turn into drained of every ounce of energy in her body. When she woke sometime in the night, she was hungry, so she rummaged in her purse for the packet of crackers she had stuffed in it the day before to be handy if nausea hit. It wasn't what she wanted, but it would do. That and a glass of water from the bathroom sink subdued the discomfort, and she slept once again.

Dawn was breaking when Uma woke once more. Pulling the covers up around her neck, she planned her course. She had to locate Tommy. After that, she could set her sights on finding a job. It would have to be one she could do from home, wherever that might be. No one would hire an unwed pregnant woman to work in a college or university anywhere. Possibly in New York City, but not in Texas, or anywhere else, like as not.

She could pretend to be widowed—buy a wedding ring and wear it. Concoct a story about a tragic death. If worse came to worse, or—if truth be told—long before it got to worse, she would do it. Uma was not willing to suffer the shame of unwed motherhood or fall apart and grasp for the first man who came along, either. The history of her mother wasn't for her. Neither was marrying the wrong man, like Cindy.

But first came finding her beloved brother. He had been her rock growing up. With him by her side, everything was OK. When he left for college, he told her she could do it too. "Don't quit, Uma. Get a degree in something that pays well—something you enjoy doing. Always be able to support yourself, to make more than a just a living. Make a life and have fun at it."

So she did. And she had enjoyed her life, until now. Once she saw Tommy again, she would throw her organizational skills into forming a new one. A life that included a baby.

Climbing from under the covers, she turned the air conditioning to a more reasonable setting and proceeded to don one of the summer dresses she bought when she returned to Texas. She had only purchased three because she knew she would soon outgrow them. After breakfast at the motel coffee shop, she hit the road again.

She pulled the map close and set her sights on College Station, near Bryan. Uma thought of it as a research project—something she had to find in order to substantiate the facts in an important study. *Start at the beginning and go from there. One step at a time, Uma. One step at a time. Don't get distracted by emotion.*

Two hours later, she arrived at the sprawling Texas A&M campus. She drove around the university grounds and finally decided to start at the Administration Building. Finding a parking place close by, she tackled the enormous flight of steps that led to the entrance of the splendid structure, which had fourteen columns gracing the façade. As Uma entered the hall, she was stunned by the grandeur of the building and stood agape for a minute before she pulled herself together.

Let's see. Which one of these offices would have information on former students? Looking across the expanse, she saw the words "Admissions Office" in gold on the glass of a door. When she entered the office, a woman behind a counter said, "May I help you?"

"Yes. I hope you can. I'm trying to locate the address of a former student. Would you have that? Or would that be a different office?

The woman frowned. "A former student?"

"Yes. He graduated from here about . . ." She stopped and did some mental math. "I guess it was in 1955."

"And you want his current address?"

"Yes. That's right. Or his phone number."

"I don't know if we can give that out. Some people don't want their addresses or phone numbers made public."

"It's my brother. I'm sure he wouldn't mind."

"You don't know how to contact your brother?" The woman's eyebrows raised.

"No, I don't. I've been working in Alaska, and we lost touch," Uma explained. That wasn't quite the way it had happened, but strangers didn't need to know any more than that.

"I'm afraid I can't give out any information, even if I had it. This office is for current and incoming students. Not former ones." She turned away from the counter, effectively dismissing Uma.

Going back out into the hall, Uma pulled her thoughts together. *I can't get Tom's address, at least from the admissions office. Maybe I could try a different department . . . Wait! I do have his address! Big B Ranch. Now how do I find out where that is?*

She spotted another flight of steps, but she didn't want to tackle them, not knowing where she was going. Looking around, she saw an elevator, and beside it a large glass-enclosed board. *Maybe that will give me a clue where to go next.*

Standing in front of the list of office numbers for all the departments in the Administration Building, Uma wondered which one might possibly give her any information about the location of the Big B Ranch. *Think again like this is a research project. If I had to find out facts or figures about a certain ranch, where would I go?*

As she read the board, she became aware of someone approaching the elevator and pushing the call button. Slightly balding, wearing dress pants and a wrinkled white shirt, his tie hanging loosely around his neck, he was too old by a decade to be a typical student. He had what appeared to be textbooks clutched to his chest. *Aha! A professor.* Uma knew professors. She knew how to handle them. She knew how to get information from them.

She took a step toward him, smiling. She was glad she hadn't pulled her hair into a pony-tail, making her look like a coed. "Can I help you?" he asked.

"I hope so," Uma said and extended her hand in anticipation of a similar response. "My name is Uma Thornton, and I'm an editorial assistant." *That's not a lie. I am what I say I am. I'm just not on a paid job right now.* "I was standing here wondering which of these offices might be able to give me the information I need."

As she had thought, he accepted her offered hand, holding it slightly longer than he would have had Uma been a man. She held her smile, happy she had donned lip gloss before getting out of the car.

"I'm Dr. Epson," he said as he continued shaking her hand. "That depends on what information you are looking for."

"I need to find the location of a ranch that is somewhere in this part of the state."

"I might be able to help you with that," Dr. Epson said as he finally released her hand. "What ranch is it?"

"The Big B."

"Oh my, yes. The Big B is well known around these parts. Are you an Aggie student?"

"No. I must admit that I'm a Longhorn. I graduated several years ago."

"That's probably why you didn't know about the Big B. It is big into oil and cattle, something A&M specializes in."

"That's why I came here. I knew that this was the place to find out." She smiled again.

"What kind of research are you doing, may I ask?"

Uma wiped the smile off her face. "I'm afraid I can't answer that." She looked around as if she expected spies to be listening to their conversation. "Some projects, you know, have to be kept quiet until they are released."

"I understand," Epson said, almost whispering. "I understand," he repeated.

"So how do I find the Big B?"

When she left College Station she knew which county it was in, the nearest town to the ranch, and what highway to take to get there.

Chapter 10

When she drove under the iron arch announcing the Big B Ranch, she could see a group of buildings in the distance. On both sides of the drive, there were cattle grazing among pump jacks that were busily bringing up liquid gold, as oil was called. As she drove closer, she saw a two-story white house surrounded with several barns and outbuildings. They stretched over the landscape almost like a small town one might come across on a dusty Texas road.

Parking on the gravel drive that circled in front of the house, she sat for a moment and admired the wide porch encompassing three sides, well-appointed with wooden rocking chairs, wicker furniture adorned with brightly colored cushions, and hanging flower baskets. *This is surely the owner's home. It's too nice to be anything else, but the way Dr. Epson described the Big B, I expected a lavish mansion. This is more of a home than a showplace.*

As she approached the front door, a yellow cat walked over to her and watched with golden eyes, observing her every step. "Hello, kitty," she said as she reached to ring the doorbell. A series of four chimes sounded; a minute later, she could see through the etched glass that someone was coming.

The woman who opened the door was tiny—a couple of inches shorter than Uma. She had dusky skin and black hair and was wearing jeans and a tee shirt with Mighty Mouse in flight across the front. At first Uma thought she might be a young teen, but a closer look revealed a woman in her twenties. Uma didn't know what she had been expecting, but the person before her wasn't it. "Can I help you?" the woman asked.

"My name is Uma Thornton, and I was told that my brother, Tom Thornton, works on this ranch. Do you know—"

"Oh my God!" Mighty Mouse squealed and threw both hands over her mouth. Her scrunched up brown eyes shone with tears. Taking her hands from her face, she reached out and grabbed Uma's arm. The cat brushed against Uma's bare leg as it hurried inside.

"He is going to be so glad to see you!" She pulled gently as she urged Uma into the foyer.

A masculine voice from farther along the passage called out, "Lovie? Was that someone at the door?"

"It's Tom's sister, Uma!"

"Really?" The voice sounded closer, accompanied by a clomping sound. Then a figure appeared from the hall beyond where the stairs ascended to the upper floor. A tall, handsome man maneuvered his crutches, swinging one leg in a cast as he made his way into the vestibule where the two women stood. His sandy brown hair stood every which way, and his face was scrunched into a scowl. She couldn't tell if it was pain or anger. Then he broke into a smile, and his demeanor changed.

"He's going to be happy to see you."

"I'm going to be happy to see him as well," Uma said. "Is he here?"

"Unfortunately no," the man said, "but let's go into the parlor and sit down." His face reflected pain once again as he turned toward the wide arch on the right. He led the way into a pleasant room, full of comfortable-looking chairs, an overstuffed sofa, and a television set. "Have a seat," he said as he collapsed into a chair, placing the crutches on the floor beside him. "How did you know to come here to find him?"

Uma hardly knew where to start the story. She went to the sofa and settled at the end closest to the yet-unidentified man. "Well, I went to visit my mother, and my sister . . ."

"You went home?" the woman said. "To Freeport?"

"Yes," Uma replied. "Look. You have the advantage over me. You seem to know about Tom's family . . . his life. I mean, you knew my name, and you know about Freeport, but I know next to nothing about you." She reached into her purse for a tissue, which she wiped across her face. The room was cool, but the heat from outside clung to her.

"Lovie darlin', Uma looks like she could use a cool drink. Could you fix us something?" The man was looking closely at Uma, frowning, as he spoke. Uma wondered if she looked like she was about to faint.

Lovie jumped up from the chair where she had been perching. "Of course! We have sweet tea, colas, or lemonade," she said. Whatever you would like."

"Sweet tea would be nice," Uma said. She hadn't had sweet tea in months. Coffee had been the drink of choice in Seattle, and anything hot in Alaska.

"I'll be right back," Lovie said as she rushed out of the room. "Don't talk. I don't want to miss anything," she added. Uma noticed that she was barefooted.

"I apologize," the man said. "Of course we know more about you than the reverse. My name is Bix Crandall. Tom and I were best friends at A&M—still are best friends. My parents own the Big B Ranch, but they bought a house in Galveston and have moved down there. They left me in charge of everything, and as you can see, I promptly screwed up but good. I had to take part in an impromptu rodeo, 'had to' being my point of view, and the bull I was riding got the better of me." He grimaced as he adjusted his leg. "This has always been like home to Tom, and I guilted him into coming to live here and taking over all the things I can't do right now. I've sent him on a business trip. He's negotiating a contract."

"When will he be back?" *Now what will I do? I guess I'll have to find a motel somewhere nearby and wait for him to return to the ranch. I'm so close, I can't leave without seeing him.*

"It depends on how long it takes him to get some things straightened out and come to an agreement." He stretched out his long legs and eased his torso into a more comfortable position. "You can stay here and wait for him, can't you? We have plenty of room, and Tom has been concerned about you. He said he hadn't heard from you in a long time." He smiled at her. "And I want to hear about all your travels as well. Tom has told me about what you do. It sounds interesting."

"I wouldn't want to put you out," Uma said, although the prospect of spending some time in a peaceful setting sounded wonderful to her. She glanced around at the room that exemplified the word 'home.' The house was surrounded by large live-oak trees, and the sunlight shining through the leaves caused shadows to flit around the room. Serenity enveloped them.

"I promise you, it wouldn't. This is a big house. You wouldn't be depriving anyone of a bedroom if you stay. And you'd be here when Tom gets back."

"Your wife might say differently. You need to consult with her before offering room and board to a stranger."

"My . . ." Bix looked at her and then at the entrance to the foyer where Lovie had exited. "Oh . . . Lovie isn't my wife. She's . . . ah, the housekeeper, I guess, for want of a better word."

Just then, Lovie walked in holding a tray with three glasses and a plate of cookies. "My great-aunt is the housekeeper," she said. "I'm the assistant housekeeper." She sat the tray on the low table in front of the sofa. In a lower voice, she said, "You'd better not let Auntie hear you call me the housekeeper instead of her. She'll tell you right off that she's in charge of this house and all that are in it." She handed Uma a glass and offered her the plate of cookies. "Peanut butter cookies, fresh out of the oven."

"They look delicious," Uma said as she took one. "I thought I smelled something sweet cooking."

"That was probably the strawberry cake Auntie is baking for dinner."

"See. Now you have to stay," Bix said. "We're having Annie's strawberry cake. You can't pass that up."

"Well . . ." Uma couldn't think of any better way to connect with her brother than to be there when he returned home, but to stay with strangers put her off a bit—even if they were friendly strangers.

"You have to stay," Lovie chimed in. "We have an empty bedroom. You can stay here at least until Tom gets back from his trip."

"Or longer, for that matter," Bix added. "There's no need to rush off."

"It'd give Bix somebody new to pester," Lovie said.

"I don't pester," Bix said, eyebrows raised in an innocent expression. This was answered by a snort from Lovie.

"If you're sure I won't be a bother."

"You won't." "Not at all." Bix and Lovie answered together as Uma looked back and forth between them, trying to judge if their banter was good-natured or not.

"Relax," Bix said. "You look all uptight. We don't allow that on the Big B."

"Enjoy your tea and cookies," Lovie chimed in. "Then I'll get someone to carry your bag upstairs."

"I can get it myself," Uma replied. "Like I said, I don't want to be a bother."

"You can't be more of a bother than I am," Bix said in an irritable voice. "I even have a hired hand assigned to me to help when I need it." He murmured, "Like I can't wipe my own—"

"Bix!" Lovie barked. "Behave yourself!"

"Sorry," he said, looking sheepishly at Uma.

Uma set her glass back on the tray. The cool liquid and the cookies had given her new energy. "OK. You've persuaded me. I'll stay until Tom gets back."

"Good!" Lovie said. "Now I'll have another woman my age around here. I've been outnumbered with Bix and Tom. They gang up on me." She stood up. "If you are ready, I'll show you to your room."

When they went up the wide stairs leading from the entrance hall, Lovie led her to a bedroom decorated predominantly in vibrant reds, blues, and greens. There were pictures of airplanes decorating the walls and a model of a plane on the dresser.

"Are you sure I'm not putting anyone out?" Uma asked. "This looks like it belongs to someone who likes airplanes."

"I'm sure," Lovie said. "This used to be Bix's big sister's room, but she lives up in Waco now. Her name is Sarah. She's a pilot."

"Really? You don't hear about many women pilots."

"No, you don't. Sarah is someone special all right."

"Is your room up here?"

"No. I have a little cottage behind the big house. The gardener used to live there until he died some years ago. My Aunt Annie has a cottage back there as well. She's been the housekeeper on the Big B Ranch for a long, long time— probably fifty years or more."

"That *is* a long time."

"She was just a young woman, a recent widow, when she came to the ranch. It was when Bix's mother, Dorie, was a little girl. A few years ago, when it became obvious Auntie couldn't keep up with physical chores, the family sent one of my cousins down here to help her. They used the excuse that

Sulla needed training in keeping a house. The Crandalls, you see, had offered Aunt Annie retirement, but she refused. She did accept Sulla's help, under the pretense of training her."

"That's a graceful way to handle it."

"It worked until Sulla wanted to move back home."

"Where is home?"

"Tahlequah, Oklahoma. That's the Cherokee capitol. Most of the family, the ones who haven't scattered, live around there." She smoothed the cover on the bed, then sat down on it. "So, then it was my turn to come help Aunt Annie."

"How did you get picked?"

"I had just graduated from Northeastern Oklahoma University there in Tahlequah, and I was ready to start looking for a job. This is a family thing, you understand. Annie is my grandfather's sister. I had to come. Family honor and all that." She paused, looking down at her hands, her voice almost shy as she said, "I'm glad that I did."

Uma wondered what had softened Lovie's voice and suspected there was a story to be told, but she wasn't going to ask such a question. "What were you majoring in?"

"Liberal Arts."

"That's kind of broad. What kind of job did you plan on finding?"

"Well, I minored in education. I was thinking about teaching. I was thinking about a lot of things." She looked up at Uma. "When Tom talks about what you do, I am so envious."

"Of me?" Uma was bemused. Somebody was envious of her—she who had no home, no place to go, no one to hold to or ask advice of. *Uma the wanderer has someone who envies her.*

A knock sounded at the open door, and a wiry older man carrying one of Uma's bags said, "Here's one of 'em." He sat it down just inside the room. "I'll go fetch the other one."

"Thank you, Peanut," Lovie said. Uma raised her eyebrows at the name but said nothing. Lovie noticed and explained, "He likes to eat peanuts. Most cowpokes and oil-field roustabouts go by nicknames instead of their real monikers." Uma wondered if "Lovie" was her real name or a nickname.

"Let me show you where the bathroom is, then I'll leave you alone for a while. You look like you could use a rest," Lovie said, getting off the bed. "Where did you drive from today?" she asked as they went out the bedroom door.

"From south of Houston to College Station this morning. I stopped there and asked where to find the Big B, and I drove from there after lunch."

"That's not too bad, I guess." They went to the room next to Uma's. "You won't be sharing this with anyone right now," Lovie explained. "Bix has moved downstairs since his tangle with the bull. Tom's room is down there." She waved vaguely across from Uma's room. "When he gets back, you'll share the bathroom with him."

"Everything is great," Uma said, looking around at her peaceful surroundings. Cool, calming colors, everything in its place, silence throughout. Welcoming and sheltering. Everything a home was supposed to be. Everything she had never known.

Chapter 11

Uma woke from her nap when Lovie rapped on the door. "Dinner's in half an hour," she called out. "Come on down when you're ready."

I must have been more tired than I thought. I only laid down to rest a minute. She looked at the Timex watch on her wrist. *An hour ago!*

In the bathroom, she splashed cold water on her face, and when she looked in the mirror, she saw the wrinkle marks from sleeping so soundly on the fold of the bed covering. Returning to her room, the reflection in the looking glass over the dresser showed that her face wasn't the only thing that was rumpled. Uma was glad she had put her other two dresses on hangers before she decided to rest a bit. She hoped some of the creases from being packed had fallen out.

After donning a pink floral-print shirtwaist dress, she tied a ribbon she used as a sash loosely around her waist. Taking a brush to the abundance of honey-colored hair, she attempted to control it by tying it away from her face with another length of the same ribbon. She had abandoned the belt that came with the dress soon after buying it, since it was already too tight. Looking at her reflection, she decided it was the best she could do on short notice. Her cheeks were still pink from being pressed on the bedspread. She had no need of blush or powder—not that she was used to wearing makeup all the time anyway. *It's time to see what I'm getting myself into.*

Reaching the bottom of the stairs, she followed the sound of voices through the arch across the hall from the living room. No one was in the large dining room that held a long mahogany table surrounded by ten chairs. It wasn't set. *They must not be eating here.*

Uma pushed the door on the rear wall. It swung open to reveal a large kitchen where two women were busy preparing the meal.

"Ah . . . you're up," Lovie said. "I was afraid you were so sound asleep you didn't hear me."

"Yes," said Uma. "I had a nice nap."

"Auntie," Lovie said, turning to the woman at the stove. "This is Tom's sister, Uma. She'll be staying with us a while."

The woman who turned toward Uma showed every sign of her Cherokee heritage. Hair that was once black but now salt and pepper gray, was braided and wound into a crown around her head. Her ample form was dressed in a calico dress covered with a voluminous white apron. She turned, holding the bowl she had been spooning food into and handed it to Uma. One nod of the head was the only greeting Uma got. "Put on table," the woman said. Uma obeyed. She got the idea everyone obeyed her.

"Uma, this is my great-aunt, Annie Runningdeer," Lovie continued the introduction.

"I'm pleased to meet you, Mrs. Runningdeer," Uma said as she placed the bowl of mashed potatoes on the table.

"Get salad from refrigerator," came the command.

Uma did as told.

"Louvinia, you put on shoes. Is not proper to come to the table bare foots."

Uma looked at Lovie, eyebrows raised in question. "Louvinia?" she mouthed.

"That's my name . . . Louvinia," Lovie answered. "But when I was a baby people started calling me Lovie, and it's been that ever since. Except for Auntie."

"Uma, you go call Bix to eat," the older woman said.

"If he is hurting, he may want to eat in his room," Lovie commented, "like he has been."

"He will come," Annie said.

"Yes, Mrs. Runningdeer." Uma started toward the door into the dining room. She stopped, holding the swinging door open, and asked, "Where is his room?"

"Oh . . ." Lovie said as she picked up a platter of fried meat. "Go through that door," she said, using her elbow to point to a different door. "That's the back hall. Turn right and knock on the second door on the left. That was the office until Bix broke his leg in that stupid stunt. Now it's his bedroom, at least until he can get up and down the stairs again."

Uma followed the directions, finding herself in a shadowy hallway. *This must be where Bix came from when I first arrived.* Rapping lightly on the heavy door, she heard his growl. "What do you want?"

"Dinner is on the table."

Silence, then the sound of clomping crutches, followed by the opening of the door. Bix's hair stuck every which way, as it had when she first saw him. Behind him she saw a hospital bed pushed against one wall, a reclining chair next to it, and piles of newspapers, magazines, and books on the floor. On the opposite end of the room was a large desk, piled with papers and ledgers. A bookcase to the side was packed with books and framed photos. Under all the clutter was an ornate rug. Uma couldn't see enough to really judge but thought it might be old and very beautiful. She kept *her* surroundings neat, a result of living her young years struggling to make some sort of sanctuary in the place she called home. She felt an itch tingling inside—an itch to get into all those papers and do something with them. She felt a real need to exercise her forte: put everything in order.

"Dinner, huh?"

"Yes, and it looks delicious."

"Lovie's been bringing me my dinner."

"Mrs. Runningdeer told me to call you to the table."

He sighed. "Well, if Annie said that, I guess I'd better come, or else I won't get anything to eat." He clung to the door with one hand and a crutch with the other. "I'll wash up and be there in a minute."

Chapter 12

There were four places set at the big kitchen table, so Uma wasn't surprised when both Lovie and Annie sat down to eat. Bix clumped into the room just as the women were taking their seats. His hair was damp and combed into order, and he had changed from the rumpled outfit he had been wearing previously. Now his jeans—missing one leg—and shirt looked as if they had been pressed. The smile on his face indicated he was in a better mood than when Uma had knocked on his door a few minutes earlier.

As he sat down and pulled the napkin over his lap, Annie spoke. "We will thank the Great Spirit for the food and for this one He has sent to this house." Lovie and Bix looked surprised but bowed their heads. Uma followed suit. They had never prayed in their home growing up, but *when in Rome,* she thought. When Annie picked up the bowl of potatoes and started serving herself, Uma opened one eye, then the other. Seeing the other two looking around, she came to the conclusion that they, too, were uncertain of what to do. Soon, the food was being passed from one to another.

"Was that the telephone I heard earlier?" Lovie asked Bix.

"Yes. It was Tom," he replied. "Checking in."

Uma almost choked on the sip of tea she had just taken. "When will he be home? I'll bet he was surprised to hear I was here."

"I didn't tell him," Bix said as he put salad on his plate.

"Didn't tell him!" Lovie exploded.

"Why not?" Uma asked, caught between tears and anger.

"Well . . ." Bix chewed on his food and swallowed before continuing. "For one thing, he has some important deals to take care of before he comes home. If he knows Uma is here, he either might quit and come home right now—which is no good—or he might be so distracted he can't negotiate the best contract."

Both Lovie and Uma sat back in their chairs and looked at him. Although it hurt her heart to think about it, Bix was right. If Tom was in charge of something important, he needed to tend to that before thinking about his sister. Both she and Tom had learned a lesson from their upbringing: you need to take care of what needs taking care of. Not doing that can lead to all sorts of things, like missing the field trip at school or the electricity or water being turned off. And if Bix told him she was there, he might start worrying about why and . . . She took her napkin from her lap and placed it beside her plate, her appetite gone.

"But I told him I had a surprise for him when he came home." Bix grinned.

"But you didn't tell him what it was?" Lovie said.

"No. Didn't even hint at it." Bix took another bite. "He tried to make me tell, but I told him it would be waiting for him when he got here." He looked at Uma and smiled. "And you will be, won't you?"

Uma could only stare at the man sitting across from her. He wasn't her stepfather playing mean tricks on her. Although there were lessons from the past she carried with her, she knew she shouldn't let suspicion cloud her judgment of everyone and everything. Nobody was trying to take something from her, cheat her of seeing her brother. She wasn't being manipulated into doing anything. *Take a deep breath!*

Lovie giggled. "Boy, is he going to be surprised."

"He will be pleased to see his sister," Annie said.

"And she will be pleased to see him," Bix said. "I could see the fire shooting from her eyes when I said I hadn't told him she was here." He reached over and put his hand over hers where it lay on the table. "You'll see him, darlin', I promise." He gave her hand a gentle squeeze.

"They do that all the time," Lovie said. "Play tricks and torment each other. They are just alike—big teases, both of them."

Uma thought back to when they were kids. There wasn't much to tease about, but Tom did have a sense of humor that wasn't as strong in Uma. She was always waiting on the worst, and it often happened. Tom expected the worst, too, but he still joked about it.

She picked up her napkin and spread it in her lap again. At first picking at the food then savoring the home-cooked meal on her plate, she soon discovered her appetite kicking in. Staring off into space, her fork held in her hand, she thought, *This is the first time I've really felt like eating since Alex died.* Her stomach wouldn't let her ignore the steak, mashed potatoes, salad, and corn. She took another bite, thinking how good it tasted.

"Uma . . . Earth to Uma! Come in Uma!" Lovie was trying to get her attention.

"Oh . . . sorry!" Uma wiped her mouth with her napkin lest a bit of gravy had missed the mark. "I was just thinking how good this is."

"I was asking what places you have been to," Bix asked. "Tom told us you move around for your job."

"Exactly what is your job?" Lovie asked.

"I'm an editorial assistant."

"Which means what?" Bix shot back.

Uma picked up her biscuit and reached for the butter. "Well, when a professional person, say a college professor or researcher, a doctor of some sort, wants to publish a paper or a book in his field of study, it needs to be put together so it reads logically, whether for the public or for a set of professionals in that field. There are things to be concerned with, like footnotes, endpapers, forwards, attribution of quotes, references to previously published studies, all sorts of things. Added to that, you have to worry about where it is being published, in America or Great Britain, in a book or magazine or journal."

"And these smart people who are going to be published can't do it themselves?" Bix asked.

"Oh, they probably could, but while they are writing the core of what they want to say, I can be putting it in order in half the time. And it will be right." She took a sip of tea. "The first time."

"It looks like that is something a college professor would know how to do," Lovie said, frowning. "A couple of my professors had articles published."

"They can handle articles, usually. It's when you get to books that it gets more complicated. And one of the biggest problems is explaining what is going on in language everyone can comprehend. It's a fine line between using words other experts know and those that the reading public understand. Assuming you want to make sales over a large buying base, and most do."

"You were in Seattle for a while, weren't you?" Bix asked. "What were you working on there?"

"A volume on the flora and fauna of the Pacific Northwest and its importance to America, especially in the past."

"The past?" Lovie said.

"Yes, and in the future. And how logging, owls, salmon, and so forth, not only influenced elections and business trends, but exploration and politics in the past century and prior to that." She stopped talking to take another bite of potatoes. "The professor who wrote it knew what he was talking about but putting it down so other folks could understand it was another thing. He skipped from one thing to another, and nobody could follow his train of thought."

"Until you came along," Bix said.

"Until I came along," Uma agreed. That was one thing she could speak out about. She was good at her job, but she wouldn't get a new one if she didn't let people know. Although, how an oil and cattle man in Texas could help her get a new assignment, she didn't know. "His work kept being rejected by publishers until I made it sound interesting. We got a contract immediately after that."

Lovie spoke up. "You said 'we.' Do you get credit?"

"I get paid. That's good enough." But somewhere deep inside, she had hoped for more. Dr. Abernathy hadn't given her any recognition, but Dr. Bellows had done so when his book about renegades and outlaws from New Mexico was published. Something inside Uma urged her not to be prideful, that she hadn't done all that research and writing, but then came the twinge of vanity that she had a hand in getting the work out in public.

"Where did you go from Seattle?" Bix asked. "Tom didn't hear from you after that, and he began to get worried."

Uma placed her fork on the table and folded her hands in her lap. This was the part that was going to be hard to talk about. "I went to Alaska."

"Alaska?" Lovie said, her voice raising a pitch. "Really? What's it like up there? Did you see any polar bears?"

"It was cold," Uma said, glancing toward the exuberant woman. "I saw one bear. It wandered by the cabin one day, on its way to someplace else, but it wasn't a polar bear."

"What kind of project were you working on?" Bix asked.

"A compilation of Eskimo, Aleut, and Inuit folktales," Uma answered.

"That sounds interesting. When will it be published?"

"I don't know," she answered. Taking up her fork, she began to poke at the remains of her salad.

"Did you live out in the wild somewhere?" Lovie asked. "Or in a town?"

"At the edge of a village. There were stores and a café." She laid the fork down again. "A doctor. People."

Annie was watching Uma intently. She pushed back from the table and said, "Time for cake. Louvinia, help serve, please." When everyone was eating their cake, she said, "Louvinia should write book of Cherokee stories. Not many of us old ones left who remember the tales of our grandparents." She turned to her niece. "You write it now while I'm still alive."

"I'd rather be writing mysteries," Lovie said.

"Oh, you write?" Uma asked.

"I play at writing sometimes."

"Fiction? Mysteries?"

"Yes. Only fiction. Anything else bores me."

"Put Cherokee stories in your mysteries," Annie said. "So they do not die." Lovie was quiet.

"Actually, that's a good idea," Uma said. "Something to set you apart from other writers."

Everyone was silent, enjoying the strawberry cake, when Lovie said, "Could you help me? That is, help me get started? If I decide to try to write, that is?"

"I'd be glad to," Uma said. "But I'm not familiar with fiction. I've never had time to read just for the pleasure of it." She'd talk about it now though—anything to keep the discussion off Alaska.

"Bix and Uma, you go sit on porch," Annie instructed. "Louvinia will help with dishes."

"I'll help as well," Uma said.

"No. First night you guest. Tomorrow you help," Annie said.

"Come sit outside with me," Bix said. "It's cooler now that the sun is setting."

"I'll be out directly," Lovie said. "It won't take long to load the dishwasher. I'll bring tea out when I come."

"Dishwasher?"

"Yes. My father bought it before he and Mom decided to move to the coast." Bix said.

"It's like a cabinet," Lovie explained, "hooked up to the water. You put the dishes in it, and it washes them for you."

"I've never heard of such a thing," Uma said.

Annie sniffed. "Aunt Annie doesn't think much of it," Lovie said. "But she uses it," she added in a whisper.

Chapter 13

The western sky was streaked with hues of pink, gold, and orange as Uma and Bix settled into rockers on the front porch. "This is lovely," Uma commented, more to break the silence than to start a conversation.

"Yeah," Bix agreed as he adjusted a pillow under his leg. He sighed and rocked back a bit, looking around the landscape. The yellow cat rubbed up against his other leg, and he leaned over and lifted it onto his lap. "See that line of trees over there?" He motioned toward the left. "That's Rio de los Brazos de Dios. The Brazos River."

"It's quite different than where it runs into the Gulf," Uma said.

"That's what Tom says," Bix replied. "River of the Arms of God. That's what the name means."

"We learned that in Texas history class in high school," Uma said. "Or maybe it was elementary school. I don't remember."

"It means the river can give life or take it away. It's all up to God."

"I guess everything is all up to God, when you get right down to it," Uma said. *Is God sending me this baby?* she wondered as she placed her hand on her growing belly.

"I guess." He leaned his head against the chair back. "They found a body in it a year or so back, down near the Gulf."

"Some poor soul drowned. It happens from time to time."

"No. Actually it was some gangster from back east. He was shot."

Uma shivered. "Does your leg hurt much?" she said to change the subject. She didn't like to think of death in any form. Death had taken away her papa and Alex.

"It's a bit better. At least now one pain pill makes it bearable. It has been a . . . uh, it's been bad." They sat in companionable silence as the sun sank farther into the horizon. The cat jumped down and walked away. "This is the first time in months I've sat out here and watched the sun go down," Bix said. "Mom and Dad liked to come out here after supper, and when everyone was home and us kids were little, we would sit out here and watch the fireflies." The little dots of blinking light were beginning to show themselves under the massive live-oak trees that were scattered about the yard. "We kids would try to catch them in jars, and Mom would make us turn them loose before we went to bed. She said if we tried to keep them, they'd just die, and then we wouldn't have any fireflies."

The ringing of the telephone sounded faintly inside the house, and a moment later Lovie stuck her head out the front door. "Bix, Vicky Powell is on the phone for you."

He shook his head. "Tell her . . ."

"I'm not going to lie for you, Bix," Lovie said.

"Tell her I really don't feel up to talking on the phone right now."

"OK. I guess I can say that without lying, but I'm getting tired of fending off your women. You need to do that yourself," Lovie said and withdrew into the house.

His women? Uma thought it best to ignore that whole exchange. "Tell me about your family. You have brothers and sisters?" Uma asked.

"One sister and one brother," Bix answered. "Sarah is eight years older than I am. Actually, she is my dad's niece. He and Mom adopted her before I was born."

"She's a pilot, right? Lovie mentioned her. I'm staying in her room, I believe."

"Yeah. She's something else, Sarah is. Then there's my younger brother, Barnett. We call him Barney. He's . . . different from the rest of the family."

Uma didn't know if she should ask different how or not, but Lovie was coming out the front door at the time and heard Bix's comment. She provided the answer.

"Barnett isn't interested in cattle or oil, which is what this family revolves around. Barnett has gone to California to make movies." She placed the tray she was carrying on the small table between the two rockers. Taking one glass of tea, she moved to the swing at the end of the porch, putting it in motion with a push of her foot. "To Bix and his parents, there is something wrong with anyone who doesn't live for cattle and oil."

"Oh Lovie. It's not that bad," Bix protested.

"Just about," Lovie countered.

"Those are two diverse things," Uma said, hoping to ward off a tiff between the two, who seemed to act like a brother and sister themselves.

"Mom owned this ranch before she married Dad," Bix answered. "It was a cattle ranch, and after her father, 'Big B' Barnett, died and both her brothers died, she ran it by herself. Not long after they married, oil was discovered on Big B land. So now there's both. Cattle and oil."

"So you were named after your grandfather," Uma said.

"No, I was named after Mom's brother, Bix, short for his mother's maiden name, Bixley."

"So he is Bix Junior," Lovie said.

"I assume that since your parents live in Galveston, your sister is in Waco flying airplanes, and your brother is in California making movies, that you are the one running the Big B now?"

Bix sighed. "It looks like it. Not that I'm happy about it."

Uma didn't know what to say about that. It seemed to her that she was finding out far too much about the Crandall family business. *Why should an outsider—and that's what I am—need to know whether Bix is or isn't happy about running the family business?*

"That's where Tom comes into it."

So my brother fits into this wealthy oil and cattle empire in some way. Maybe I do want to know about the Crandall family.

"Actually, there is more to Big B Enterprises than just cattle and oil. The corporation owns property all over the state: storage facilities for grain, cotton, oil, whatever." He shifted his leg once again, and Lovie rose from the swing and went to the other end of the porch. She returned with a low stool, which she placed in front of Bix, moving the pillow onto it.

"Here. Prop it a little higher and see if that helps."

Bix swung the cast up, grimacing when he placed it on the stool. Uma stood up and took the pillow that had been behind her back. She carefully lifted his foot and placed the cushion on top the other one.

"Thanks. That's better," Bix said. He leaned back, took a swig of tea, and continued his story. "Thanks to Dad's brother, Thomas, and Sarah, we are now heavily invested in aeronautics, but Tom thinks we ought to diversify more—put more resources into various areas. We had a professor at A&M that stressed putting your eggs in more than one basket. If the price of cattle is down and the price of oil is down, have other sources of revenue.

"Tom thinks that's the way to go. I agree it's a good idea, but I don't want to be in charge of doing it. I'm interested in the cattle part of the business. The oil pretty much takes care of itself—the company that holds the leases pays us our part, and all I have to do is keep records. Or really, look over the records the accountant keeps. I don't want to run all over the state buying more property."

"So you have Tom doing that?" Uma asked.

"Yep."

"So you didn't want him to quit and come back if he knew I was here." It was a statement, not a question.

"You got it."

Uma was silent only for a few seconds. "I totally agree with you," she said.

Bix looked at her, eyebrows raised. "I'm glad you do," he said. "I wouldn't want to be the cause of any trouble between the two of you, but I needed this business taken care of, and I'm in no condition to do it myself." He swung his foot down and rose to his feet. "And now, ladies, if you will excuse me, I think it is time for me to take another pain pill and go to bed."

Uma agreed. "I'm tired too. This has been a long day for me." *After a long and tiring week.*

Lovie rose and picked up the tray of glasses. "Me three. I'm on my way to bed. I'm reading a good book, and I want to find out what happens next."

As the women followed Bix to the front door, Uma held the screen open for Lovie, and as she passed, Uma asked, "Were you serious about writing books? Is that something you are considering?"

"I've been thinking about it. It's something I could do wherever I am, and for now I am here with Auntie." They entered the foyer, and Lovie paused on her way to the kitchen. "I'd like to talk to you about it tomorrow, see what you think, if you don't mind," she said.

"I don't mind at all," Uma responded. As she ascended the steps, she thought, *I can see how Tom became so close to this family. They make you feel like you are a part of it.*

Chapter 14

The next morning the smell of coffee drew Uma down to the kitchen. The pungent aroma had been unsettling to her stomach for several weeks, but suddenly it stirred her taste buds, and she craved a cup.

"Good morning," she greeted Annie as she entered the room. "How are you this morning, Mrs. Runningdeer?"

"I am good," the stout Cherokee woman answered. "You call me Annie, like rest of family."

Rest of family? So I'm a member of the family now? Funny she should say that. After only one day, this household is beginning to feel like family to me. I'm more at home here than I was with Mom and Cindy.

Uma took a cup from the stack setting near the coffee maker and filled it. Sugar and cream sat nearby, and she laced the brew liberally.

"You drink coffee like your brother," Annie observed. Uma smiled. She couldn't comment. She hadn't been around Tom enough to know how he took his coffee.

"Good morning," Lovie said as she entered from a door at the back of the kitchen. "It's a beautiful day, isn't it?" The slim young woman was dressed much as she had been the day before, in jeans and a tee shirt. This day her gray shirt displayed a logo, green wings on each side of the words "Waco Airport."

"Good morning," Uma replied. Lovie saw her reading the words on her tee and, pulling it taut to make it more legible, said, "It's my latest shirt—a gift from Sarah."

"Very nice."

"I'm glad you got comfortable today. You were so dressed up yesterday," Lovie said.

"Me? Dressed up?" Uma looked down at her jeans. She had on a tee shirt as well, but it was mostly covered with an unbuttoned long-sleeved cotton shirt.

"Yes, you. I seldom wear a dress. Only when I have to go someplace special."

"You ought to see me when I'm at work in an office on campus," Uma said, adding a little hot coffee to her cup.

"More dressed up than yesterday?" Lovie asked, "Or more casual?"

"Dresses like yesterday's, cotton shirtwaists, would be fairly casual. Usually I'd wear a suit or a dressier outfit."

"Why?"

"To make myself seem . . . well, older, more experienced, important, maybe."

"Doesn't the fact that you know what you are doing and your recommendations prove you're up to the job?"

"You'd think so, wouldn't you?" Uma said. "But you have to look the part as well."

"I'll bet if you were a man you wouldn't have to dress just so," Lovie commented.

"I don't know about that. They have their own dress code." Uma took a spoon from the counter and stirred her coffee. "Maybe someday I'll have a big enough reputation that I can dress any way I darn well please."

Annie opened the oven door and pulled out a big pan of biscuits. The aroma reached all the way to Uma's stomach, which growled. "Louvinia, you cook breakfast. I be back to fix lunch." She started out the back door. "Don't forget Fran is coming to clean house today. See if you can get in Bix's room this time." She closed the door behind her.

"What can I do to help?" Uma asked. Normally she disliked cooking, having had to do it from the time she was a little girl until she left for college.

"You can set the table. The dishes are in that cabinet," Lovie said, motioning toward the right. "There'll be the three of us." She went to the refrigerator and retrieved a bowl of eggs and a plastic container. "And put the butter and preserves out as well."

As Uma worked, she decided to ask, "Who is Fran?"

"She lives in town. She's the housecleaner."

Uma continued working, but finally gave in to her curiosity. "There's a housekeeper, an assistant housekeeper, and a housecleaner?"

Lovie, who was spreading slices of bacon in an iron skillet, laughed and said, "Yeah! It's something, isn't it? See"—she wiped her hands on a brightly colored kitchen towel—"Aunt Annie was first. She came when she was first widowed, when the Barnett kids were small and Mrs. Barnett needed help. Soon after that, Mrs. Barnett became very ill—her heart, I think—and Auntie took care of the household. Mrs. Barnett, she died.

"The sons went off to war, the first war that is, and one didn't come home. The other one, the first Bix, he came home, but then he died, and the father as well. That just left Dorie running the ranch and Auntie taking care of the house. Soon, Dorie married Jonah, and he brought his sister's orphan, Sarah, to live with them. Then they had Bix, and a couple of years later, Daniel Barnett Crandall—Barney—so of course Aunt Annie stayed to take care of the kids.

"Now she is much too old to still be working, but don't tell her that. That's when they worked up this—this charade—with the family, who send her a niece to 'train' how to keep a house."

She turned the bacon in the skillet and, pulling a platter from the cabinet next to the range, covered it with paper towels and started placing pieces across it. "So now Fran comes from town twice a week to vacuum, dust, straighten, do the laundry, anything that is needed." She took an egg from a blue bowl. "You eat fried eggs?" she asked Uma.

"Yes, please. Over easy."

"How many?"

"Just one, thank you."

"Three for me," a voice sounded from the doorway.

Uma looked up from placing eating utensils beside each plate. Much to her surprise, her heart gave a little jump at seeing the tall, handsome cowboy enter the room. His tan cheeks were freshly shaven, and his brown hair neatly combed. The blue checked shirt he wore looked pressed, and his jeans had a crease on the leg that remained intact. The foot not in a cast was clad in a boot with ornate designs running down the side.

"My, my," Lovie commented. "You look like a new man!"

"Peanut helped me shower without getting the cast wet," he said. "And I put on clean clothes."

"I can tell," Lovie said. "You smell better."

"It wasn't that bad," Bix said, frowning. "I didn't stink. I just took a shower a few days ago."

"Well, you smell better now." Lovie cracked an egg into the hot grease. "You and Uma sit down."

Uma took the same seat she had occupied the night before. The aroma of his aftershave reached her, but it wasn't overpowering. It smelled like freshly cut grass mixed with herbs. Not sweet like many men wore.

"Fran is coming today," Lovie said as she scooped grease onto the egg. "We need to put fresh sheets on your bed."

"Have at it," Bix said. "Can I have a cup of coffee?" He sat and waited. Lovie turned, lowered her head, and looked at him, frowning. "Please," he added. "Can I have a cup of coffee, please, Lovie?"

"I'll get it," Uma said, and rose from her chair.

"No, you're a guest," Bix said, reaching for her arm, but he was too late. "You don't need to be waiting on me."

"I need to do my share," Uma insisted. She returned to the table with a mug and carefully set it in front of him. "I'm sure you would get it yourself, if you were able."

Lovie snorted.

"Of course I would," Bix said with an innocent look. "And I'd get one for you if you needed me to." He smiled. Looking at Lovie, he said, "You tell Fran not to touch anything in my temporary room except to change the sheets. Last time, she threw away some important papers."

"Bix, you know Fran did no such thing. She knows not to get rid of anything. With that pile of . . . stuff in there, no wonder you can't find what you want." Lovie slid the platter of bacon onto the table and set a plate in front of Uma. "There you go. Dig in while it's still hot. I'll have Bix a plate in half a minute." She went back to the stove.

"Actually, I have another favor to ask of you," Bix said.

"Anything I can do," Uma answered.

"Would you drive me over to the barn after breakfast?"

"Why can't Peanut do that?" Lovie asked.

"Because, *Louvinia*, I want Uma to do it."

Lovie looked back and forth between them as she put the plate of eggs in front of Bix. She shrugged and went back to the stove to tend to her own eggs.

"I'll be glad to," Uma answered, "but are you sure you feel up to it? It won't be too much?"

"I'm sure," he replied as he took two biscuits from the basket Lovie placed on the table.

"We have orange juice," Lovie announced as she looked in the refrigerator. "Anybody besides me want some?"

"Yes, please," Uma said.

"Yes, please, Louvinia," Bix said. Lovie shot him a dirty glance. "Actually, I'm not hurting much this morning. I slept well, and I took a pain pill before I took my shower. I'm doing good." He used his knife to break the biscuits into layers and put a large dollop of butter inside each. "I just want to be sure everything is going all right over there."

"I'll be happy to drive you," Uma said.

When the three had eaten their fill, Bix said, "I'll meet you back here in the kitchen in ten minutes. OK?" and left the room.

"I'm glad to see him feeling better," Lovie said as she and Uma cleared the table. "His appetite is back to normal, and he must not be in as much pain to want to go visit the barn. It's been hard on him to be laid up like this."

Uma wiped the table with a damp rag as Lovie loaded the dishes into a strange cabinet with racks inside. *That has to be the dishwasher that was mentioned last night.* "I'll just run upstairs to freshen up," she said, rinsing out the cloth and spreading it over the divider in the sink.

Back in her room, she looked at herself in the mirror. She'd have to do something about clothing soon. Her jeans were unbuttoned, her growing waist covered with the blue tee-shirt she wore. Unfortunately, that item of clothing fit tightly over her rapidly expanding breasts, so she disguised that embarrassing feature with a plaid shirt, left unbuttoned since it no longer reached far enough to be worn as it was intended without gaps showing. *Maternity clothes aren't far away. I thought I could make it longer than this. I need to figure out where I'll be and where I'll be working before I spend any more money on clothing.*

She brushed her hair and tied it back with a ribbon. At the last minute, she applied pink lip gloss before returning to the kitchen.

"There you are," Bix said as she entered the room. "I thought you'd ditched me."

Uma blushed. "Oh, no! I'd never . . . I said I would . . ."

"Bix," Lovie said, "stop teasing her. Can't you tell she's not used to your bull?"

Bix looked at Uma, then at Lovie, then back at Uma.

"I remember you telling me," Lovie said, "warning me really, that Tom was like that when you first met him. He didn't know how to take teasing. He wasn't raised with teasing that wasn't hateful or mean. Well, this is his sister. She's not used to it either."

Bix looked abashed. "I'm sorry," he said to Uma. "I knew you wouldn't go back on something you said. I was just joshing you." He picked up a large western hat lying on the kitchen table, put it on, and grasped the crutches under his arms. "I'll try to do better." He swung toward the back door. "And if I do it again, you just bat me down." He took a couple of steps. "Just treat me like Mighty Mouse does. Like I'm her pesky older brother." As he reached the door, he stopped, looked at Uma, and smiled. "No. That's not right. I definitely don't want you to treat me like I'm your brother."

Chapter 15

When Uma followed Bix through the door, she expected to find herself outside. Instead, she was in a room that appeared to be a combination of mud room and laundry room. Against the left wall was a long bench, underneath which were several pairs of boots in various colors, sizes, and types. Behind the bench, on the bead-board-covered wall, there were hooks, some of which held raincoats or jackets. To the right of the door were a washer and dryer, both busily performing their respective tasks. Beyond them was a deep sink, and across from the group, under windows looking out onto the backyard, was a large table. At the far right end of the room was an ironing board, set up ready for use.

Bix proceeded to the next door, flung it open, and started down a wooden ramp topped with a rubber mat.

"My car is parked out front," Uma said as she followed him.

"*My* car is parked out here in the car barn," Bix shot back. "You can drive a stick shift, can't you?"

"No."

"No?" Bix came to a stop. "You can't drive a stick shift?"

"No," Uma said. "I don't drive a stick shift." She wasn't about to admit that Tom had taught her how when he was teaching her to drive, back when they both were teenagers. That was a long time ago, and Uma didn't know if she could remember how. She wasn't about to embarrass herself trying to do it now.

"Darlin', your education is sorely lacking," Bix said.

"Your *manners* are sorely lacking," Uma retorted. She immediately regretted the remark. It wasn't like her to say such a thing, but she wasn't going to apologize. If she had talked like that when she was younger, it would have earned her a beating. When Tom finally came home and she was able to talk to him about her situation, she was leaving, getting away from Bix, a complete smart aleck.

"I guess you'd better go get yours, then," Bix said.

Uma cut around the side of the house, pulling the car keys from her jeans pocket. When she pulled around to the backyard, Bix was standing on the grass next to the dirt drive that led to the building across the yard from the house. She parked next to him and killed the motor. Opening her door, she slid out and went around the front of the car to help him manage getting into the low vehicle. By the time she had reached him, he had pulled off his cowboy hat and tossed it on the dashboard, gotten himself into the passenger seat, and swung the cast into the vehicle. Uma helped him get the crutches inside, slammed the door, and returned to the driver's seat.

"It's down that drive," Bix pointed to their left toward a large barn about a quarter mile away.

"How do you like your car?" he asked, patting the dash as if it were a dog—or a horse.

"I've only been driving it a few days," Uma said. "It's a rental. It's OK."

"A rental, huh?"

"Yes. I sold my last car in Seattle. I won't buy again until I'm settled somewhere."

"We're thinking about putting a car rental place in one of our airports," Bix said.

One of our airports?

"But it doesn't really fit in with our other businesses. Park there," he said, pointing to a spot by the large opening at the end of the enormous barn.

Uma pulled up between two pickup trucks, only a couple of many parked in no particular pattern. It looked like people just stopped wherever they were and got out. She opened her door with the intention of helping Bix with the crutches, but when she got to the other side of the car, he was already out and adjusting them under his arms.

Entering through the high, wide opening, Uma saw all kinds of equipment in the cavernous building. She could see now why the entrance was so large—so that the tall or wide pieces of the gear could fit through it.

"Let's go in here," Bix said, veering to the left toward a room with several plate-glass windows looking out into the main part of the building. The word *office* was on the window of the door. A large oak desk sat directly in front, and it had stacks of papers, a cup of pens, and a typewriter on it. It was not what Uma would have expected in a cattle or oil operation. A bookcase sat against the wall to the right, half filled with books. A window air conditioner hummed, filling the space with cool air.

"Uma, darlin'," Bix said in a low drawl, laying his hand on her shoulder, "let me introduce you to my foreman, Ellis Ponder."

Uma stuck her hand out, determined to be businesslike, but each time Bix used the word *darlin'*, she was nearly undone. She knew it was a Texas expression and didn't mean anything like the word *darling*, but it was still hard to take.

"I'm pleased to meet you, Mr. Ponder," she said as he took her hand.

"Ellis, this is Uma Thornton. She's stayin' up at the big house for a spell."

Uma was speechless. *Should I explain that I'm Tom's sister and I'm just waiting for him to come back? Bix makes it sound somewhat inappropriate.*

"Pleased to meet you, Miss Thornton. I hope you enjoy your visit to the Big B."

Uma didn't know what she thought a foreman ought to look like, but this man looked more like an accountant than a cowboy. *Maybe this is what a foreman looks like these days.*

Bix must have read her mind. "Ellis can get out there on the range when it's necessary, but mostly he keeps track of everything that's going on in the cattle part of the Big B," he explained. "He keeps records on every cow on the place. Ellis, where are you keeping Ranger?"

"He's in field B, Bix. We keep check on him. He's got some other horses to keep him company. That little stream runs through the corner of it, and the grass is high. He's doing good."

"Better than I am, probably," Bix said.

"Glad to see you up and around, Boss. The boys were gettin' worried about you. Thought maybe you were broke up worse than we thought."

"I'm mendin', Ellis. I'm mendin'." Bix grinned. "Can't keep a good man down, ya know." He moved the position of his crutches and started to turn. "I'm going to go pay Ranger a visit," he said. "Let him know I haven't forgotten him." He put his arm around Uma's shoulder. "Let's go, darlin'. I want to show you my horse."

He had to remove his arm to manipulate his crutches, and Uma was able to breathe again. They left the barn and walked some yards away, to where a fence marked off what looked to be a couple of acres. Several horses grazed contentedly. Bix raised fingers of both hands to his mouth and gave a loud whistle. In the distance, a chestnut horse raised its head. Bix whistled again, and it came toward them at a fast trot.

"Hey, big boy!" Bix said as the horse nuzzled him. "Did you think I'd forgotten about you?" He rubbed the horse's neck vigorously. "I should have brought you a carrot. Next time, I will." He ran his hand over the glistening neck. "This is Ranger," he said to Uma. "Ranger, this is Uma."

"Hi, Ranger," she said, and tentatively put her hand on the beast's nose.

"Do you ride?" Bix asked.

"No," she answered. "This is the first time I've even touched a horse."

"You're kidding!" Bix stepped back and looked at her. "You're from Texas and you've never touched a horse before?"

"I know. I know. My education is sorely lacking," Uma said.

"May be," Bix said. "But you're learning!"

Chapter 16

Uma suspected Bix had overdone it. On the way to her car, his steps lagged, and his brow was knitted in concentration. When they started back to the house, his hands were curled into fists, and one tapped against his leg the entire way. They rode in silence.

Uma pulled her car onto the closest spot to the ramp and hurried to open the passenger side door for Bix. He managed to get out and started toward the door as Uma noticed Peanut coming across the lawn carrying a peck basket filled to the brim with corn, tomatoes, and squash showing at the top. Since she was behind Bix, and he couldn't see her without turning, she motioned to Peanut to assist Bix. He set the basket down and hurried to Bix's side.

"I've got it!" Bix snapped.

"I know, Boss. I see you do," Peanut answered, but he kept one hand close behind the larger man's back and the other to his side, ready to catch him if he started to topple. They went through the back door as Uma picked up the abandoned basket of vegetables and hurried to catch up.

In the laundry room, Lovie stood at the table, folding towels. "You look like you've been rode hard and put up wet," Uma heard her say as she entered the back door. Bix responded with a grunt as he continued into the kitchen, Peanut still behind and beside him. Lovie quit her task and followed the men. "I'll bet you could use a cold glass of sweet tea," she called out as the two men went into the back hall on their way to Bix's room.

"I was afraid he was doing too much," Uma said as Lovie retrieved large glasses from the cabinet. She picked ones circled with green, red, blue, and yellow rings.

This family even has dishes that make you feel happy. I remember we had glasses like that when I was little, back when Daddy was alive and everything was . . .

"Yeah, but nobody can ever tell Bix what to do," Lovie replied, reaching into the freezer for ice cubes. "You look like you could stand some refreshment too."

"Yes. Thank you. It's getting hot out there, and we did some walking."

"Walking?"

"Up to see Bix's horse, Ranger, and back to the car."

"Bix is a typical cowboy," Lovie said as she poured tea into the two glasses. "He dotes on that horse."

"I'll take it to him," Uma said as she reached for the happy glass. When Lovie stopped pouring and looked at Uma with raised eyebrows, Uma said "What?" and gave a shy smile.

When she reached the bedroom, Bix was sitting on the side of the hospital bed. Peanut had the one boot in his hand. "Just toss it anywhere, Peanut," Bix was saying. That rubbed Uma wrong, but looking around, she couldn't see anywhere that would be a good place to set it. Everything was covered with either clothing or newspapers and magazines.

"Here's your tea," she said, looking for a place to set it.

"Thanks," Bix said as he reached for the glass. "Hand me two of those pills from that bottle." He pointed toward an amber bottle on the desk.

"Two?" Uma questioned. She studied the label, wanting to ascertain whether one or two was the proper dose.

"Yes, two, busy-body. The doctor said I could have two if I needed them."

When the label verified what Bix said, she flipped open the lid and shook two into her hand. She slid them from her palm into his large, calloused one, and he tipped them into his mouth in one quick motion, followed by a swig of sweetened beverage.

"Ahh. That'll do the job," Bix said.

"I was concerned that you were trying to do too much," Uma said.

Bix moved back against the elevated head of the bed and sunk into it contentedly.

"But I did what I had to do," he said.

"Which was?"

"Let the men know that the boss was OK, that a little ol' bull wasn't going to knock me out for long."

"Today did that?"

"It did."

"How?"

"When I appeared on my own two feet, even with a cast on one, with a beautiful woman on my arm, everyone knew I was on the mend." He closed his eyes. "Think I'm gonna take a nap," he said.

Chapter 17

When Uma returned to the kitchen, the phrase "beautiful woman" was floating around in her head. Any time she looked in the mirror, she saw a reasonably attractive woman in front of her. *Clear skin. Hazel eyes. Good hair—long and blond. Not ugly, but . . . beautiful?*

Lovie had a glass of tea in her hand and was headed toward the laundry room. "I have just a little more folding to do. Why don't you go sit on the front porch, and I'll join you in a few minutes?"

"That sounds good to me," Uma said. Picking up her frosty glass, she went through the door into the dining room, then into the foyer and out the front door. Choosing a comfortably cushioned wicker rocker, she settled herself to wait. She looked around the yard and marveled at the towering live oak trees scattered about, limbs bending toward the ground. This was where the fireflies were flitting about the night before. Taking a swallow of cool tea, she let her head fall back farther as she noticed the ceiling was painted a pale blue shade instead of white like the rest of the porch.

Lovie came out the door, her glass in hand. Seeing Uma looking at the ceiling, she said, "I'll bet you're wondering why it's blue, aren't you?"

"Well, I don't know that I was wondering, exactly, just noticing it. But as long as you mentioned it, why *is* it blue?"

"According to Aunt Annie, who is the expert on all such things, Cherokee or not, the porch ceiling is blue to keep the haunts away," Lovie said as she took a seat in a high-backed wooden rocker.

"Haunts?"

"Ghosts. Spirits. Things that go bump in the night."
Lovie took a swallow of tea.

"Huh!" Uma studied Lovie, who didn't look like she
was joking. She looked back above her. There was a certain
connection in her mind between this story and the Alaskan
tales she had been listening to and typing during her last
months. "How does it do that?"

"According to Auntie, they think the blue is water, like an
ocean or something, and haunts don't like water, supposedly.
So they won't cross it to get into the house."

"I'm very glad to hear," Uma said wryly, "that I don't
have to worry about haunts while I am visiting here." She
looked at Lovie to see how she took that statement. You
could never tell how people felt about such things. Lovie
might be a believer in all sorts of mystical beings.

"We've never had a ghost," Lovie said, the corners of
her mouth twitching, "or any other kind of spirit that I know
of. Auntie says that's because the blue ceiling works."

"Uh-huh," Uma murmured and took a sip of tea. She
wasn't going to get into a conversation about ghosts.

"So," Lovie said, "do you think I really could write
fiction? Good enough to publish, I mean?"

"I really don't know," Uma said, thrown by the change
in subject. "I've never read any of your work." She paused
to gather her thoughts. "I've never read much fiction—only
what I was required to read for school. It's not that I didn't
like it, but I had to study so hard that I didn't have time for
reading for pleasure alone."

"That's the opposite than I am," Lovie said. "I love
fiction and only read non-fiction when I had to for school."

"I'm guessing that there is some non-fiction reading an
author would have to do when writing fiction in order that
everything you write is accurate. Facts, that is."

Lovie frowned. "I hadn't thought about it like that, but it's true." She sat rocking as they both looked out over the yard, lost in their own thoughts.

Uma broke the silence. "So what are you thinking of writing? Genre, I mean."

"Mysteries are what I like to read." She wiggled and readjusted herself in the chair. "And when Auntie suggested I include Cherokee stories, it got me to thinking." She leaned forward and placed her glass on the small table at her elbow. "Not that I want to do that, exactly, but I could have a Cherokee hero. I know the culture."

"That sounds like a good idea to me," Uma said.

"And I know the problems of American Indian and white interacting. The different opinions. My family is a mix of races. Sometimes it causes problems."

"There is a saying, 'write what you know'," Uma said. "You would have inside information, so to speak." She took another sip of tea as she thought. "Your protagonist, your detective or police officer or whatever, doesn't have to be male," Uma said. "You could have it be a woman."

Lovie's eyes lit up. "Yes, I could, couldn't I?"

They rocked some more. After a couple of minutes, Lovie said, "You could help me, couldn't you? Help me get started?"

"I don't know how much help I would be. What I do isn't writing, it's organizing what someone else has written. I don't think fiction needs what I do." She set her glass beside the one Lovie had placed on the table. "Besides," she said with a firm voice, "I'm only going to be here until Tom gets back. After I visit with him, I'll be moving on."

"Where will you go?" Lovie asked.

"I don't know yet," Uma said. "Wherever I can find a job." Deep inside her, sadness crept in. *Somewhere there has to be a place for me and my baby.*

Chapter 18

"Lunch, it is on the table," Annie announced, pushing the screen door open. "Time to come eat." She disappeared back into the house.

As Uma walked through the hall she heard the sound of a vacuum cleaner coming from upstairs. She was startled until she remembered that the cleaning lady was scheduled for that day.

The kitchen table was laid with platters of meats and cheeses; white, wheat, and rye breads; mayo and mustard; several kinds of pickles; sliced tomatoes; and a large bowl of salad.

"Go ahead and sit down, Uma," Lovie said. "I'm going to refresh our tea."

"Bix, he sleep," Annie said. "We eat without him." She took her place at the table. When Lovie sat down, Annie said, "We give thanks to Great Father," and lowered her head. A moment later she raised it and reached for the bread.

"A long time ago," she said as she made a sandwich, "many bad things come upon the Big B. Many heartbreaks happen here. But the Great Father sends those who are needed. He sends Bix's father, Jonah, and things gets better. He send us Sarah, who gives us future. Ever since that time, I give thanks to the Great Spirit who watches over us all for sending us those who need to be here." She reached for the bowl of salad. "He send us Daniella." Uma had no idea who Annie was talking about but figured Daniella must be an important member of the family to be mentioned in prayers. "He send us Tom, to be a brother for Bix when his own brother goes far off to California. He send us Louvinia." Annie fixed a piercing gaze on Lovie, who looked away from it. "And now he send us Uma, for this to be her sanctuary, her home."

Uma didn't know what to say to that, so she said nothing. Lovie, too, seemed to be speechless. They were sitting silently eating when a gray-headed, plump older woman stuck her head in the door from the back hall.

"I'm all through, so I'm going now. I didn't do a thing for that pigsty Bix calls a room. He took onto me something fierce last time when all I did was stack the newspapers all neat for him. I did change the sheets on his bed and brought some dishes and glasses to the kitchen." She turned to leave. "I'll be back next week," she said and disappeared.

"Thank you, Fran," Lovie called out.

"You're welcome," came the muffled reply, followed by the sound of the front door closing.

"I go now and take nap," Annie announced. She picked up her plate and put it in the sink. "There is ham for dinner, and potatoes and eggs boiled to make potato salad. Baked beans be good with it, and sliced tomatoes." She left by the back door, but promptly opened it and added, "Jell-O with fruit and whipped cream for dessert." She closed the door once again.

"Sounds like you are really in training to care for this family," Uma said. "Especially after what she said about God sending you here."

Lovie sighed. "I know, I know. But . . ."

Uma looked at her quizzically. "But?"

"I came with the idea I would stay a few months, a year maybe, and move on. Make a life somewhere. But now . . ."

"But now you might stay?"

"No, I won't be staying, I don't think. But everything has changed."

"How so? If I may ask."

"I can't really talk about it right now, Uma. But when we . . . when I'm sure, you'll be one of the first people to know."

Uma used her fork to take another piece of cheese from the platter and place it on her plate. She cut it into bites with her fork as she said, "Like what she said about me. That this was to be my sanctuary and home. But I'll be leaving as well. As soon as I talk with Tom, I'm leaving. So Annie will be disappointed with me too."

"Why will Annie be disappointed with you?" Bix said as he came through the hall door. "Is there anything left? Or have you two eaten it all?" He took his place at the table.

"There's plenty left," Lovie said. She got up and pushed all the food closer to him and went to fix him a glass. "Are you feeling better?"

"Yes indeed. Pain pills and a nap fixed me right up," Bix said and filled his plate.

"Fresh sheets on your bed probably helped you sleep," Lovie commented.

"I slept better because Fran didn't touch my stuff," he retorted. Lovie snorted.

"I'm curious," Uma said. "What's with all the newspapers and magazines?"

"It's like this," Bix said as he assembled a tall sandwich with several layers of meat, two kinds of cheese, slices of tomato, and lettuce he picked out of the salad. "Tom and I think that Big B Enterprises ought to diversify. Go more directions." He paused and took a big bite of his creation. When he could talk again, he said, "I've subscribed to several business magazines and to newspapers from all over with the idea of being ahead of trends, seeing where the world is headed." He took another bite, and tomato juice rolled down his chin. He picked up his napkin and wiped his face.

"So, I've got all these magazines and newspapers, and since I got hurt, I haven't been able to keep up with them, so they're piling up."

"Be honest, Bix," Lovie said. "You weren't keeping up with them before you and the bull got into that tussle."

"Well . . ."—he took a swallow of tea—"there is that, of course." He continued eating.

"You need a system," Uma said. "How do you find something now when you want it?"

Bix looked sheepish. "I rummage through the papers until I find it . . . *if* I find it."

"Throwing the ones you aren't using to one side?" Uma guessed.

"Yeah." Poking the meat and cheese that was trying to escape back between the bread, he took another bite.

"So, you need a way to find what you want easily."

"Easier said than done." A full mouth made it sound like "e-er ad tha un", but Uma deciphered it.

"That's your job, isn't it Uma?" Lovie asked. "Organizing projects?"

"Well, I organize the parts of a project for putting it into written form."

"Maybe you could figure out something for Bix. You have to admit it, Bix," Lovie said, turning to him. "It is beyond anything now. You couldn't find anything if you tried."

Bix wiped his mouth. "Could you?" he said, looking at Uma. "That is, would you? Take a look at what I have and make some suggestions?"

"I'd be glad to," Uma said. The piles of debris she was seeing anytime his bedroom door was open had set her organizational skills into alert mode. "I could see what might be done."

"Great!" Bix said and grinned.

"But I can't promise," Uma hurriedly added, "to be able to do anything usable. I've never worked on anything like this before." *But in a way, it is like the enormous amounts of notes in all forms that Dr. Abernathy presented me with. Could this be any harder?*

Chapter 19

Uma's head swirled with the amount and variety of all the printed material Bix was hoarding. "Can we stack these according to some category?" she asked him when they started.

"How do you mean?" he asked.

"At the very least, to start with, stack newspapers together and magazines apart from the papers."

"Yeah, sure. We can do that. They just got all mixed up when I was trying to follow a thread of information. Like finding something in a ranching magazine and then trying to go to the newspaper for that same area to cross-reference it." They worked together for half an hour, stacking magazines by name and placing the piles neatly in front of the bookshelves that covered most of one wall.

"The newspapers are the worst," Uma said as she looked around the room. "Do you really need to keep every one of these papers? What parts do you need?"

"Well, I guess I don't need all the papers. Maybe."

"You don't need the obituaries. You don't need the wedding announcements. You don't need the funny papers. Do you?" Uma was relentless.

"No, smart ass. I don't."

"So, why are you keeping everything?"

"Because I don't know what to do with what I do want."

"Hmm. Let me think about that," Uma said. "What is it that you do want?"

"Articles about business in an area, and I need to be able to go back and see that they may need more warehouses, or grain silos, or . . . or anything Big B Enterprises could provide and collect rent on."

"OK. What else?"

"The classifieds, along with any special ads about property for sale. We might want to see about buying in various parts of the state."

"Wouldn't that be only current listings? Once the property was sold and gone, or you had decided you didn't want to buy it, couldn't you throw the paper away?"

"No, because I need to keep up with whether it comes back up for sale months later, or compare it to other property that comes on the market."

"I see."

By late afternoon, they had the newspapers stacked by city. Bix had several arriving daily: Houston, Dallas, Fort Worth, Amarillo, San Antonio, Lubbock, and smaller cities as well; Waco, Beaumont, Marshall, Mexia, and others that were on the outskirts of the large metropolises.

"Bix, there has to be another way to do this," Uma said, tired of sorting papers. There would never be an end to it with more arriving daily. She pushed her chair back from the desk. "This isn't working now, and it isn't going to work in the future."

"You say it isn't, but this is the way we found property for sale in Lubbock and in Houston that Tom is checking on right now. He's looking at a warehouse in Lubbock as we speak," Bix argued.

"Let me think about it," Uma said. "You can't overwork me. It's in my contract." She stood up. "I'm getting a glass of lemonade and going to the front porch."

Bix got on his crutches and followed her out of the room. "You just think I can't overwork you," he said. "I'll tell you something. You don't have a contract, so I can work you all I can get away with."

Uma held in a laugh. "You won't get away with much." They went down the hall and into the kitchen. Uma went to the cabinet and retrieved a glass. "Do you want something to drink too?"

"Yes, please," Bix said.

"Lemonade or tea?" Uma asked as she pulled a pitcher of lemonade from the refrigerator.

"Whatever you are having is fine with me," he answered.

She poured two glasses of lemonade and asked, "Do you want to sit in here, or do you want to join me on the porch?"

"The porch sounds good."

Uma led the way through the dining room, into the front hall, and pushed open the screen door. She expected to find Lovie there, but she and Bix were the only ones to take advantage of the lowering of the sun and cooler temperatures. She led the way to the corner of the porch, where it made the turn to run down the east side of the house. Placing one glass on a wicker table, she took the other and sat on the swing, pushing it into motion with her foot. Bix settled himself into a wooden rocker next to where his glass sat. "Didn't want to sit next to me, huh?" he asked.

"What do you mean?"

"You put my glass clear over here where I couldn't reach it if I sat next to you."

"Oh . . . I, uh . . ." Uma didn't know what to say. She was sure her cheeks were red. She didn't know how to deal with Bix and was afraid she'd hurt his feelings.

"I'm sorry . . ."

"Relax," Bix said, grinning. "I'm just teasing. You really don't know how to take a little playful banter, do you?" He leaned far forward until he could reach her leg. He placed his hand on her knee and squeezed it. "If I'd really wanted to, darlin', I'd have set next to you, even with the glass clear over here." He released her and sat back, reaching for his cool drink.

"So here you two are," Lovie said as she came through the front door. "Got it all straightened up, have you?"

"Not hardly," Bix said. "I think Uma is overwhelmed."

"I'll get a handle on it," she countered. *And you.*

Lovie walked over and took a seat in another rocker. "I think I need to buy a typewriter," she said.

"What for?" Bix asked.

"To write books."

"You're going to write books?"

"Yep! I'm going to try anyway."

"What kind of books?"

"Murder mysteries, or something like that. With a Cherokee woman detective."

"Wow!" Bix looked at Lovie, eyes wide. "What brought this on?"

"Well, I was talking to Uma and Aunt Annie, and the idea came up."

"That's a big idea to come up with," Bix said.

"I've been playing around with the idea of writing fiction for some time now. I've written some short stories and really enjoyed the process. Aunt Annie was saying I ought to write Cherokee stories, and I said I was thinking more along the lines of mysteries. Uma suggested I combine the two with a Cherokee . . . protagonist? Is that the word?" Lovie turned toward Uma.

"Yes. Protagonist. That's the word."

"So, I've been making some notes about a plot. But I need a typewriter to do it right. When I was in college, I could use one in the library. I need to buy one of my own." She turned to Bix. "Can I use a car in the morning to go to town and look for one?"

"Sure," Bix agreed. "Any one you want."

"Or I can drive you in," Uma said.

"Oh! Would you?" Lovie said. "I'd love your help in picking one out. That's something I know nothing about."

"I'd be glad to," Uma said.

"I thought you'd help me with my papers and stuff," Bix said petulantly. Uma couldn't tell if he was serious or teasing her again.

"Well, you can't have her all to yourself, Bix," Lovie protested. "You have to share her."

"OK," he drawled. "I guess. If I have to." He looked at Uma. "If you come up with an idea to make order out of my chaos, you may go with Lovie to town tomorrow."

"Gee, thanks," Uma said sarcastically. "That's so nice of you."

Bix and Lovie looked at each other. "I think she's catching on," Lovie said.

"Yup! Pretty soon she'll be picking at me just like you do," Bix said.

Chapter 20

The next morning at breakfast Uma quizzed Bix, "Do you have plenty of file folders in your office?"

"Probably not. Only a few, maybe. Why?"

"And paper clips. And small note-size paper?"

"No and no. Are we going to need them for our project?"

"We'll need them for *your* project."

"Then you'd better get them when you are in town with Lovie. You'll be in the office supply store anyway. That's the only place in town to find a typewriter." He took a bite of his eggs. "Or file folders."

Later, as she and Lovie were leaving, Bix pulled her aside to say, "Be sure Lovie gets a good typewriter—the best she needs. I'll call Stewart's Office Supplies and have them put everything on the Big B tab. Both yours and Lovie's. Get everything she needs and everything we are going to need as well."

When they pulled into Cottonport, Uma saw a bustling small town. The courthouse sat in the middle square, and the streets that surrounded it accommodated all sorts of businesses, especially those having a connection with county dealings. Several attorney's offices and a title company were on the east side. Everything a person might need was available somewhere around the square or on the side streets that branched off at each corner. On the south section was a business displaying the words Stewart's Office Supplies and Printing. Uma found a parking place directly in front and angled in.

"I like it that they still have angle parking in Cottonport," Lovie said. "I can parallel park but pulling in like this is so much easier."

"Yes, these wide streets make pull-in parking convenient," Uma agreed.

When they entered Stewart's, the smell of fresh, new paper combined with the pungent tang of ink filled the air. Through a large opening in the back, the sound of a printing press rumbled. "Good morning!" said a pleasant woman behind a counter where she was putting brochures into a box. "How can we help you?"

"I'd like to look at typewriters," Lovie said.

"They're up front to your far right," the woman said. "If you go browse, I'll be there just as soon as I finish packing these in boxes. The Kiwanis folks will be here to pick them up shortly. Getting ready for their pancake breakfast, you know."

Lovie and Uma wandered toward the direction the clerk had indicated. The selection was larger than Uma had anticipated. For a small town, there was a varied assortment of brands and sizes to choose from.

"You'll want an electric model," she said to Lovie. "That's the latest thing, and they do a better, quicker job."

"Won't they be a lot more expensive?"

Uma knew she wouldn't be able to keep it a secret. Might as well say it up front. "Bix said to see that you picked out the best that they had." She had been wondering if Bix and Lovie were a couple—if they cared for each other in more than an employer-employee relationship. This seemed to indicate they were. A typewriter was an odd gift for a lover, but she didn't want to judge.

Lovie's mouth dropped open. "He said that?"

"He sure did. Just before we left."

"My goodness. He pays me well for working on the Big B, and you can see that I don't have much to do. This is very generous of him." She ran her fingers over the keyboard of an IBM model.

"That's a good one you are looking at," Uma said. "It would be an excellent choice."

By the time they left, in addition to the typewriter, they had accumulated a box of paper, two boxes of file folders, paper clips, pads of smaller paper suitable for notes, sticky labels for marking the folders, index cards, and pens. Just to be safe, in case there wasn't one on the ranch, Uma bought a large map of Texas, one that would fit on the wall where the hospital bed sat, along with tape to attach it to the paneling. When she picked out the map, it nudged her to buy pushpins with little flags on them. She bought boxes in several colors. What, exactly, they would be used for Uma didn't know, but it was handier to have them than to have to come back into town when her mind worked out all the details of her organizational plan.

"I guess we'd better get back," Lovie said. "I don't like to leave Auntie there alone to do any work, otherwise I'd suggest we eat at the café before we go home. She'll be fixing lunch, though, and I need to be there to help her."

"She's a worker all right," Uma said. "But I can see why you'd feel that way. I imagine her age is on up there."

"She's in her eighties," Lovie replied. "She still gets around well, but she tires easily. Bix's mother, Dorie, has tried to get her to retire, but she won't even think about it. It's not that she doesn't have any place to go—she has lots of places she could go—but the ranch is home to her."

As Uma pulled into the yard at the Big B, she saw a black pickup truck to the side of the drive at the front of the house. It was parked in the same place Uma had taken when she first arrived, handy to the front door.

"Oh!" Lovie said, her voice rising. "Oh!" she repeated, "He's home!" She opened the passenger door as soon as Uma came to a stop.

On the front porch, a tall man walked out the front door and down the steps. Lovie was out of the car and running toward him before the engine was off. Uma's fingers were still on the keys as she stared at the figure descending from the porch. *Tom!*

Uma opened the driver's door and stepped out of the car. By the time she had closed the door with a slam and looked over the top of the hood, Lovie had reached him. Jumping, she wrapped her arms around his neck and her legs around his body. Tom's arms held Lovie close as they kissed. One of his arms held the slight figure off the ground, while the other worked its way to her head, and his fingers twined into Lovie's black hair, pressing her lips closer to his.

I sure was off about that! Uma thought. *Lovie never gave a clue that she and Tom . . .* Just then, the couple broke the kiss and stared into each other's eyes. Uma started around the front of her car. The movement caught Tom's eye, and he let Lovie slide to stand on her feet.

"Uma? Is it really . . .?" He turned Lovie to one side, his arm still around her shoulders.

"Yes. It's me!" Uma said. Tears began to form at the sight of her beloved brother.

"Bix didn't tell me, the scoundrel," Tom said.

"He wanted to surprise you," Lovie said.

"He sure did that," Tom said as he dropped his arm from around Lovie and started toward Uma. She was almost running when they met and threw their arms around each other.

"I've been worried about you for some reason," Tom said quietly. "It's been so long since you've written."

Uma pulled back and looked him in the face. "And just how was I supposed to write to you when I didn't know where you were?" she accused.

"Well, there was that," he said, grinning. "The last time I wrote you were in Seattle. Are you through with that job?"

Lovie had come to stand by his elbow. "She's been in Alaska," she said.

"Alaska?" He looked from Uma to Lovie and back to Uma.

Uma tried to grin, but the tears grew closer to the surface. "Yes, Alaska."

"What in the world were you doing in Alaska? Do they actually have research projects and book publishing jobs in that part of the world?"

Lovie slapped his arm. "That part of the world, as you call it, is one of the forty-nine states now."

"The project was about Eskimo, Inuit, and Aleut folk stories." Uma got that much out before her throat clogged with unshed tears.

Tom frowned as he looked at his sister. "Let's all go in the house," he said. "We can sit down and hear all about it. Annie is putting lunch on the table." He put one arm around Uma and the other around Lovie as he guided them toward the steps.

As they reached the kitchen table, Bix stepped through the door from the back hall. "How do you like my surprise?" he asked with a grin.

"I love your surprise," Tom said, "but you could have warned me. I might have had a heart attack."

"Naw," Bix countered. "You're young and healthy. I wouldn't have risked my chief negotiator." He took a seat at the table. "And Annie's glad to have you back. Look at this spread she's put on for you." The table was filled with fried chicken, ham, biscuits, and half a dozen bowls of vegetables.

"I've missed your cooking, Annie," Tom said, patting her on the shoulder as she placed a bowl of butter beans between the platter of sliced tomatoes and the bowl of corn on the cob. "They don't cook like this in Lubbock."

"Sit down, sit down everyone," Bix said. "Annie, you too."

Tom took a place between Uma and Lovie, and Annie sat at the far end of the table as she had other times. As Bix's hand reached for the platter of chicken, Annie said, "We give thanks to Great Spirit for bringing Lovie's Tom safely home. Everyone bowed their heads. After a moment of silence, she added, "And for sending us Uma to be part of our family." They remained silent until Annie raised her head and proclaimed, "Is time to eat now."

Chapter 21

When everyone had eaten their fill, everyone but Bix started clearing the table. "Sorry I can't help," he said.

"Yeah, I'll bet you're sorry," Lovie replied.

Bix became serious. "I'd rather be helping than to have tangled with that bull."

"You're plum lucky you weren't hurt any worse," Tom said as he scraped the residue from the plates into the garbage. "You could have been killed."

"Yeah, for a couple of minutes I thought I was going to be," Bix said, "when I couldn't scramble out from under that animal."

Annie pulled off her apron and hung it on a hook by the door to the laundry room. "I go to my room and rest. I come back and make a cake later."

"Her golden boy is home so she's going to make a cake. How come you don't bake me cakes, Annie?" Bix teased.

Annie stopped in the doorway. "All you my family. I bake cakes for everyone. This house needs to be full. Miss Dorie and Mr. Jonah go away to live by ocean. Barney go to live in Hollywood, California, and make movies. Little Bird go to fly airplanes. Daniella come from across the sea, then go to make her own family. Tom come, and then Uma come. House is filling up again. Soon we will see little one come. House be happy to be full again." She went out the door, closing it gently behind her.

"A little one?" Tom murmured and looked at Lovie.

"Do you two have something to tell us?" Bix asked, pointedly.

"No!" they replied in unison.

Uma ducked her head. *How could Annie know?* She couldn't look at anyone, fearing that they would guess her secret. She had to talk to Tom and get his advice. She had to make plans about where to go and what to do. Her pregnancy would begin to show before long, and she needed to decide whether or not to start staging the charade of being a recent widow, and where to settle so she could find a job.

"Sis," Tom put his hand on her shoulder. "You look deep in thought. How about we find some place, and you catch me up on your life?"

Uma shot a watery smile at him. *I never cry, so why am I constantly on the verge of tears these days? Is the baby making me this way?*

"That sounds good to me, but I don't want to take you away from Lovie."

Lovie saw the tears hovering in Uma's eyes and said, "That's OK. You and Tom visit. I'm sure you have plenty to tell each other. I'm going to find Peanut and have him unload the typewriter and the other things we bought."

"Other things!" Bix said. "What did you two do? Buy out the store?"

As Uma and Tom started toward the front porch, he stopped, his hand on her arm. "You look very serious. Do we need a more private place to talk?" Uma nodded her head. "Come on. I have just the right spot." He led her down the steps and to his truck, pulling the keys from his pocket as they went.

They wound over a rutted track leading to the band of trees Bix had pointed out the first night she was there. Snaking among the trees that lined the river's bank, they came to a clearing that eased down to the water. The remains of a campfire indicated the place was a regular meeting place. Several Adirondack chairs surrounded the ashes, and long lengths of coat hanger wire gave evidence of wiener roasts in the past.

"Here we are," Tom said. "No one will bother us here. The track to it is on Big B property, and only the family comes down here."

"And you're part of the family now," Uma said.

"Looks like," Tom replied. "Ever since Bix and I were assigned to be roommates that first year at college, we've been like brothers."

"That's nice," Uma replied. "It's good to have a brother. I would never have made it through those terrible years if not for my brother." She smiled at him as she took a seat.

"I didn't really have a family to go back to after you left for college," Tom said as he picked the chair next to hers. "Even Mom, she didn't seem like family anymore. Her family was that drunk and Cindy. You were my only family."

"And then I was gone as well."

"Yep. Then you were gone as well. So tell me, where have you been? We haven't had a good talk in years. Not since you left Austin to go to Albuquerque. Start there."

Uma told him of New Mexico. Of desert and mountains and clear, starry nights. Of hot-air balloons and fiestas and working on a project she knew nothing about but grew to be fascinated with.

"What about friends? Did you make friends there?"

"Yes. I had friends, but not close ones, like you and Bix. And not many of them."

"Was there a reason for that?"

"Sort of. In my position, I wasn't a member of the faculty nor was I part of the student body. Younger than one group and older than the other, I didn't fit in with either. I shared an apartment with a graduate student, but she spent most of her time either at work or in the library. We were friendly, but not pals. I did have some friends among the secretaries and staff, but most of them were married or had a boyfriend.

"I volunteered at the local animal shelter on Saturdays. I enjoyed that." She was quiet for a few seconds. "I liked working with the dogs. I couldn't have one, not in an apartment, but it seemed like I was making up for . . . for Trixie."

Their minds went to the fox terrier that was the beloved pet of their childhood. Until the night Grady Miller was slapping their mother around and Trixie tried to protect her. Grady's foot sent the small dog flying across the room into a wall and ended their companion's life. They never had another pet, fearing it would meet the same cruel end. *But someday I will,* Uma promised herself. *Sometime, somewhere, when it is safe, I'll have a dog.*

"You didn't have a boyfriend?"

"Not really. I dated a few times, but nothing serious."

"And from there you went to Seattle?"

"Yes. My boss in Albuquerque heard about the search for an editorial assistant for a professor trying to get his book published and recommended me."

"Was it interesting work?"

"In a way it was. The subject matter wasn't all that interesting to me, and getting the job done was complicated and not stress-free. Dr. Abernathy wasn't the easiest person in the world to work with."

"How so?"

"He was disorganized, changed his mind in midstream, didn't know how to structure his work, wouldn't trust anyone else."

"Wouldn't he trust you?"

"Not at first. He had some bad experiences with assistants in the past. He was sure I was going to lose his notes or change something. It took a while before he could put his trust in me." Uma leaned her head against the back of the chair and looked at the fluffy clouds sailing by. "But he finally did, and we got the job done."

"Nothing you've said so far seems to be anything that would put that sad look on your face that I've seen since I first saw you this morning," Tom said. "So, it must have to do with something outside of your work." He paused, waiting for Uma to comment. "Or your next assignment," he added when she didn't respond.

Uma was still silent. She was afraid when she started telling her brother about her situation she would begin crying. She didn't want that. She wasn't—refused to be—a crier. But it had to be done, no matter if she held in her emotions or not.

"How did you get to Alaska?" Tom finally asked. "And what was the project there?"

Uma looked down at her lap, playing with the hem of her shirt. "My last day—the day I was clearing out my office, I ran into a professor who invited me to a cocktail party at her place. She said I might hear of another assignment—perhaps something in development. And I did."

She took a deep breath and sat unspeaking until Tom asked, "What was the job?"

"A professor at the party was on his way to Alaska. He was gathering folktales, stories from the Eskimo, Inuit, and Aleut cultures. Since Alaska was made the forty-ninth state, there has been a demand for material from there, and he had the promise of publication for his book. Then there was the possibility of more research and publication on tie-ins with Russian culture or even American folktales."

"Sounds interesting," Tom said.

"It did to me as well," Uma responded. "We spent dinner discussing it, and I gave him advice on how to record everything he did. He would be so far away from home, and it would be difficult to get materials when he was there. On the other hand, when he went back to Chicago, he wouldn't be able to clear up questions or gather any other information he needed."

"Chicago? That's where he was from?"

Uma nodded her head. So far, it hadn't been hard to tell the story.

"Yes. He taught at Northwestern."

"So . . . what happened next?"

"He offered me a job. Come with him and keep up with all his notes while he was in the field recording the stories told in the villages. Catching the holes—the questions that needed to be asked while he was still there in Alaska."

"So you did?"

"Yes. Alex flew on up there, while I stayed a few days in Seattle and settled all my business. Sold my car. Vacated my apartment."

"And then you went up to . . . where?"

"I flew in to Fairbanks, and from there we took a small plane into a little village northwest of there. A few hundred people, a couple of dozen stores and shops. Lots of snow."

"Where did you live while you were there?"

"Alex was using a cabin that belonged to a friend of his, a professor at the University of Alaska at Fairbanks. I stayed there."

"With him? With this professor?" Tom's eyebrows were raised as he looked at Uma. She saw the question of more in his eyes, and it was difficult for her to meet his gaze. She knew what he was silently asking. She could put it off no longer.

Tears poured down her face, and she looked up at the endless blue sky before closing her eyes. "I'm pregnant." She choked back a sob.

Tom let her cry for a couple of minutes before he asked in a grim voice, "Is he going to marry you?"

"Oh, Tom! He's dead!"

"Dead?" Tom leaned forward. "How?"

"He had been to a settlement to get more interviews and

coming back there was an avalanche. It pushed his truck off the road and killed him."

"Oh, Uma," Tom said. "I am so sorry."

"That isn't the worst of it," Uma said.

"No?"

"No." She took a deep breath. "The worst was when his wife showed up to get his things: his research, his clothes." She took a deep breath. "And she was quick to let me know that I was just one of many coeds who had succumbed to his charms."

Tom frowned. "Did you know he was married?"

"Of course not! I wouldn't . . ." Uma's voice was laced with hurt. *How could he ask that?*

"OK. OK. I had to ask." His voice was soothing. "Did she know you are pregnant?"

"No. Nobody knows but me."

Tom rose from his seat and walked to the river's edge, muttering expletives under his breath. He bent and picked up a handful of pebbles. One by one, he threw a rock as hard and far as he could, fury giving energy to each pitch. At one point, he turned toward Uma and said, "If he was still alive, I'd kill him." He turned back and resumed his rock-throwing activity.

Uma sat and watched the river flowing by, throwing off an occasional wave where it bumped over a stone. *Like life, it can look so serene, but underneath there are bumps that mar the peaceful surface. You just think life is smooth until you hit one of those bumps. Nothing is as it seems.*

Turning, Tom asked, "Have you given any thought to what you want to do?"

"I've had plenty of thoughts, but I seem to be stifled, unable to move. Unable to make some kind of definitive plan for my future." She used the tail of her shirt to wipe her eyes. "I thought when I talked to you, I'd suddenly know what I needed to do."

"I meant, are you going to have the baby? Are you going to keep it?"

Uma stared at her brother in horror. "Of course I'm going to have it! How can you ask that?"

"How can I ask that? How can I not?" He dropped the remaining pebbles and dusted his hands on his jeans. "If Mom hadn't had Cindy, she would never have married Grady. And Cindy, remember, didn't have the first baby she was pregnant with at the tender age of fourteen."

Uma remembered, and there had been times she had wondered how differently their lives would have been with no Grady for a step-father and no Cindy for a sister, but . . . "Yes! I'm going to have the baby!"

"Are you going to keep it?"

This time, Uma paused. She had weighed that solution, if only briefly, of giving the child up for adoption. "I'm going to keep it," she told him. "I'm educated. I'm experienced. I'll be able to support myself and a child." She rose from her chair and walked closer to the river's edge. "My problem right now is deciding where to go. Where to look for a job. And what to do about the problem of being an unmarried pregnant woman looking for a job."

Tom sighed and ran his fingers through his hair, pushing it away from his eyes. When he looked at his sister, his look was filled with anguish. He walked to her and gathered her into his arms. "We'll work it out, Sis. I'll help you with whatever you need." He set her away, holding to her shoulders. "We're family. We'll always be family." He gave her a little shake. "No more going away. You can find a job here in Texas somewhere. I want to always know where you are and how you are doing." He smiled an unsteady smile. "I want to be close to my niece or nephew. I want to be the uncle I never had."

"I was running away," Uma said. "I was running away from everything I had known from the time I was six years old. From a family that didn't work, that fussed and fought. From a step-father who was drunk all the time. I was angry at Mom—angry at her for getting pregnant in the first place and marrying Grady." Tears rolled down her cheeks. "And I thought I had found love. True love with a man who thought like I do and was solid and substantial with a career that I could help him in, and who loved me the way I loved him." She took a deep breath. "I was disdainful of Cindy for sleeping around, for being a tramp from the time she was old enough to notice boys. And I didn't . . . I didn't sleep around. I was a good girl. And here I am in the same predicament. Pregnant and no husband in sight."

Chapter 22

Both brother and sister were silent on their way back to the big house—lost in their thoughts. When Tom parked where he had earlier, he asked, "Your car?" motioning toward the sedan at the edge of the drive.

"A rental," she replied.

"Unless you are plush with money . . ." he started, looking to her.

She shook her head. "Not hardly. I have savings. I'm not broke, but not plush either."

"I think you need to stay here while we figure all this out. I've missed you more than I can tell you. You can use one of the vehicles on the ranch, at least until you decide where you are going. No need to spend money when you don't need to."

"You are offering room and board and use of a car, but this isn't your ranch, big brother!" Uma looked at him. "Not your house and not your vehicles."

"No, but I'm an employee of Big B Enterprises, more than that, really, and I have a certain say-so over some things."

"Really? An employee?"

"Really. An employee. Paychecks and perks and everything that goes with it."

"So what are you? I mean . . . what do you do for the Big B?"

Tom settled back with a satisfied grin on his face. "Well, see, there is more than one entity called the Big B. There's the Big B Ranch," he gestured in all directions. "It's the cattle operation. That's what Bix is mostly concerned with.

"Then there is Big B Oil." He pointed toward a pump jack working away in the distance. "We don't have any actual, physical work to do with that. Big B just deposits the checks from the big shot oil company that drilled and pays us for the oil."

"Us?"

"Yes. Us," Tom said in a deliberate tone. "Dorie and Jonah, Bix and Barney and Sarah's parents, set all this up as a family endeavor, and they included me."

Uma's mouth dropped open. "They counted you like family?"

"Yes, with the provision I work for Big B Enterprises. I draw a salary, like any employee, but I also have a share." He saw the amazement on Uma's face. "Look at it this way, they would have to pay anyone who does what I do, and they can count on my loyalty. They know that I'll do the best I can because I will share in the profits. Bix draws a salary for running the cattle operation, and I draw one for running Big B Enterprises."

"So what is Big B Enterprises, exactly?" Uma asked.

"Lots of things. Cotton warehouses, grain silos, storage facilities. Anything we figure can make a profit. Here lately we've been investing in airport facilities."

"Lovie told me that Sarah flies airplanes."

"Sarah flies airplanes, and Barney makes movies. This is a very diverse family."

Uma gave a wistful smile. "Why couldn't we have come from a family that worked together like that? They sound like the perfect family."

"Maybe now, but not at the beginning, but that's not my story to tell." He put one arm along the back of the seat. "I feel comfortable offering you the use of a bedroom and a vehicle for as long as you can stay. After all, Bix invited you to visit in the first place, didn't he?"

"Yes, he did."

"And I have a feeling that he has been trying to rope you into helping do something about his office." Uma looked away. "You have seen it, haven't you?"

"Yes, I've seen it." She grimaced. "It's a mess."

A voice came from the direction of the front porch. "Are you two going to sit out there all day and talk? And me up here dying of boredom?"

They looked toward the figure in the rocker at the far corner. Tom grinned and said, "I guess we'd better go amuse him." He reached toward the door handle. "I won't say anything about . . . anything. All that's up to you." He opened the door and swung out.

Chapter 23

Uma tried to disappear to her room as soon as they topped the steps. "Wait a minute," Bix called out to her. "What am I supposed to do with all those file folders and cards that Lovie put on my desk? And that map? What's that for?"

Uma knew her red eyes would give away the fact she had been crying, and she wanted to get away from Bix before he commented. Tom saved her by saying, "Bix, let me go over some things with you first. You can talk to Uma later." He waved his hand at her, as if shoeing her away. As she went up the stairs to her room, she thought about the times when Tom had helped her avoid the wrath of a drunken Grady by distracting him. Her beloved brother was still rescuing her.

She put a cool, damp washcloth over her eyes and stretched out on her bed. She hadn't intended to fall asleep, but the drama of the day wore her out. When she awoke, she could tell some time had passed by the way the light shown in the window. *It must be almost supper time.* She went downstairs to help. It had become her job to set the table before meals.

"I was getting ready to come call you," Lovie said. "Did you have a good nap?"

"Yes, I did. I didn't realize I was so tired. I haven't been doing anything to wear me out."

If Lovie or Annie noticed her red eyes, they didn't comment on them. Uma hurriedly put plates, silverware, and napkins on the table, and it was soon filled with platters and bowls of food. "Louvinia, you go call Bix and Tom," Annie commanded. Soon the room was full of hungry people.

"Tom, you tell us of your travels," Annie said.

"First, I went to Houston," he said, "and talked with the accounting firm that has been handling the Big B Enterprises accounts." He stopped to eat a bit. "From there, I checked out a couple of deals in Dallas." He took a sip of tea. "Then Sarah flew me to Lubbock to check out some properties for sale there."

"I'm happy that we put in that landing strip here on the ranch," Bix said. "It sure has come in handy." He turned to Uma and said, "Sarah flies him just about everywhere he needs to go and brings him back home. It saves a lot of time and hassle."

"Did she bring you home today?" Uma asked her brother.

He nodded, his mouth full of food. When he swallowed, he added, "I left my truck at the landing strip. She just touched down, let me out, and took off again for Waco."

"I can see where that would be very handy," she agreed.

"Bix, I told Uma she should use one of the ranch vehicles while she's here," Tom said. "No use her paying for a rental car she's barely using when there's a whole barn full of cars and trucks of one sort or another."

"That's right," Bix said. "That's a waste." He looked at Uma. "You can use any one you want—except my mother's. She's picky about her cars." He reached for the basket of biscuits. "I can't even drive them."

"Especially you can't drive them," Lovie said. Bix shrugged his shoulders.

"And I hope you are planning on staying for a long visit, Uma." He picked up his knife and reached for the jar of apple butter. "I'm counting on you to help me with my papers and stuff in my office. You must have an idea of something because you bought all those supplies today."

"I'll be glad to help if I can, Bix," Uma said. "I've never done anything quite like this before, so I don't know how much assistance I'll be. I have some ideas."

"Anything is better than what it is now," Lovie said.

"What should I do first?" Bix asked Uma. "In case I wake up in the night and want something to do?"

"Are you awake much?" Tom asked. "Is it the pain?"

"Actually, it's getting better every day. Most of the time it is more uncomfortable than painful, and I have pills when I need them. No, I think I wake up at night because I don't get any exercise in the daytime. I'm used to being active on the ranch. All this sitting around is getting to me. Maybe if I get more involved in the office work—in what we had been talking about—I could sleep better."

"Not to mention that your dad wants you to be more involved in all aspects of the Big B businesses, not just the cattle," Tom said.

"Yes, there is that," Bix agreed.

"To start with," Uma said, "we've already separated the magazines from the newspapers. You can stack all the magazines together by title and all the newspapers by city. I'll need you to tell me what, exactly, you are wanting out of each category."

"Well . . ." Bix began.

"Not now," Uma cut him off. "I'll come to your office and you can explain and show me."

Bix smiled. "Yes. You come to my office. I'll show you what I need."

Chapter 24

After supper, the women cleaned up the kitchen and put the dishes on to wash. Bix and Tom had disappeared into the office, and when Uma went to the front porch, Bix walked out right behind her. She expected Tom and Lovie to join them, but when she kept glancing at the screen door, Bix finally said, "They aren't coming."

"No?"

"They've gone to Lovie's cabin for some alone time."

"Oh."

"You won't see your brother 'til tomorrow, most likely."

Uma was silent. She had seen the welcome home that Lovie had given Tom that afternoon, but she had been so focused on telling her brother about her own situation that she hadn't thought any further about Tom and Lovie's relationship.

"Do you have someone, somewhere? A boyfriend who is waiting for your return the way Louvinia was waiting for hers?"

"No. No I don't." Uma leaned her head back and looked away into the pink and orange sunset.

"That's good," Bix said.

Uma thought about that statement for a moment, then replied, "Good?"

"Yes. I'd hate to think I was moving in on someone else's territory." When Uma couldn't think of what to say to that, he added, "But I'd do it. In a minute." He looked at her and grinned.

In her chest, her heart gave an extra hard thump. *But if he knew . . . He wouldn't be interested in me. Not at all.*

"It's hopeless," she finally said. "You and me . . . it's not going to happen."

"Why? Don't you like me?" Bix asked.

Uma shrugged. "I like you just fine." *I like you more than fine. If I wasn't pregnant . . . if, if, if.* "It's just the situation right now." She stood and started toward the front door. "It's just not going to happen," she repeated.

Chapter 25

When Uma came down to breakfast the next morning, Annie was at the stove and Bix at the table. There was no sign of Lovie and Tom.

"You sit," Annie commanded. "I cook." Uma did as she was told. She looked at Bix, who was almost finished with his eggs and biscuits.

"Looks like someone slept in this morning," he commented.

"I guess I was more tired than I thought," Uma replied.

"I was talking about Lovie and Tom," he answered.

"Oh." She glanced down as Annie placed a plate of ham and eggs in front of her.

"Of course, they probably aren't sleeping," he added.

Uma was sure she blushed. Although the talk around the table when she was a teenager was sometimes coarse, she never liked it, nor did she participate in it. Whatever people did or did not do in bed was not for casual conversation, in her opinion. She was sure Bix was staring at her.

"They're probably . . ." he started.

"Bix, you not embarrass Uma," Annie instructed. "You be gentleman in front of your guest."

Bix averted his gaze and reached for another biscuit. After spreading it liberally with butter and jelly, he changed the subject. "So, are you ready to help me with organizing my office?"

"Sure. As soon as I eat and help Annie with the dishes," she said. She finished her breakfast without any more bantering from Bix. She had just finished and was pushing her chair back from the table when Lovie and Tom came in the back door.

"Good morning, everybody," Tom said. Lovie was smiling but said nothing.

"Morning, bro, Louvinia," Bix said, grinning at the two. "Sleep well?"

"Sure did," Tom replied, giving Bix the evil eye. Lovie poured herself a cup of coffee.

"Come on, Uma. Let's go work in my office. Lovie and Tom can help Annie clean up in here." He stood up and put his crutches under his arms. "Your brother isn't the only one who can have a good-looking woman at his side." He swung toward the door to the back hall.

Uma looked helplessly at Tom and followed Bix to his office. She could tell when she entered the room that he had made some progress with the clutter, but there was much more to be done. *At least the newspapers are all together in neat stacks . . . and the magazines.* Bix walked behind the large desk and took a seat in the high-backed leather office chair. He propped his crutches against the wall next to the window and swung the chair toward the work surface.

"OK, you're the boss," he said. "What do you want me to do first?"

Uma took a seat in the wing-backed chair facing the desk. "Before we start to work, the first thing is for me to understand what is going on here. I can't take on a project without knowing what we—what *you*—are trying to accomplish, besides making all this clutter into some sort of order. What are you doing here? What is the end objective?"

"Besides getting it neat in here?"

"Right. Besides getting it neat in here."

Bix leaned his head against the back of the chair and looked at the ceiling fan as it lazily stirred the air. He swung the chair slightly to and fro as he thought. After a heavy sigh, he began to speak.

"For you to understand what I'm trying to do, you have to understand the businesses the family is involved in. And to understand the businesses, you have to know the people in the family and how they fit into the various dealings we have." He looked at her to see if she was following.

"OK."

"My parents have been married—let's see—I guess over twenty-seven years now since I'm twenty-six." He grinned. "And they had been married a year or so when I came along. My mother, Dorie Barnett, was the only surviving child of Bigelow, Big B, Barnett. He built this ranch into a mighty brand in the beginning of this century. It was cattle then—no oil—and some storage places he owned in southeast parts of the state, like Houston and Beaumont and other places. It was always planned that his son, Bixby, for whom I am named, was to take over. But without getting into too much detail, both the Barnett sons, Bix and Danny, died during or right after the first World War. That just left Dorie, my mother, to run the ranch when her father died. And she did. As well as Big B Enterprises.

"So my father and mother married. There's a lot more to that story too, but I won't get into it. Mom brought the ranch and Big B Enterprises into the marriage. Dad, Jonah Crandall, was heir, along with his brother, Thomas, to a ranch and banking interests up around Waco. He also brought his niece, Sarah, who was the daughter of his late sister."

"Sarah that flies airplanes?"

"That's the one. Mom and Dad adopted her, so she is legally my big sister. Dad's brother, Thomas, is into airplanes and airports and all things aviation. He's the one who taught Sarah to fly. So now, through Dad and Uncle Thomas and Sarah, we have more business interests in those areas."

"You own shares in . . . in airports and such?"

"Airports, hangars and airlines, parts companies and more."

"My goodness. It gets more complicated."

"Tell me about it. I won't even get into who owns shares of what. That's really convoluted. Anyway, a year or so ago Mom and Dad decided they wanted to retire. That's when they bought a home on Galveston Island and moved down there. Dad said it was time for me to start taking care of the family income. By that he meant all the businesses, particularly the ranch and Big B Enterprises. He told me he expected me to build the enterprises to at least double what it was. Enterprises being everything except cattle, oil, and airplane related."

"That's a big expectation!" Uma said.

Bix swung away and stared at the wall behind the hospital bed. "I knew when I went to college at A&M that I was being prepared to take over the business end of things. After all, Barney had made it plain that he wasn't interested in anything except making movies. Somehow it just didn't sink in, though. Let me tell you," he said, turning back to look at Uma, "it was Tom who saved my hide. When I wanted to party, he convinced me to study. Finally, I started catching on—listening to what my professors had to say about everything. Ranching, the oil industry, diversifying businesses, the whole shebang. It finally began to sink in that at some time in the future Big B Enterprises as well as Big B Ranch was going to depend on me. I buckled down and studied. I began to understand what was going on. So when Tom and I graduated, Dad offered Tom a job here at the Big B."

"He did?"

"Yes, but Tom turned it down."

Uma was puzzled. "He turned it down?"

"Yes. Back then he did. He got a job in Dallas, an office job for a multifaceted company much like Big B is, but not family. He wasn't happy there, and when he got the chance, he took a job in Beaumont with a similar outfit." Bix leaned forward in his chair. "But I guess I'm telling you things you already know."

"No. I don't know any of this. While he was doing this, I was still in college in Austin, then in my jobs after that."

"Anyway, time went on, and when Bix was here one weekend, Dad offered him the job again. Told him he could have a share of Big B along with his salary if he'd help me run it the way it needed to be run." He picked up a paper clip and started bending it, his forehead wrinkling into a frown. "Dad said he couldn't trust an outsider the way he could trust Tom, that he was like family and ought to be treated as such. Told him back then that he and Mom wanted to retire and move away from the ranch—at least for part of each year— and although I was the heir to the operations, I needed help. With all of Big B holdings it was too much for one person."

"Did Tom accept this time?"

"Yes," Bix threw the paper clip on the desk. "He accepted." He leaned back. "Dad worked with the two of us for over a year before he and Mom took a couple of trips, then bought the place in Galveston." He crossed his arms and rocked back. "Tom and I were supposed to look for opportunities to grow Big B Enterprises. Invest so that if cattle and/or oil income fell, we would have other sources of support for the family. After all, we have a lot of people depending on Big B, in all of its forms, for their livelihood."

They were both silent. Bix leaned back with his eyes closed. Uma wondered if he was in pain. She closed her own eyes as she mulled over what Bix had been left to accomplish.

"So . . ." Uma raised her head and opened her eyes. "All this"—she waved her hand around the room—"has to do with locating business opportunities?"

"Yeah!" Bix placed his arms on the desktop and leaned forward; a wide grin spread over his face. "You've got it. I subscribed to the newspapers from the major cities in the state and to the magazines I thought would give me some ideas. I don't want to look anywhere outside Texas, at least for now."

"And did they? Did they give you leads?"

Bix's smile faded. "Not really. All this is overwhelming. And when I wanted to refer to something I had read, I couldn't find it again." He leaned his chin on one hand as he surveyed the piles. "And I got bored. That's when I decided to organize a rodeo of sorts."

"Of sorts?"

"Yeah. Just the Big B hands and me. Bronc riding. Bull riding. The usual."

"The usual?" She thought she was beginning to sound like a parrot.

"Have you ever been to a rodeo?" he asked.

"No."

"We'll have to do something about that," Bix said.

"I doubt if I'll be here long enough for that," Uma said. "Besides, I think you would have had enough of rodeos for a while."

"Well, there is that, of course," he said, and suddenly became serious. "But you'll be here, won't you? I mean, you'll stay and help me with this. You wouldn't have bought all these folders and things if you didn't have some ideas."

"I do have some ideas," Uma said, "A few. But I have to find a job. A real job. I have to support myself."

"This is a real job," Bix said indignantly. "I'll pay you."

"No. You won't pay me. I mean, I won't take pay from you. After all, I'm staying here and eating your food. I won't take pay for helping you straighten up this . . ." She looked helplessly around the piles.

They went to work on the pile of newspapers, some of them a couple of months old. "What did you hope to gain from these?" Uma asked before they started.

"Two things," Bix replied. "Trends and upcoming business development in the locations and, secondly, businesses for sale we might be interested in buying."

"Did that work well for you?"

"Not so much," he replied. "By the time Tom checked out the companies or locations we might think about buying, either they were already sold or they weren't what we were looking for."

"It looks like there would be a better way to do it," Uma said.

"That's what Tom said."

"Can't you contact what appears to be the top commercial real estate brokerage in each area, present your needs, and ask them to be on the lookout for anything you might be interested in? Maybe they'd even give you a heads up before the property is even on the market."

Bix looked sheepish. "Yeah, that's what Tom suggested as well."

"Bix, when I was at A&M trying to find someone who could tell me how to get here to the ranch, I got the impression that Big B is well known. It's an important concern. A commercial real estate firm would be lucky to work with you."

"You're right. So how do I find a company to work with?"

"That's where your newspapers can be helpful. Look at the ads and see who is listing the most commercial property in each area. Call and talk to the head person—I think they are called brokers—and introduce yourself: Bix Crandall of Big B Ranch and Enterprises." Uma reached over and picked up a package of index cards. "Keep a card with the broker's name, company name, town, address, phone number, and anything else you think is important. Keep a card file so you can pull it at a moment's notice if the broker calls. If he does, make a note on the card . . . or another one. You might even want a folder for each company if you end up doing business with them, or getting a lot of calls, so you don't forget what was offered before."

"I have a Rolodex," Bix said, reaching for the revolving card file. "I can put them on here."

"Yes, you should do that as well, but you need a larger card so you can make notes about phone conversations and what properties you have discussed. Things like that."

"That's a good idea," Bix said. "But there are also articles in some of the papers about things that are going on in the area that might influence our decision to buy property there."

"Cut out the article, make a file folder for it, and make an index card."

"More index cards? I'm going to get them mixed up."

"No, you aren't. I'll be sure they are easy to deal with," Uma said. "You may have extra files and extra cards so you can find what you are looking for. Say you want to see what is going on in . . ." She sputtered to a stop.

"In Longview," Bix said. "Or Tyler."

"So you might have a folder for Longview and one for Tyler. And you might have a card saying 'new . . . whatever,' going in next fall. And then you know to look in the Longview folder."

Bix's forehead wrinkled as he thought. "That might work," he finally said.

"Then you could throw away all the extra parts of the paper," Uma said. "You're taking up lots of space with what you don't need, like the wedding announcements and comics."

"I like the comics," he retorted, grinning at her.

Uma smiled back. "Just throw them away after you've read them."

"Good. Let's get started." Bix enthusiastically grabbed a pile of papers. "Move your chair over here—no, it's too big to fit here by me—move it to the end of the desk."

"Why?" Uma asked.

"So we can look at the same thing at the same time."

"And why do we need to do that?" Uma's eyebrows were raised. *What is he up to now?*

"So I can understand what you are doing and why," Bix said innocently.

Uma didn't understand that rationale, but she did as she was told, and Bix wheeled his chair to the corner of the desk next to her. Armed with folders, index cards, pens, scissors, and labels, they went to work.

As they worked the next several hours, Uma saw why Bix wanted to sit close to her. He was absolutely right that he needed to see what she was writing on the cards and labeling the folders. Another motive also became clear. He was close enough to touch her, which he did often.

"Let me look at that." He laid his hand on her arm, and his fingers played on her skin as he read what she had written on the index card. "OK. I understand," he said then lifted a strand of her hair and moved it a bit. He put his hand on her shoulder as he explained why they were looking at the town mentioned in the article. His hand covered hers as she placed a file in the growing pile and held it there while he studied another clipping before saying, "Here. Put this in the same file." Every excuse he could think of to touch Uma, he did. Nothing out of line. Nothing exactly provocative, but Uma grew used to the warmth of his touch. It seemed they were constantly connected.

She had never had a boss do that before—touch her in any way. Except for Alex, and that was different. That was mutual. And if one had, she would have stopped the practice immediately. But Bix wasn't her boss, even if it was his business she was working on. *This is just a friend helping a friend, isn't it? I'm just Tom's sister helping his friend. His good-looking friend.*

Being touched was an old bugga-boo from childhood, when a touch from her stepfather often signaled a slap or pinch was coming. This was entirely different. She wasn't sure what it was. That was the problem. If it was clear he was coming on to her, then she could shut it down. But he wasn't coming on to her. At least she didn't think he was. So, she endured his touches, and she grew used to them.

When Tom came to tell them lunch was ready, they had been working several hours and the stack of papers was greatly reduced, and the trash basket was full to overflowing.

The conversation over lunch revolved around the work Bix and Uma were doing.

"This is just what we needed," Tom said. "I think what you are doing will be very helpful."

"Me, too," Bix said. "Your sister is getting me on the right track, all right."

"I'd like to sit in on this," Tom said. "At least when you start talking about the real estate companies and people in the various towns. I think I could give suggestions on that part, since I've been working in that area for a while now."

"Certainly," Bix said. "After all, you're part of Big B. You have input, probably more than I do about that part."

After lunch, they left Lovie and Annie to clean up and started toward the office.

"When we get finished, I'm going to my house," Lovie said. "I've started outlining my novel, and I want to work on that."

"Write a bestseller," Bix said as they left the room.

Bix, Uma, and Tom spent the afternoon discussing and making notes about various towns and whether they ought to search out possible investments in those areas. "I think we ought to rule out Lubbock and west Texas," Tom said. "It is too far away. I know Sarah can fly us there, but it is going to get inconvenient for her to do that—drop everything to haul one of us out there and back. We can look at that avenue again in a couple of years. If and when we decide to invest in west Texas, we need to be ready to hire someone to manage that territory."

"Agreed," Bix said. "We'll just concentrate on east and central Texas, from Oklahoma to Mexico."

"Maybe," Tom said. "At least from Oklahoma to Houston and vicinity. That's plenty of territory for the two of us to tend to, and we may have to hire at least one more person, depending on how much property we end up buying."

Three hours later, they had a list of towns, along with the name of what they had determined—by looking at newspapers—was the major commercial real estate company in each.

"Bix, you probably need to cancel the newspaper subscriptions to the places you are no longer interested in . . . at least for now," Uma suggested.

"OK."

"And you might want to subscribe to others in the area you and Tom have talked about."

Bix grunted and continued reading an article that diverted his attention from the conversation.

"Make yourself a note so you don't forget." *I'm sure getting bossy with the boss,* she thought.

"Nag, nag," Bix said as he pulled a tablet closer to him. "I can see right now I need a secretary." He added to the list he had started. "How am I going to keep up with the cattle operation when I get back on my feet if I have to do all this cr . . . stuff?"

"That's what Ellis Ponder is for," Tom said. "Keeping up with the cattle operation. You just want to hang out over there with him or out on the range with the men."

"Yeah. You're right," Bix said. "I don't much like this office stuff. If I can hire Ellis Ponder to help keep the ranch operation going, why can't I hire a secretary to keep all this in hand?"

"I'll think about it," Tom said. Uma wondered if he had to give his approval for hiring people.

"One thing you haven't explained," Bix said, looking at Uma. "What's the map for?"

"I thought you might like to put it on that wall"—she pointed behind the hospital bed—"and put a flag wherever you have a property. It might help you envision territories and how far apart or how close your holdings are."

"That's a good idea," Tom said.

"You could have different color flags for different kinds of property. Red for air-related. Blue for grain storage. Yellow for cotton warehouses. Whatever."

"As soon as I get a walking cast so I can make it up the stairs, this bed is gone. We can put it up then."

"Or maybe we can put it up now, and when you can't sleep in the middle of the night, you can lay there and look at the pins," Tom suggested.

All Uma could think about was Bix moving upstairs and being right down the hall from her room. She didn't know why that made her nervous. Bix was a gentleman. She didn't believe he would ever intrude on her private space, but there was something inside her that was stirring her up. *Forget it, girl,* she thought. *You are out of the market for a man for a long, long time.*

Chapter 26

The next morning at breakfast Bix announced, "I need everyone's help today."

"You've got it," Tom said. "What do you need?"

"Uma," Bix said, "are you still planning on turning in your rental car?"

"Yes, if I can use one of the ranch cars to go to town when I need to. I'll figure out what to do about a vehicle when I get a job and leave here."

"We can cover that," her brother said. "I'll get you where you need to go, and you can make arrangements for a car there."

"Yes," Bix said. "We'll get you where you need to be."

"So, what's your plan for the day, Bix?" Lovie asked.

"We will help Uma take her car back."

"Why does it take everyone to do that?"

"Because, *Louvinia*," Bix said in his snarky voice, "Uma will drive her rental car back. Tom will drive my car so we'll have a car to get back to the ranch. You will go along to keep Tom happy, and I will go along to check out the car rental place." He looked at Tom. "We had discussed investing in car rental places at the airports Thomas is buying or building. This is the perfect opportunity for me to ask questions. I'll have a good excuse for being there."

"You're right. We were. It sounds like a plan," Tom agreed.

"Besides, I'm bored staying at home all the time. This is the longest I've ever stayed here in the house. I'm ready for a day in the big city. We'll eat lunch in Houston before we start back home." He looked at Uma. "You did say you rented your car at the airport in Houston, didn't you?"

"Yes, I did."

"Sounds like fun," Lovie said. "Let me help Annie clean up, and I'll go get ready."

"I'll help too," Uma said. She stacked the plates from the table and put them in the sink. Lovie followed, wiping the tabletop with a damp cloth. A day with her brother and friends was something she had never done before. She agreed with Lovie. *It does sound like fun.*

An hour later they met in the living room. The men were in dark, pressed jeans, neat western shirts, and white Stetsons. Uma thought they looked like brothers. Bix was a couple of inches taller than Tom's six-foot height, but both were lean, muscled, tan, and looked like they were ready to take on the world. The fact that one leg of Bix's jeans was missing didn't detract from his good looks. Until a person noticed that it was a cast on his leg instead of denim, his apparel looked totally normal.

Both Uma and Lovie wore dresses. Uma had to leave the snap at the waist undone and covered with the belt, extended to the largest hole. She took a large silk scarf and tied it around her middle, the point hanging to one side. It looked very fashionable, not like it was covering a baby bump. She wore a necklace in colors that matched the silk.

"Well, look at Mighty Mouse," Bix exclaimed when Lovie came from the back of the house. "All dressed up!"

"Did you think I never wore dresses?" Lovie asked. "I can dress up when I need to."

"You sure can," Tom said, never taking his eyes off her. "You look beautiful."

Lovie blushed and ducked her head. "Thank you," she said simply.

Tom turned toward Uma and said, "You look nice too."

"Thanks."

"Let's get this show on the road," Bix said. "When Peanut finished helping me get ready, I had him move my car by the back door. Let's go out that way. Tom, you'll have to drive. Lovie, you ride in the Caddie with Tom. I'm going to ride with Uma."

As the group piled into the cars, Bix called out, "Meet at the car rental place at the airport." Tom, driving the big, black Cadillac sedan, pulled down the driveway toward the road before Bix could get his crutches situated in Uma's vehicle. As they pulled out, Bix patted the dashboard and asked, "How do you like this Impala? Does it drive good?"

"Yes. I like it fine," Uma answered. "You have a perfectly good car yourself—much nicer than this one. Why did you really have me take you to the barn in my car the other day?"

Suddenly Bix was serious. "Sometimes it's OK to show off a little bit, and sometimes it's not. I don't like to take the Caddie down there. Seems like I'm trying to look better off than the men."

"Even though you are and they know it?"

"Yes, even then. No use rubbing it in that the head boss has a better vehicle than they do."

"What would you normally drive around the ranch?"

"My old truck."

"Is that your old truck instead of your new truck?"

Bix grinned. "You got it."

"And your trucks, either or both of them, have standard shift?"

He looked over at her. "Yep."

They talked all the way to Houston. He told her of a couple of scrapes he and Tom had gotten into at A&M and asked her more about the jobs she had the last couple of years. He was especially interested in the time she had spent in Albuquerque. "I'd like to visit there some day," he told Uma. "It sounds like an interesting place. There was an article in the paper the other day about people going there to fly hot air balloons. The landscape is so wide open it's good for that. I'd like to see it."

"Yes, when I was there, I'd see one fly over from time to time."

Bix reached over and took the end of a strand of Uma's hair and played with it. "Tell me about Alaska," he said. "From hot to cold. Two extremes."

Uma tried to keep her mind off everything that went on in Alaska. If possible, she would have erased it from her past entirely, but she knew she couldn't avoid talking about it altogether. "Well, I typed up Alaskan folk stories."

"Eskimo, you mean?" Bix asked as his fingers wrapped a small section into a curl. "That kind of folk stories?"

"Eskimo, Inuit, Aleut." Uma diverted his attention from that subject by asking, "What are you doing with my hair?"

"Looking at it," Bix answered. "I like to look at it. It looks like spun gold."

Uma couldn't think of anything to say to that, so she was silent, and when they began to talk again, the subject was Houston and the properties Big B Enterprises owned in the region.

When they reached the airport, Uma parked in the area set aside for rental cars, and they went inside. Tom and Lovie were in the customer waiting area. "About time for you two to show up," Tom said.

"You drive faster than your sister," Bix said.

"We're going to find the nearest place to get a cold drink," Lovie said. "We'll wait for you there. Come find us when you are ready to go."

"Don't eat anything," Bix said. "I plan to take everyone out to lunch. I'm ready for a big steak."

"Sounds good to me," Lovie replied as she and Tom headed toward the concourse.

"I'm going to wander around here—maybe ask some questions," Bix said. "I have a good excuse for being here since I'm with you. I'm going to be nosy. You go ahead and check in your car. I'll come find you."

"OK. I'll wait out here if you aren't back," Uma said, indicating the seats in front of the rental counter.

She approached the check-in desk and filled out the proper paperwork. "We'll have to check the vehicle for cleanliness and damage before we can tell you your final bill," the clerk told her. "You can wait over there." She motioned toward the row of seats where Tom and Lovie had been seated.

Thirty minutes later, the bill was presented, and Uma wrote them a check. "I need to verify the information on this check," the clerk said. "Do you still live at this address in Seattle?"

"No, actually I don't," Uma replied.

The clerk frowned. "What is your current address and phone number?"

Uma hesitated. "I don't know the actual address, but I'm staying at the Big B Ranch."

"The Big B?" the woman repeated.

"Yes. Have you heard of it?" Uma asked.

"Of course," the woman replied. "Everyone has heard of the Big B."

"Well, I'm staying there for the time being."

"Staying there?" The woman seemed to be stuck repeating everything Uma said. "Living there?"

"I work different places," Uma tried to explain. "At different universities, usually. When I get hired on a new project, I'll go to wherever it is. For now, I'm staying at the Big B Ranch. My brother works there."

Suddenly, a man rushed up behind the clerk and said, "Everything's all right, Mary. Her check is fine." A few yards behind her, Bix stood, his usual grin on his face.

"OK," the clerk said. "I guess you're through then." She handed over several sheets of paper. "Thank you for renting from us."

Uma turned and joined Bix, and they began walking down the concourse, keeping an eye out for Tom and Lovie. "Did you find out any information about car rental agencies?" Uma asked.

"Sure did. I found out a lot. I'll share at lunch," he said as they spotted their friends at a table at a fast-food place. "Let's go get lunch," Bix called out. "I'm hungry."

As they started out the entrance, Tom said, "We're parked over here." He stepped in the direction of the next lot.

"We need to go to the rental car lot," Bix said.

"Why?"

"I bought a car from them," he answered. The whole party came to a stop.

"Bought a car?" Lovie exclaimed.

Tom shook his head. "What for?"

"Well, see, I didn't know car rental places sell the cars too. They sell them toward the end of the model year. They sell the older ones and buy the latest models. Folks want to rent new cars, not older ones. It's getting that time, and they offered me a good price, and we can always use another car at the ranch, and . . ." He stumbled to a stop.

"What car did you buy?" Lovie asked. Tom just stared at his friend.

"The one Uma was driving. The Impala."

"The one I was driving? I didn't ask you to buy me a car!" Uma was mad.

"Who said I bought *you* a car, smarty?" Bix said. "I bought the Big B a car. You'll just happen to be the one to drive it." He paused. "Or maybe I'll drive it. You don't know." He turned as rapidly as he could on the crutches. "Let's go eat. You drive." He stopped and pulled a set of keys from his pocket. "When we get back to the ranch, I'll have to get my secretary to take care of the registration and insurance."

Chapter 27

Bix directed Uma to the steakhouse he and Tom had agreed on earlier. When they had ordered, the conversation turned to the potential in owning a string of car rental agencies. "The manager back there told me that the major airports were pretty much tied up with either Hertz or Avis or both," Bix told them. "There is a new company making a stir, but they don't know if it will make it or not. They claim to be cheaper than the ones out there already. Easier on the budget, they say. That's what they call it—'Budget.'"

"Sounds like we don't need to try to buck the market," Tom said. "We could spend a lot of money and still be third . . . or fourth."

"Yes and no," Bix said. He paused as the waiter delivered glasses of iced tea. After the server left, Tom questioned him.

"What do you mean by that? Yes and no?"

"The existing rental agencies are located in major airports." Bix paused once more as the waiter delivered their salads. A minute later he took up the subject again. "I think we ought to look at the feasibility of smaller car rental agencies in small and medium-size airports." He stopped talking to take a bite of salad. "We need to talk to Thomas and Sarah about this. What about towns the size of Waco or Tyler?" He paused to take another bite. "Longview. Galveston. Marshall. Do people flying in and out of those towns need to rent a car? I don't know."

"Hmm," Tom mused. "That's a good question. That might be a valuable market . . . or not. It might be a market that the larger agencies don't want to fool with. Let's have a meeting with Thomas and Sarah to talk about it."

The conversation turned to the map and flags and how that would be a visual reminder of exactly where the assets of Big B Enterprises were located. "That could show you where it might be best to locate other investment properties, including a car rental agency," Uma said. "If you or one of your employees is going to be flying into a town to check on properties or to check out more opportunities, then it would be handy to have a car there. And if you have a car there for yourself, you might as well have three or four or more to rent out to other people," she suggested. "How do you get around now when you go to another town?" She looked at Tom.

"I drive there," he answered. "And that takes hours out of my day." He stopped to cut a bite of the steak the waiter had placed in front of him. "I'd love to fly and be there in no time. Sometimes I get Sarah to fly me. She used to like to do that, but she is so busy now that I hate to ask her."

"Maybe we need to hire a pilot for Big B," Bix said. "Somebody to be on call."

"And when you get to wherever, what do you do for a car?" Uma asked.

"Call a taxi," Tom answered.

"Yep. We have a lot to think and talk about," Bix said.

Chapter 28

When they were on the road back to the ranch, Bix settled into the seat, leaned his head back, and put his Stetson over his face. "I hope you don't mind," he said, "but that lunch put me in the mind to take a nap."

"I don't mind," Uma replied. "Thank you for the lunch. This was my chore to get done—returning this car. You didn't have to pay for it."

Bix raised one side of the hat and looked at her. "You're welcome," he said. "It was my pleasure." He settled the hat back over his face.

She thought he was asleep when his voice, muted but still deep and smooth, said, "I've figured out why I like you so much."

He likes me? All the mocking he does is because he likes me? Cautiously, she asked, "Why?"

"Because you don't put up with any guff from me. You give as good as you get."

In no time, soft snores came from underneath the wide brim, but Bix didn't offer any more opinions, about their relationship or anything else. The occasion of being close to him without the necessity of fending off his verbal jousts left Uma free to let her mind explore exactly what she thought of the tall cowboy stretched out beside her.

Uma was surprised that she had been able to hold her own in conversational battles with Bix. She had grown up withdrawing from any verbal exchange that held the likelihood of a disagreement or disparagement of herself or others. Such exchanges were apt to turn into full-scale verbal battles, which in turn led to distracting her from what was important: doing what was necessary to finish school and get out of the tumultuous home.

When Uma finished college, she was immediately immersed in a boss-employee relationship, which, while friendly enough, didn't involve verbal parries of the kind Bix threw at her every day. The first couple of days she was at the Big B Ranch, she was at a loss for words whenever he acted a smart aleck. Uma simply dropped her gaze and didn't respond. Lovie's warning to him had slowed his comments but hadn't stopped them altogether, and Uma finally began to deflect his prods with her own. At first, she worried that she had gone too far at times, but his earlier comment confirmed that was not the case.

She repeatedly glanced at the masculine form beside her. Long legs were enclosed in the denim that stretched tightly over muscular thighs. *I bet he got those muscles holding onto his horse as he rides the ranch.* Bix's arms were crossed over his waist, and the rolled shirt sleeves displayed tanned arms ending in large, calloused hands. *You can tell he's a working man. All this office work has thrown him off course. He's used to being out doing physical work.*

Uma pulled her eyes away from the man beside her, but it wasn't so easy to pull her thoughts from him. *Get a grip,* she told herself. *There's not a way in the world I can have a relationship right now. It will be a long time before I can think of such a thing.*

As she entered Cottonport, her speed slowed, and Bix woke up. He sat up straighter, tossed his hat onto the backseat, and ran his fingers through his hair. "Almost home," he commented. "Let's take the back way."

"Back way? I only know one way."

Bix directed her through the heart of town and onto a dirt road that ran along the side of the Brazos River. "All us kids learned to drive on this road," he said, "and I can show you some good spots to catch some brim or catfish." He turned to face Uma. "Do you like fish? To eat, that is."

"All I've ever had is sea fish, like grouper or sea bass, but I liked it. Mom used to wait tables at a seafood place, and sometimes she brought a meal home. It was always a treat to get something special like that."

"I'll have to take you out to eat fish sometime soon."

"I'd like that," Uma replied, before she could stop the words springing from her mouth. *Don't encourage him. Nothing can come of it.*

When Uma pulled into the backyard close to the ramp that led to the back door, Peanut was there and opened the door for Bix. As he maneuvered his crutches out of the car, Bix said, "Park this car in the big barn, Peanut, right handy to get to. It's our newest transportation."

"Will do, Boss," Peanut replied. "You done bought yourself another car?"

"I did, Peanut. I did. Thought we needed one for Uma and Lovie to tool around in."

"That's a good idea," the wiry man said as Bix dug in his pocket and came up with a key.

"Uma, darlin', you keep that key you've been using. The car place gave me another one. We'll keep it on the board in the barn." He took a few steps toward the back door. "That's something else I learned today: always have an extra key that the agency keeps, just in case you have to repossess the rental or if the person who rents the car loses theirs."

"That's a good idea," Uma replied. "If you don't mind, I'm going to lie down a bit. I'm tired."

"That's a good idea," Bix said. "I've had my nap, now it's your turn."

Chapter 29

When Uma woke from her nap, she felt hot and sluggish. A cool shower invigorated her but trying to find something to wear had her despairing. Nothing fit any longer. It was time to shop for maternity clothes, or at least things that fit loosely. And that meant making her condition public knowledge. There was nothing to be done about it except face up to the feeling of shame that washed over her. Expectant mothers who were not married were ostracized from society, as were their families. Uma didn't think it would be wise for her to remain at the Big B much longer. She didn't want her condition to mar the community's opinion of the Crandall family.

As she donned the same dress she had worn all day, she vowed to make a move forward. She decided to write letters to all her former employers, informing them of her availability for a new project. She would drive in to Cottonport and buy new clothing that fit; along with that, she would purchase a cheap wedding ring. She could think of no other option than to present herself as a widow. There was nobody who could disprove it. The simple lie might make the difference between being hired or not.

When Uma entered the kitchen, she found Bix standing in front of the refrigerator, staring into the cold depths. He looked up as she entered the room.

"It's suppertime, and there is no supper," he complained.

"Are Tom and Lovie back?"

"No. They found something else to do, I guess, rather than come home."

"Is Annie OK? Usually she fixes supper."

"Yeah. She left a note." He waved toward a piece of paper on the counter.

Uma picked it up and read, "I do not know when you be home. You fix own supper."

Walking over to stand beside Bix, she surveyed the contents of the fridge. "Hmm. Plenty of sandwich makings. That OK with you?"

"That's fine with me. I ate such a big lunch I don't want much."

When Uma had spread out the cheeses, meats, bread, mayo and mustard, sliced fresh tomatoes, set jars of pickles and olives, and a dish with gelatin and fruit on the table, it looked like a feast.

He ate two thick sandwiches, a mound of pickles, tomato slices in addition to those on his sandwiches, and drank a large glass of iced tea. *If this is what Bix's appetite is like when he doesn't want much, what it would be like if he had worked hard all day?*

He leaned back with a satisfied expression on his face. "This has been a good day," he said.

Uma agreed.

"I obtained a good car for the ranch—despite what you may think, we did need one. I gained information about car rental agencies. And . . ." He paused and looked intently at Uma. "I got to spend the day with an interesting, beautiful woman."

"And slept while you were with her." It popped out before Uma could stop herself.

Bix broke into laughter. "Touché," he said. "You got me." He stood and reached for the crutches on the floor beside his chair. "I'd help you clean up, but I don't think I'd be much help."

"That's OK," Uma said as she got to her feet and started clearing the table. "I don't mind doing it."

"I'll be out on the front porch," Bix said before he left the room.

When Uma had the kitchen back in shape, she took paper napkins and wrapped two cookies in one and one cookie in the other. Peanut butter, she knew, was Bix's favorite, and they appeared to be freshly made. The fragrance floated out when she took the lid off the cookie jar.

When she reached the front porch, she found Bix standing at the far left corner, leaning against a post, looking off to the west in the direction of the Brazos. "Would you care for some fresh peanut butter cookies?" she asked as she approached him.

"I always care for peanut butter cookies," Bix said. Uma stood next to him as she handed him the larger bundle of sweets. They watched the pink, orange, and purple of the sky as the sun sunk below the tree line. When he was finished and dusted the cookie crumbs from his hands, Bix put his arm around Uma, his hand resting lightly on her shoulder. *I should move. I should pull away.* He squeezed her gently, and moving his hand to her back shoulder blade, he started turning her toward him.

Uma had to summon her resolve. *It can't go like this. He doesn't know . . .*

"Stop, Bix. Stop."

It didn't stop him. He pulled her closer to his chest. "I don't want to stop. I want to kiss you. Are you saying you don't want to be kissed?"

"Yes . . . no . . . there's something I have to tell you."

He looked into her face, eyebrows raised.

"I'm pregnant."

Chapter 30

Uma arrived in the kitchen the next morning to find Annie frying bacon. "Good morning, Annie," she said, although it wasn't one—not for her, anyway. She had slept restlessly, waking often during the night only to toss and turn before falling back asleep. When she finally gave in and got up for the day, she took a shower, thinking it might help revive her spirits and give her much needed energy.

"Good morning, Uma," Annie replied. "You do not look like you sleep well. Your eyes look tired."

"I didn't, Annie. I didn't." She poured herself a cup of coffee before she started her usual morning task of setting the big table.

"It will get better," Annie pronounced.

Uma hoped the woman had some ancient Cherokee knowledge that could see the future and that the prognostication was correct. "That bacon smells good," Uma said as she placed the knives, forks, and spoons beside the plates. The weeks of morning sickness and queasy stomach had passed, and Uma had become ravenous at mealtime and often hungry in between. It was having an effect on her body. She couldn't put off a shopping trip any longer since she had no choice but to wear the same dress she had the day before when she discovered it was the only thing she had that could be fastened around the waist.

Bix entered the kitchen. Uma had been dreading that moment—facing him again after the night before. *He might ask me to leave the ranch,* she thought. *He might not want me here any longer now that he knows. Maybe Tom will have an idea of where I can go.* Although Bix's behavior had been sympathetic, Uma's imagination led her to a deep, dark place. She could easily conceive being shamed about her unwed pregnancy. *Don't be ridiculous!* she told herself. *He was caring, even compassionate, last night. He's not going to turn on me now.* She told herself that, but deep down she wasn't too sure.

When Uma had announced, "I'm pregnant," Bix stared into her eyes, and she was dismayed to find tears forming in her eyes. She didn't want to cry. He didn't speak but pulled her against his chest and wrapped his arms about her. As they stood there, unspeaking, his hands rubbing her back slowly, a comforting feeling came over her, and she relaxed against him.

"Want to tell me about it?"

It poured out as if it had been dammed, awaiting a time to let the pressure release into the atmosphere. She told him the story—the whole story. Of the job she valued, the handsome professor she thought she had bonded with. Their shared interest in the project. The love—what she had thought was love—that formed between them. Then the horrible time. The avalanche and Sheriff Bear coming with the news that his body had been found. Followed by the arrival of a wife she didn't know existed and—even worse—being made aware that she wasn't that special after all. She was only one in a string of lovers he had taken. Nothing special at all.

Bix held her long after her tale had been told. Soothing and kind, he listened, not commenting either on her naivety or the situation she had found herself in—a baby on the way and no husband—then just stood there holding her. Uma even told him the ultimate shame: she had turned out just like her mother and half-sister. She had tried so hard to escape the lifestyle she had been raised in, only to find herself repeating those same patterns. "I don't want to be like them! I don't!" she had said, and Bix pulled her tighter and murmured, "You aren't. Believe me, you aren't like them at all."

"Good morning, Annie. Uma," Bix said as he entered the kitchen, and Uma was pulled back to the present. "What's for breakfast?" The words were what might be expected from him, but his tone was quiet, subdued.

"Pancakes," Annie answered. "How many you want?"

"I'll start with four," he replied. All the time he spoke, he was looking at Uma. Their gazes met, but then she dropped hers to the task she was doing.

"How many for you, Uma?" Annie asked.

"Umm . . . two will be plenty."

"I can cook more if you finish and want more."

The back door opened, and Tom and Lovie came in. "Good morning, everyone" came their mingled greetings. Both Bix and Uma's voices were subdued as they answered, "Good morning." The newcomers looked at them, then at each other.

"Is something wrong?" Tom asked.

"No," Uma answered at the same time Bix said, "Nothing's wrong."

Tom stared at Uma, and she met his gaze and held it. A look of comprehension came over him, and he nodded his head slightly, looking away as he pulled his chair from the table. He looked at Bix thoughtfully.

"What's going on?" Lovie asked, glancing between Uma, Bix, and Tom.

"Nothing's going on, *Louvinia*," Bix replied. His snarky tone as he said her name wasn't up to its usual quality.

She didn't answer back, but frowned as she turned toward Annie, taking the plate of pancakes thrust toward her, turned back, and put it in front of Bix.

"Lovie, I wonder if I might use your typewriter after breakfast," Uma asked. "And some of your paper."

"Sure thing," Lovie replied.

"There's a typewriter in the office," Bix said as he slathered butter on his pancakes. "You can use that one. And there is paper, too. Letterhead paper for the Big B."

"There is?" Lovie said. "Where?"

"In the closet," Bix replied. "I can get it out." He frowned. "Or maybe Tom can do it."

"May I use it?" Uma asked. "I want to get some letters in the mail."

"Letters?" Tom's voice had a question in it.

"Yes. I need to get started looking for a job. I only agreed to stay here until you returned and I had a chance to visit with you. I'm going to contact my former employers and notify them that I am available for a new project. They may know of someone who is looking for an editorial assistant."

Bix looked at her pointedly. "I think that is a terrible idea," he said. "I'm sitting here needing a secretary in the worst way and offering you the job. Besides, you never know what kind of a . . . a pervert might contact you and offer you a job. You don't know what you might be getting into." His forehead wrinkled, and his eyes narrowed as he spoke, conveying the seriousness of his words.

"Well, that's my business, isn't it?" Uma retorted. "And for your information, I'm an editorial assistant, not a secretary. If you want a secretary, call the employment office."

"I don't want just any secretary. I want a secretary who knows how to organize my office. I want a secretary who understands my businesses." He threw his napkin on the table and reached for his crutches. "I want *you* for my secretary!" He hobbled toward the door to the back hall, leaving his breakfast barely touched.

"Well, maybe I don't want to be your secretary!" Uma yelled at his back. "You're too hard to work with."

Bix turned his head. "At least I wouldn't . . ." He paused and started over. "At least I'd be honest with you."

Tom put his hand over his eyes. Lovie looked bewildered. Annie smiled.

Chapter 31

By late morning, Uma had letters ready to mail to Austin, Albuquerque, and Seattle. When she shoved them through the slot at the post office in Cottonport, she said a little prayer that one of them would lead to a job suitable for her talents.

She had used the letterhead paper Bix had offered. It looked elegant and furnished the return address and telephone number, which would be memorable and also make it easy for anyone to contact her. The old typewriter he had offered for her use was a pain. *If I were the secretary, I'd insist Bix get a new typewriter,* Uma thought. *Now where did that thought come from?* She looked up from the letter she was folding, startled to find that even a small consideration of accepting Bix's job offer had sneaked into her thoughts.

With the letters on their way, Uma went in search of new clothes. Several hours later, she entered the front door at the Big B, arms full of sacks. Lovie was there, polishing the mirror above the side table in the foyer.

"My goodness, Uma! It looks like you've been doing some shopping."

"I have. Come up to my room," Uma suggested. "I'll show you what all I bought." She paused. "And I want to tell you what's going on."

An hour later the story had been told. It was getting slightly easier, Uma found, to relate how she ended up in Alaska and the sad ending to her adventure there. It was the third time she had said *I'm pregnant*; this time she did it without tears. Although her eyes filled when Lovie hugged her, they didn't spill over. Uma counted it a step in the right direction.

Her bed was covered with clothing she had bought in town. There were two pair of jeans and two skirts with soft, stretchy fabric covering the belly; several tops that were interchangeable with the jeans and skirts; two dresses, loose and flowing; plus underwear.

"I love this print," Lovie said, fingering one of the tops. "Why don't you change and put it on with a pair of jeans? I'll bet you'd be more comfortable."

"I think I will," Uma answered. She was tired of the dress she had been wearing for several days. She took off the belt that was holding the gap shut and reached for the buttons running down the front of the cotton shift. Pulling on the jeans, she looked in the mirror above the dresser and ran her hands over the soft panel covering her belly. "Oh, yes. This already feels better." She picked up the navy print top from the bed and slid it over her head.

"I can't believe I didn't figure it out," Lovie said. "I just thought you were gaining a little weight, not that you were pregnant."

"People don't assume an unmarried woman is pregnant," Uma said as she tugged the fullness of the shirt into place.

"I'll bet Annie did. She knows everything without being told."

"I think so, too." Uma studied herself in the mirror.

"So . . . what are you going to do? I mean about the baby," Lovie asked. "Or is that being too nosy?"

"No, it's not too nosy," Uma answered. She turned and went to sit on the side of the bed beside Lovie. "For sure I'm keeping the baby. No way am I going to give it up for adoption. I have a good education, which is the base to find and keep a good job. I make good money when I am working. The only problem is keeping a job. When a project is finished, I am out of work. Hopefully, those letters I sent out today will bring results.

"The ideal thing would for me to find a job at a university that could use me in some capacity full time, while loaning me to whichever person or department needed my special services at the time. It will be harder to pick up and move with a child."

She stood and started picking up the clothing from the bed, an item at a time, and putting it on a hanger from the closet. "This is the first time since I graduated from college that I haven't been employed—or at least on my way to the next project."

"And each time you have to find a new place to live," Lovie said. "Now you'll have to find childcare as well."

"That's true," Uma said, picking up the stack of underwear and putting it in a dresser drawer.

"For your sake, I hope you hear about a job soon. But I'm also selfish, and I wish you could stay here. I like having another woman my age around. I mean . . . I love Tom and all . . . but . . ."

"I caught on about you and Tom right away," Uma said. "It's hard to miss, but this is the first time I've heard you say anything about it. It's serious, then? I mean, not just another romance?"

"It's serious," Lovie said, looking down at where her fingers were playing with the pattern in the bedspread. "He's asked me to marry him, and I've said yes. The only hold up is Bix's broken leg. When that happened, it stopped some of the business things going on." She looked up at Uma. "The other problem has been resolved."

"What was that?"

"Tom refused to get married until you knew about it, and he didn't know how to find you."

Uma smiled. "Really?"

"Really," Lovie said. "He loves you very much. He feels like you are the only family he has. I'm so happy you've come back to Texas. I hope the next job you find is somewhere here in the state, or at least nearby. He wants to stay close to his sister, and now I know he'll want to be near his niece or nephew."

"Do you have any idea where you will live after you marry? Will you stay here on the ranch?"

"No, definitely not here on the Big B. Bix will live here and manage the cattle operation, as he is now, and receive the reports and oversee the oil. Whenever they—Bix and Tom—buy whatever businesses they are going to add to Big B Enterprises, then Tom will supervise all that, with input from Bix. We'll live wherever is handiest. Your map will help show us where. We're thinking possibly Houston or somewhere thereabouts."

Lovie rose from the bed and walked toward the door. "I'd better go see if Annie needs any help starting dinner." She turned back to face Uma. "Oh! I didn't ask. Did you have lunch in town? Do you need something to eat?"

"Thanks, but I got a milkshake at the Dairy Cone in town. It had been a long time since I had one, and the thought of ice cream just pulled me in. I'm not hungry now, but I imagine I will be by dinner."

"OK," Lovie said. She had the door open a crack when she released the knob and threw her arms around Uma to hug her. "I'm so glad you are going to be my sister," she said before she rushed out the door.

Wow! A sister! The thought startled Uma so much she went to the chair beside the bed and sat there to think about it. When Tom and Lovie married, Uma would have a sister-in-law. She would be delighted to have Lovie as family . . . absolutely delighted.

Chapter 32

Uma gladly went back to the project of organizing Bix's office. Now that the letters to her former places of employment were in the mail, there was nothing more she could think of to do on that front. Her secret was out in the open, so she was no longer worrying about the reaction of anyone in the household. Not one to stay idle, Uma spent her time with the piles of newspapers, magazines, and stray notes that cluttered the room that Bix occupied.

At first, Bix was a different person around her: gentle, polite, totally un-Bix-like. But gradually he returned to the teasing, joking man he had been before. As Uma became more familiar with the Big B businesses and what Bix needed to be able to find in his office, she took the initiative. It took a little over a week to have the office neat and organized.

"Bix, have you ever thought about having the telephone company redo your phone system—set it up like a business?" Uma asked one day.

"No. Why?"

"Because half the time I answer, it's for the household, not Big B. It may be a store or Fran or someone else, and I have to go find Annie or Lovie. It seems like it would be handy to have a business phone with more than one number and tie the new number in to a phone in the kitchen. You could tell by which light was blinking who needs to answer. Are there phones upstairs?"

"Yes, there is a phone in the master bedroom."

"Is that where you usually sleep?"

"Yes, it is. And I will again before long."

"When will you get that cast off?"

"I see the doctor next week. Maybe he'll tell me."

"In any case, give some thought to what a good setup for phones would be. The number you have now could be for Big B, with a second number for the household. How does the barn operate, phone-wise?"

"They have a separate number," Bix answered.

"The telephone company could tell you, but I think you could have a phone on your desk with all three numbers coming in, and you could answer any of them, if you wanted."

The next week the system was in place. "This feels like a real business," Bix said, running his fingers over the buttons on the phone.

"It ought to," Uma replied. "It *is* a real business, after all."

"Yeah, I'm beginning to get the idea," he responded.

~ ~ ~

The doctor had told Bix he had to stay in the cast a couple more weeks, although the pain was all but gone. Bix spent a lot of time in the barn working with Ellis Ponder, or in conferences with Tom about the possibilities of storage facilities in Texas towns in the eastern half of the state.

As Bix contacted real estate brokers in various towns, Uma made folders with all the information about both the broker and the locality she could find. One day, as she was working in the office, Bix was on the phone with a broker in Longview.

"Well, if you have a listing you think the Big B would be interested in, you can call me at the number I gave you. You can speak to Tom Thornton—he's my manager for Big B Enterprises or, if he's not here, talk to my . . ." Bix looked up at Uma, who had stopped what she was doing and frowned at him. "Talk to my assistant. Uma. Yes, that's right. Uma.

She knows what's going on—she's my right hand . . . er . . . person. You can talk to her anytime."

"So I'm not your secretary?" Uma asked after he hung up.

"Certainly not," Bix looked away. "You are much more than a secretary. You are my assistant. My *executive* assistant."

"Executive assistant?"

"That's right. You've been promoted."

"From general flunky to executive assistant?"

"That's right."

"What's the difference?" Uma asked, grinning.

Bix frowned. "A raise," he said. "You get a raise in salary."

"But I don't get a salary."

"Starting today you do." Bix reached for his crutches. "Enough working for nothing."

"I've told you, I don't expect pay. You are furnishing me room and board, so to speak. I don't expect nor want any pay." Uma gathered a stack of papers from her lap and frowned at him.

"Well, missy, you might as well get used to taking it." He stood in front of where she was sitting in the wing-back chair. "I would be paying, big time, for someone who could do what you are doing for me, and I probably couldn't find anyone in Cottonport or vicinity that could do the job you are doing. You've organized me and got me on the right track. You have furnished a huge service to Big B—a service no one else could do. I couldn't begin to find someone who could match your skills." He shifted on the crutches. "So you'll take a salary or else."

"Or else what?" Uma couldn't resist asking.

"Or else . . ." Bix frowned as he thought. "Or else I'll fire you!" He clumped out of the office.

Does that mean I couldn't work on any of this? When she came to the realization that she was truly interested and involved in Big B business, the phone rang.

"Big B," she answered. "Yes, this is Uma Thornton, Mr. Crandall's executive assistant, and I can help you." She realized she had accepted Bix's offer of employment.

Chapter 33

Uma spent little time dwelling on the results, or lack thereof, from the letters she had mailed to her former employers, although every few days she was clutched by the fear that nothing would come of them. *What if it comes time for the baby to be born, and I still don't have a job by then? Big B isn't my home, and I can't bring a baby here as if it were.* She mailed in an insurance payment each month and finally made an appointment with a doctor in Cottonport. She couldn't keep on ignoring the fact she needed to make arrangements.

Then Uma put thoughts of the upcoming birth to the back of her mind and returned to taking notes about the grain elevator for sale in Texarkana, the cotton warehouse that would come up for auction in a month in Beaumont, and she would contact the broker in Tyler concerning the property he had called about the week prior. It was up to her to ask all the questions before Tom flew off to check it out. She felt much more connected to the work than she had ever done when organizing and editing books for publication, and it was satisfying to her.

One day when the phone rang, she answered it as she always did. Bix was in the barn, conferring with the foreman about the fall sale of cattle. "Big B. Yes, this is Uma Thornton speaking." She expected it to be concerning one of the many calls they had out to real estate companies across the state, or perhaps even an individual who had heard they were buying. When she hung up, she sat stunned.

"What is it? What's happened?" Bix, who had just walked in the office door, asked.

"It was . . . it was the publishing company," she said.

"What publishing company?"

"McDutton-Parker Books," Uma replied. "They are publishing the book on Alaska."

"The one you helped write?" Bix asked.

"I didn't help write it." Uma pulled herself together. "I just organized and typed it."

"Yes, well, the one the jerk wrote." Bix leaned his crutches against the desk and took a seat in the wing-back chair before it. "The jerk that . . ." He quit speaking and pressed his lips together tightly, as if to hold in the words.

"Alex wrote it. Dr. Alexander Keillor is . . . was . . . was his name."

"Whatever. So, what did the publishing company want?"

"They are having a big release nationwide. What with Alaska becoming the forty-ninth state and Alex dying like he did, there is big talk about the book. They have rushed the printing and are having release parties in major cities around the country. They want me to come to the one in Dallas and talk about how the folktales were gathered."

Bix simply stared at Uma. Finally, he asked, "Are you going to do it?" His voice was low and raspy, and he dropped his gaze.

"I suppose so," Uma replied. She placed her hands flat on the desk, unable to think of what she should do next—unable to think of anything except Alaska and the prospect of pulling her thoughts away from the Big B and back to the subject she had been trying so hard to forget. "I told him I'd think about it."

"Are they going to pay you?" Bix looked up.

"Yes." She picked up a pen, twirling it among her fingers. "And it would be great publicity for finding another job. I haven't had much luck with that."

"You have a job," Bix said.

"But not the kind I am trained to do."

"It seems to me that you are trained just fine," Bix said, and anger flared in his voice. "You are doing just fine. Better than fine. You are the best assistant I could have." He stopped speaking and rubbed his face with both hands. After a moment, he took them down and asked again, "Are you going to do it? Go to Dallas?"

Uma didn't speak as she rolled all the emotion around in her mind. "Yes," she finally answered. "I think I need to."

Bix snorted.

"It's the last thing I can do to finish that project. When I do that, I'll be through with it." She ran her fingers through her long, blond hair, pulling it away from her face. "In every case, the job I finish has led me to the next one. Maybe that's why I haven't found a job yet. I haven't finished the last one."

Bix shoved himself to his feet, and muttering an obscenity, he left the room.

Chapter 34

The trip to Dallas was to take place in three weeks' time. A large, independently owned bookstore was hosting the event. They had a special room that was used to accommodate book signings, lectures, and author meet-and-greets. Although Uma was nervous over the prospect of speaking before a crowd of people, the publisher's representative assured her that her talk could be short—as little as fifteen or twenty minutes. "The main thing," he said, "is to create interest so the public will be aware of the book and then buy it. Only you can answer questions about how Dr. Keillor gathered the information to write the book. Tell about him going to the remote villages to gather the stories. Explain how you got to town to buy supplies. People want to know about Alaska and how people live up there." He hinted that Alex's death and the manner in which it occurred added to the interest, but he didn't come out and say that. In fact, he said, "You don't have to talk about Dr. Keillor's death if it upsets you. I wouldn't want you to be uncomfortable."

Uma hadn't definitely said yes when the representative first called, but after thinking about it for two days, she decided she could do it without losing control of her emotions, so she called the phone number he had given to her and told him she would come.

Bix was finally out of his cast. Able to wear trousers with both legs in them, he hobbled around the house with the help of a cane, daily growing more steady and pain free. He could make his way up the stairs, one step at a time, and he resumed occupancy of the master suite at the end of the hall. Uma hoped that the proximity wouldn't be a problem, and it wasn't. They seldom met upstairs. Bix was up and out of the house long before she stirred each morning, and since the master bedroom had its own bath, there was no problem with sharing the facilities.

The downstairs room that had accommodated him was an office once again. The hospital bed went back to the rental agency, the recliner was returned to the living room, and the map went up on the wall, over time gaining more and more pins marking Big B properties. Tom flew out at least once a week, visiting various towns in the eastern half of Texas. Uma kept up with the information on the several properties of interest to Big B Enterprises, and she also kept records on those they considered but rejected for the time being. She spent more time in the office than Bix did.

"This was originally the ranch headquarters," Lovie told her one day. "Aunt Annie said that when this house was built, it was the only office on the place. Then Mrs. Barnett, Bix's grandmother, became ill and couldn't go up the stairs any longer, so Mr. Barnett—the original Big B—had the bathroom added and the room furnished as her bedroom. That's when the office in the big barn was added. When she died, this went back to being an office."

"So it's made a full circle," Uma said. "Office to bedroom, to office, to bedroom, and back to office again."

"I hope it never has to go back to being an invalid's room again," Lovie said.

Uma asked Bix if she could use the Impala to drive to Dallas for the book release. "I'll get you to Dallas and back," he informed her. "Don't worry about it."

"I'm not worrying about it," she replied. "I can drive myself there and back."

"Darlin', you don't know your way around Dallas," he said. "I do."

"But I don't expect you to furnish transportation for me. This is a job I'm going to, and I need to provide for myself."

Uma thought he was going to lose his temper when his face muscles tensed up, but then he relaxed and reached out to smooth a strand of her hair behind her ear. "I'm going to start calling you, instead of Louvinia, Mighty Mouse. You are so determined to refuse any help from me." He cradled one side of her face in his hand. "I have business I can transact in Dallas as well," he said. "And I'm familiar with the town. You might as well give in. I'm planning this trip for the both of us." He smiled, dropped his hand, and hobbled to the kitchen to fix himself a glass of iced tea.

Bix told her to be ready just after lunch the day before she was to speak. Uma borrowed a small bag from Lovie to pack for the trip. "Thanks, Lovie. I didn't want to go buy luggage, and all I have are the two big suitcases, one of which is still filled with work clothing and cold weather garb." As she packed for the trip, Lovie sat on the bed and watched. "I guess I can get rid of the Alaska clothes. I doubt that I'll ever go back there again."

Inside, a little tremor ran through her body. At one time, she had looked forward to seeing more of the newest of the United States, but now the thought of Alaska left her sad. She pushed it from her mind. In two days' time, she would have to speak of it, but for now, she would thrust it to the back of her mind, and when she stood at the podium, she would think only of dispassionate parts, not of Alex, nor the baby conceived there.

"I don't know, Uma," Lovie said. "You might get a job someplace up north. Even if it's not Alaska, it can get pretty frigid in some places. You might need them if you end up someplace like Minnesota or North Dakota."

"Maybe," Uma responded. She was afraid if she dressed in the same clothing she wore when . . . *No! I won't think of him! I won't.*

Bix refused to tell her what plans he had made. "Be ready for anything," he said, so Uma was packed and downstairs shortly after they ate the noon meal. She assumed they were driving when Bix met her in the foyer with his own bag, and he said, "You drive your car." Uma had given up correcting him when he said, "your car." It was the Big B's car; she only drove it when she went to town to buy office supplies, although she had used it the one time she had made an introductory visit to the local doctor. She noticed, however, that Lovie used Tom's pickup when she went to town, and Peanut used an older, much-dented vehicle when he was sent to pick up whatever was needed by Annie or Bix.

Bix was dressed in typical western gear: dark, freshly pressed Levi's, a white western shirt with a bolo tie, ornate belt buckle, western boots, and his white Stetson. The cane in his hand was the one he was using every day—an ornately carved staff with a dragon figure curled and curved around the length of it.

Peanut was to take their bags to the car. Uma was sure she could have managed her own bag, and it seemed lazy to have someone do for her what she could have done for herself, but she didn't argue. She simply smiled and said, "Thank you, Peanut."

Uma turned the car toward the main road. At a fork in the long driveway, Bix said, "Turn here." He directed her to the ranch's airfield, situated about a mile away. She had never been there before and was surprised to see a hangar with two gas pumps beside the large door. A slim man dressed in a dark blue uniform trimmed in gold braid was standing beside a sleek jet airplane.

"Just pull inside the hangar, darlin'," Bix said, his Texas drawl strong. "We'll leave your car in there." Uma turned to face him. He smiled.

"I thought we were driving," she said.

"Nope. We're flying," Bix said as he opened the passenger door. He went to the trunk and withdrew their bags, grasping the handles of both in one hand while he held his cane in the other.

"Darlin', this is Steve. He's our pilot for this trip," Bix said as they approached the plane. "Steve, this is Uma. She's going to be speaking at a gathering in Dallas."

"Pleased to meet you," Steve said, touching the bill of his pilot's cap.

"Let's get on board, darlin'," Bix said. "We've got places to go and things to do."

When both Uma and Bix were settled into the luxurious leather seats, Steve pulled the plane onto the runway, and soon they were in the air.

"It's a beautiful day for a flight," Bix commented.

"Sure is," Uma answered, looking out the window as she watched the ground shrink away. She turned toward Bix. "Is this a Big B Enterprises airplane? That is, do you own it?"

"Not yet," he answered. "I'm just trying it out."

"Trying it out?"

"Yeah. To see what I think." He patted the arms of the seat. "Comfy, isn't it?"

"Yes, comfy."

"It's a Sabreliner." Bix looked around the cabin. "Thing is, it might not be big enough."

"Not big enough?" Uma thought she sounded like a parrot, repeating what Bix said, but when she opened her mouth, whatever he had just said fell out.

"Yeah. It only holds four passengers." He leaned forward, turning and craning his neck to see the two seats behind where he and Uma sat. "We could go somewhere with Tom and Lovie, and there is room for a co-pilot along with the pilot, but what if we wanted more folks along with us? What then?"

"Uh-huh." Uma couldn't imagine such a thing.

"But if I buy a bigger plane, say a JetStar, we could carry ten passengers. That would be enough for the whole family, but then we'd have to make the runway longer to land and take off at the ranch."

Uma couldn't take in the fact that he was planning on buying an airplane, let alone a larger one. Finally, she asked, "You're really thinking about it? About buying a plane?"

Bix looked at her, eyebrows raised. "Well, sure. You see how hard it is to get Tom around to every place he needs to be, and it takes too long to drive, especially if we spread out to more places."

"Airplanes must cost an awful lot of money," Uma said tentatively.

"They do," Bix agreed. "It just depends on how much it costs to travel by commercial airlines, and how much time we save, and how much it costs to fly our own planes, and all that."

"Uh-huh." Uma just stared at him.

"That's where you come in."

What? "Me? What do I have to do with it?"

"You can research all that. You know how to research stuff. And you can make folders and all, keep records, answer my questions when I have them." He had a smug look on his face as he faced her. "I might need to buy two planes."

"Two?" Uma was almost beyond asking questions.

"A big one and a little one," Bix answered.

The innocent expression on his face made her suspicious. The more Bix tried to look innocent, usually it was because he wasn't.

"Folks," the voice of the pilot came over a speaker, although he was seated directly in front of them. "We're fixin' to encounter a little turbulence. There's a thunderstorm over to our east. We aren't going to fly through it, just around the edge, but we might get shook up a bit. Be sure you have your seatbelts on."

Uma grasped the armrests. She had flown before: from Albuquerque to Seattle. From Seattle to Fairbanks. From Fairbanks to Houston. She had even flown on another small plane when she flew from Fairbanks to the small Alaskan village and back. But she had never flown through turbulence. The thought of it made her nervous. She looked out the window to find that the clouds had moved in close to them, touching the windows with streaks of gray and white.

"It'll be OK," Bix said. "Steve's a good pilot. There's nothing to worry about."

Uma didn't speak. At that moment, the small plane dipped, leaving her stomach topsy-turvy. She held on tightly.

Bix placed his hand over hers and squeezed. "Just think of it as a ride at the carnival," he said.

"I never liked those rides," Uma responded.

"What did you like?" Bix asked. "Did you ride any rides at all?"

"Mostly, we didn't have any money to go to the carnival," Uma said. "But I remember when my father was alive. He took me on the Ferris wheel. I liked that. I liked seeing far away over the town."

"How old were you when your father died?"

"Five," she responded. Then Bix asked another question, and another, and before Uma knew it, the clouds were gone and the flight smooth. She was no longer clinging to the armrest, but Bix was still holding her hand in his.

"We'll be landing at Love Field in about ten minutes," Steve's voice said over the speaker.

Chapter 35

"There has to be a mistake," Uma said.

"Ma'am, there is no problem with your room. McDutton-Parker Publishing reserved several rooms weeks ago," the desk clerk said. "Yours is ready and waiting for you."

"But you've lost *my* reservation," Bix said.

The clerk ran his finger over the list in front of him one more time.

"Sir, I do not see a reservation for Bix Crandall anywhere on the list."

"Or Big B Ranch, or Big B Enterprises," Bix added.

"No sir. Nothing under Big B at all. Nothing under Crandall." The clerk folded his hands together on top of the sheet of paper and looked at Bix over the top of his glasses. His words were set in stone.

"I called it in over two weeks ago. Somebody goofed," Bix said.

"Be that as it may, there is no reservation, and the hotel is full," the man behind the counter said haughtily. "There are no rooms available."

"What will you do?" Uma asked. "Go to another hotel?"

"That probably won't do any good," the clerk said. There are several conventions in town, and the good hotels are full." He looked from Uma to Bix and back again. "However . . ."

"Yes?" Uma and Bix said together.

"Your room," he said, looking at Uma, "has a king-size bed, should you wish to share a room." His glance fell to her belly, then darted back and forth between the couple. The unspoken message was clear: *You slept with him once. Why can't you share a bed now?*

"Let's go to your room and talk about this," Bix said. Uma remained silent.

"That's room 714," the clerk said as he handed the key to the bellhop who was waiting a few steps away with their luggage. Both clerk and bellboy looked relieved to have come to some sort of solution.

When they reached Uma's room, the bellhop slid the two suitcases in and exited quickly, before there was a possibility he could get pulled into a discussion about the missing reservation. Bix caught him before the door swung shut and slipped bills into his hand, while Uma looked around.

"This is nice," she said. It was the first time she had stayed in an upscale hotel. The few times she had traveled, she had chosen a motel on the side of the highway for her sleeping spot, something clean-looking, but not luxurious.

The carpet under their feet was plush. The bed took up the majority of the room, although the desk and chair didn't make it crowded, nor did the dresser with the large television on top. The color coordination of the drapes, bed, carpet, and pictures on the wall was pleasing, the furniture good quality.

"I can sleep on the floor," Bix said, moving from one foot to the other, testing the comfort of the carpet. "There's plenty of room."

"You can't—You can't sleep on the floor." *Where else is there?* She walked to the window and gazed at the busy street below and then turned back toward the bed. "That's the biggest bed I've ever seen."

"It's the newest thing. It's called a king-size. It's bigger than a regular bed."

Uma had no words.

"I'll be OK on the floor. Really I will." Bix sounded sincere. "I've slept on the ground many a time, trying to prove I was a real cowboy like the old timers who used to ride the range. This floor will be a lot more comfortable than dirt and rocks. I'll get housekeeping to bring up some more blankets and pillows, and I'll be as comfy as can be."

He looks like he's telling the truth, Uma thought. *And what else can we do? I can't just make him leave and go find someplace else.*

"OK, I guess," she said. "If you're sure it won't be too uncomfortable."

"I'll be fine. I promise." He picked up his bag. "I'll just hang up tomorrow's shirt so the wrinkles will fall out." Thinking that was a good idea, Uma hung up the dress she planned to wear.

"Let's go scout out the neighborhood," Bix said. "Didn't you say the bookstore where you'll be speaking is close by?"

"Yes, that's what the letter from the publisher said." She dug into her purse, pulled out a folded paper, and read the address aloud.

"That sounds like it's only a couple of blocks away. We could get a taxi if you want, or we could walk there," Bix said.

"Let's walk. I'm tired of sitting."

A few minutes later they found themselves in front of the wide glass windows of a bookstore. The volumes spread across the display all had some tie to Alaska, and front and center was a stack of the books Uma was most interested in: *Tales of the Frozen Frontier: Folk Stories and Legends of Alaska, by Dr. Alexander Keillor.* A small easel held a framed photograph of Alex, dressed in gear that suggested he might have been in Alaska, but Uma recognized that he was younger when it was taken. Still, she caught her breath at the reminder of him, but the longer she looked, the more the memories faded away, as if he were someone she knew a long time ago. The emotional blow she expected never came.

"That him?" Bix asked. She nodded. He looked into her face. "You OK?"

"Yes," Uma said. "I'm fine." She looked back at him and smiled. "But I'm hungry. Let's go eat."

Chapter 36

Bix drew her arm through his and held it close to his body. Grasping his cane in his right hand, he smiled down at her. "Sure 'nough, darlin'. Let's go get something to eat." They started back the way they had come. "I wish I had thought to bring a suit. I would take you someplace fancy for dinner."

"I don't want someplace fancy," Uma retorted. "I'd like a hamburger and fries."

"I reckon we can take care of that order at the hotel coffee shop. That OK with you?"

"That's fine with me," Uma said.

"I'd take you upstairs to the Skyroom, but they probably wouldn't let a poor cowboy like me in."

"You're not a poor cowboy. You're a rich cowboy, and what do you mean? This is Texas. It was built on cowboys," Uma said as they strolled along.

"Honey, this is Big D. They ignore cowboys in Dallas. They like oilmen better here," Bix said as they waited for the traffic light at the corner to change.

"Well, you're an oilman as well as a cowboy," Uma retorted.

"Yeah, but oilmen dress a bit different. If we wanted to eat in the Skyroom, I'd need to wear a suit, even if it's a western suit, not jeans."

"Really?"

"Really. I'm dressed for Fort Worth, not Dallas."

Uma looked into his face to see if he was kidding. She couldn't tell.

"Next time we come to Big D, I'll take you some place fancy," Bix said.

"I'd be uncomfortable in any place that was fancy," Uma said. "You're dressed fine to eat any place I'd want to go to." The bustle of city life was all around them, and Uma realized how much she had grown accustomed to the quiet of the ranch.

True to her word, when they were seated in the hotel coffee shop, which was much nicer than any such place Uma had ever been in, she ordered a hamburger and fries. Bix ordered a steak.

"That's a good choice," the waitress told him. "It's the same steak they serve upstairs, minus the sprig of parsley, and it's ten dollars cheaper."

After an excellent meal, it was time to return to the room where the message light on the phone was blinking. The publisher's representative was checking to be sure she was in town and ready for her presentation the next morning.

"I'm as ready as I'll ever be, Mr. Morgan," she replied.

"The bookstore is just over a block away," he said. "Should I arrange to have a taxi pick you up in the morning?"

"No. That won't be necessary. We walked to it this afternoon, so I know where it is. Unless it's raining, a taxi won't be needed."

"I'll see you about a quarter until ten, then," he said. "The program is scheduled to start at ten."

When she hung up, Bix was coming out of the bathroom. "Sugar, I didn't bring any pajamas to sleep in," he said. "So, I'll just keep my undies on tonight. You get ready for bed first and slide on in. I'll call down and get some more blankets and pillows to make me a pallet."

"Bix, I hate for you to sleep on the floor, but . . ."

"It'll be fine, darlin'. It really will."

She took her bag and went into the bathroom. When she returned, wearing the one nightgown her blossoming belly would still fit in, a flannel "granny gown," Bix was wrapped in one blanket and stretched out on the floor, his head resting on one of the pillows from the bed.

"I thought you were going to get more blankets and pillows," Uma said.

"They didn't have any."

"They didn't?"

Bix grunted. Uma slid into bed on the side farthest from him and switched off the lamp. She tried to remain still, but the thought of Bix sleeping on the hard floor—she had no doubt it was hard, even with plush carpet—made her uncomfortable as well.

"Bix?"

"Yeah."

"There's no sense in you sleeping on the floor when there is this big bed."

"I was hopin' you'd say that." She could hear him sit up and saw the dark outline of his head pop up.

"You have to promise to stay on your side."

"I promise," he said as he pulled back the covers and slipped in.

After some tossing to get comfortable, all was quiet.

"Uma?"

"What?"

"Can I have a goodnight kiss?" he asked with a chuckle.

"No."

They fell asleep, each as far to their respective sides of the bed as they could get, but when Uma awoke early the next morning, she was nestled against Bix's back, and he was snoring lightly.

Chapter 37

"Mr. Morgan?" Uma approached the man in the suit and tie who was restacking the pile of books on a table at the front of the room.

"Yes?" He peered at her over the top of his glasses, looking her up and down. His gaze lingered a brief moment on her belly.

"I'm Uma Thornton," she said as she extended her hand. His mouth dropped open, and he hesitated before accepting her handshake.

"Uh . . . yes, Ms. Thornton." His eyes widened. "You . . . you aren't what I expected."

"Oh?" She wasn't going to let him off the hook. "And what, or should I say who, did you expect?"

"A much older woman. Maybe gray hair in a bun. You see," he said, "I talked with some of the authors you have worked with, and they described you as such an accomplished assistant, that I imagined you to be . . . well, as I said, much older. Not so young. Yes. Hmm . . ." His eyes strayed once again to her belly.

Time to get the subject off me and onto the book. "*Tales from the Frozen Frontier.* I wish we could have come up with a catchier title," Uma said as she picked one off the stack on the table sitting by the podium. "This is the first time I've had a chance to see the published product."

"Really? I'll have to be sure you get one before you leave," Morgan said. "The acquiring editor I am working with said it came to him practically ready for printing. It was so completely proofed and assembled in proper order that nothing much had to be done to it."

"That's my job," Uma said. "That's what I do for my clients." *No sense in not tooting my own horn. That's what I'm here for, to find my next job.*

"And what are you working on now? Something interesting?"

"I think it is." *I'm not lying. What I'm doing is very interesting.* "One of the largest family-owned concerns in Texas. Oil. Cattle. Aviation. Widespread investments throughout the state."

"And who is the author? McDutton-Parker might be interested in a contract before the word gets out," Morgan asked. His eyes lit up. "Anything about Texas always sells well."

"We aren't at the stage to make it public yet," Uma said. "Big B Enterprises is a closely held business. There is even a Hollywood connection to the family that may be interested. Right now I'm making a lot of index cards and folders. Putting things in order and all that." *Definitely not a lie.*

"I'm very interested in hearing more about it. I'm sure McDutton-Parker would want to have the first chance at a contract." Morgan glanced at his watch. "I'll talk to you about it later, but right now it's about time to start. It looks like we're going to have a good crowd. Standing room only, maybe. Can I get you anything before we start?"

"A glass of water on the podium, please." Uma turned to face the room. Rows of chairs, enough to accommodate forty or fifty people, were almost full. She saw Bix sitting about a third of the way back, and when he saw her look his way, he grinned at her until the man sitting next to him pointed to Bix's ornate cane, and he turned away to answer. Several people were scanning the room, looking for a place to sit, and there was a line still coming in the door.

Uma mentally thanked her advisor for pressuring her to take public speaking while she was at the University of Texas. Otherwise, the thought of getting up in front of the group might have made her lose all awareness of what she was going to say. But she had spoken to several groups that size or larger, and she had her ever-present index cards to keep her on track. She took a seat in one of the chairs in the front row with a "reserved" sign on it, ready to pop up when she was introduced.

"Ms. Thornton? I'm Bill Sexton, manager of Everyone's Bookstore. We're so happy you are here today. We've been looking forward to hearing about your adventures in Alaska." The slim, balding man stopped in front of her and shook her hand. "I'll just introduce you, and we'll get started." He took the one small step onto the raised area across the front of the room and stood behind the microphone. Tapping it slightly, he frowned, flipped a switch on the side, and tapped again.

"If I may have your attention, please," he said, and the room grew quiet. "It is the great pleasure of Everyone's Bookstore to have a special guest speaker today. As you probably know, the author of *Tales from the Frozen Frontier*, Dr. Alexander Keillor, met with an untimely death in an avalanche just as he finished writing this fascinating and comprehensive book about the legends and tales that are part of the history of our forty-ninth state.

"Today, we have with us Dr. Keillor's assistant, Uma Thornton, who was by the author's side as he gathered the stories that are related in *Tales from the Frozen Frontier*. She transcribed his notes and tape recordings into written form and followed his instruction as she arranged those writings into the order in which they were published. Ms. Thornton, we eagerly await what you have to tell us about our newest state." Sexton turned to Uma, stretching his arm in her direction in greeting. He moved forward and offered his hand as she stepped up onto the dais.

She took the manager's place behind the podium. "Thank you, Mr. Sexton, for that kind introduction. You know, don't you," Uma said as he took his seat in the front row, "that that introduction will only be good for a few more days, as Hawaii will join our great nation as the newest state next week?" Everyone in the audience either laughed or acted surprised. "Alaska has had that honor only seven short months, but early on Dr. Keillor was there, on the frozen frontier, recording the folk stories that have been handed down for generations. Oral tales that were passed from father to son, from grandmother and grandfather, from aunt and uncle, to each following age."

Uma's speech touched on many of the creatures and beliefs held by the Inuit, Eskimo, and Aleut inhabitants of the far north. She told of the Qalupalik, the green-skinned, long-haired creature that might carry off children who did not stay close to their parents' side; and the sea-creature, the Tzherak; and the dog-man, the Adlet. "Unfortunately, Dr. Keillor's life was cut short before he could make plans to continue his studies of the subject. It was his interest to find out how far these tales spread. Were they the same legends told in the northeastern parts of Russia, for example, and how far east did they spread into Canada?"

Uma spoke for close to twenty minutes before she paused and asked the audience if they had any questions. She held her breath as she looked around for raised hands. One thing she learned in the class for public speaking was that questions indicated an interested audience, but the type of question that might be asked made her nervous. She didn't want to face any questions about the death of her lover. Her equilibrium was fine, so far, but talking about the avalanche and the details of his demise might be more than she could handle.

Question after question came, not about the mythical

creatures, but another kind of question. What kind of transportation did they use? Was there heat? Electricity? Indoor bathrooms? Did bears threaten them? *If I am asked to speak again,* Uma thought, *I'll lead in with this information.*

So, Uma spoke another few minutes about the village, accessible mainly by small plane.

"Dr. Keillor used a four-wheel-drive pickup truck on snow-packed trails to travel to the native settlements where he gathered most of his stories.

"No, I didn't accompany him, I stayed at the cabin we used as headquarters and transcribed the tapes, eventually arranging and typing them in the order to be published in book form.

"I drove a snow-buggy, a motorized vehicle on ski-like devices, to the village not far away.

"Yes, there was a store where I could buy most anything I needed. If they didn't have what I wanted, they would order it, and it would come by plane in a few days.

"There was a café if I wanted to eat there while I was in town.

"No, there were only a few telephones. Most people used the one at the general store.

"Yes, there was a doctor in town—a very good one, I understood, although I never needed to go to him.

"No, I was never afraid."

Finally, Mr. Sexton put an end to the questions. "Folks, any other questions you may have are probably answered in Dr. Keillor's book, which we have for sale." He signaled to a young woman with a printing calculator and a money box, who came forward to sit at the table with the books. "I'm sure Ms. Thornton would be happy to sign a book for you, if you buy one." He looked at Uma, who nodded. "But let's allow her to sit down as she does it. Thank you for coming to Everyone's Bookstore, and watch for our next event."

"I'm sure you must be ready to get off your feet," he said to Uma. "My wife's feet swelled when she was . . . uh, well, why don't you sit here on the front row? That was a very good presentation. Very interesting. Do you have a pen? No?" He pulled one from his pocket and handed it to her. "If it has a receipt sticking out of the top, it's paid for, and you can sign it."

By the time he had walked Uma to her seat, the first buyers approached her with their copies of *Tales from the Frozen Frontier*, bubbling over with accolades and more questions. A line formed, and Uma's hand quickly tired from signing over and over.

At last the crowd grew sparse. One woman had held back. Uma caught notice of someone standing in the back of the room as she finished signing, someone with curly red hair. *It can't be. It's just my imagination playing tricks on me.* A woman approached and stood directly in front of Uma; she was the person she thought she'd never have to encounter again.

Chapter 38

Uma knew her own face was molded into a disingenuous smile, as if she were a doll made of plastic. That's what she felt like—plastic. She thought she handled herself well. She said the right things to Mr. Sexton—thanked him for all he did to make her comfortable at the presentation. She also said the right things—or at least she thought she did—to Mr. Morgan. When he complimented her on her speech, she had said that she was grateful for the opportunity. When he handed her an envelope, she looked at it blankly until he said, "Your check," and she nodded her head.

Bix showed up at her elbow and guided her out of the room, out of the bookstore. He looked into her eyes and asked, "Are you alright?"

"I'm alright." But she knew she wasn't. She held onto his arm and let him lead her where she should go. She heard him ask Mr. Sexton to get them a taxi, and sure enough, when they went out the front door, there was one waiting. When she climbed into the back seat of the cab, she closed her eyes and wished she could go to sleep and wake up back on the Big B. She wished the day had never happened.

"Maybe you need something to eat," Bix said, after he had joined her and told the taxi driver to take them to the hotel to pick up their bags, then to Love Field.

She shook her head. "I'm not hungry." She sat motionless. *I don't even want to think.* She was glad Bix was quiet on the ride to the airport.

Bix helped Uma out of the car, grabbed their bags, paid the driver, and hustled her through the busy terminal to the gate where the little Sabreliner was waiting. When they were in the air, Bix took her hands in his. "When we get back home, I think you need to see the doctor."

Uma shook her head. "No, I don't need the doctor."

"Something has happened, Uma. Something's wrong."

She remained silent, but tears began to form and slowly ran down her cheeks.

"Are you sick? Is that it? Is it the baby?"

She shook her head. "No, the baby is fine."

"Then . . ." He continued staring into her face. "That woman. That red-headed woman who was talking to you at the bookstore. I was looking at you, and you turned white as she spoke. You dropped your head, and I saw you change. Who was she? What did she say to you?" His voice rose in anger.

"That was . . . she was Alex's wife."

"What was she doing there? What did she want with you?" His voice was low, and Uma thought he sounded as if he was holding himself in tight control.

"I don't know why she was there—keeping track of the marketing of the book, I imagine."

"Tell me what she said to you, Uma. Tell me what upset you."

Uma sighed. She looked out the window at the wisps of clouds they were passing through. She tried to pull her hands from Bix's grip, but he wouldn't let her go.

"She saw that I am pregnant. She said, 'So he gave you what I wanted more than anything in the world. A baby. A baby that he refused to give me.'"

"So she's angry because you got pregnant but she couldn't?"

Uma shrugged. "She couldn't or he wouldn't. I don't know which."

"It's not like you planned it," Bix paused and looked into her face. "Did you?"

"No! It wasn't like that at all. It was very . . . unplanned. The affair, I mean. And when it happened, he thought I was on birth control pills, but I wasn't. He went and bought condoms, but it was too late." She shook her head. "No, I didn't plan to get pregnant. And no, I didn't know he was married, but I wasn't trying to trap him into marriage, if that's what you are thinking."

"I wasn't thinking any such thing," Bix protested.

"Then she said . . . she said," Uma's voice quivered, and tears flowed freely. "She said that she ought to be the one with a baby—Alex's baby—to carry on his heritage. She said as his wife, she ought to be the one raising his child, instead of a fly-by-night assistant who never knew where her next job or home was going to be. She said I was going to be an unfit mother, and my child—no, she said Alex's child—would suffer because of it." With these words, Uma broke into sobs. Bix released her hands and put his arms around her, holding her close as she cried in great shuddering breaths.

"Shh . . . shh. It's not true. None of it is true."

"But it is. I don't know where my next job will be. I don't know where my next home will be. It is very true." She pulled back and looked into Bix's face. "I'm turning out just like my mother. I tried. I did. But here I am, just like her. Pregnant and not a husband in sight."

Bix let her cry until all her tears were spent. By the time they landed at the ranch, Uma was quiet. "Go get in the car, darlin'. I'll drive us back to the big house," Bix said. Uma didn't argue.

Chapter 39

It was quiet in the Big House when they arrived. When Uma walked in the front door, she closed her eyes and let the serenity wash over her. *This is what home feels like. Peace. Comfort. Safety. Love. Love?*

Once, not long after she had come to the Big B, Annie had said something about the spirit in the house. Uma hadn't understood what the Cherokee woman meant, but now she did. She felt it—felt the spirit envelope her, welcome her back, and fold her in arms of love. A wisp of air brushed by her, as if the essence of someone or something greeted her. *If I believed in ghosts . . . but I don't.*

She opened her eyes and thought about that. After her father died, the only love she had felt was from her brother. Of Tom's love, Uma had no doubt. But after he left for college, she was on her own, and had been ever since. Even her mother was so preoccupied with her own existence, she spared no time for thoughts of what Uma needed. And all Uma had needed was love and security.

She was secure unto herself, and sure that wherever Tom was, he loved her, as she loved him. But in the big sprawling house set among oil rigs and cattle and barns, situated near the River of the Arms of God, inhabited by unrelated people, Uma felt love. She was sure that any one of the individuals living there could stake their life on any one of the others and would encourage and protect them. She placed her hands over her belly. *Just as I would love and protect my child.* She smiled.

The thought she had been suppressing for months finally fought its way to her consciousness and demanded to be acknowledged. *I didn't love Alex. It was mutual interest. It was attraction. It was sex. But not love. I was a foolish girl, and now I have a baby on the way, but I'll not mourn Alex's passing. I do not miss him, and I'll not be sad.*

Bix had tossed his hat on the hall-tree and disappeared toward the bathroom. Now he came up the hall toward her. "Hey!" he said. "There you are, still standing here. I'm hungry, and I'll bet you are too. Let's see what we can find."

Before the house had performed its magic on her, when she still felt as if she were made of plastic, Uma would have said she wasn't hungry, but a twinge of hunger stirred, and a tiny ripple moved over one point of her belly. She put her hand over the spot, and her eyebrows raised.

"What? What's wrong?" Bix was immediately at her side.

"Nothing. Nothing's wrong. The baby just moved. I guess she's hungry."

"She? She? Maybe *he's* hungry," Bix said. "Can I feel?"

"Right here." Uma placed his hand where she had felt the movement, and the baby obliged by touching his hand with a tiny hand or foot.

"I felt it! He touched my hand!" Uma didn't correct his assumption it was a boy, but she knew it would be a girl.

Chapter 40

Bix and Uma went back to their usual daily routine. Uma answered letters and phone calls, made folders and index cards, and put more flags on the map. Soon, real estate brokers began calling her instead of Bix about properties that were coming up for sale. He, more likely as not, would simply refer them to "my executive assistant, Uma Thornton," anyway.

"You can find out anything I or Tom need to know. You're good at that," he would say. "I need to be busy doing other things."

"Other things" was usually riding his horse around the ranch, visiting with the cowboys, checking on the condition of the cattle, talking with his foreman about the fall sales, and even riding the fence lines checking for breaks or apprising the condition of the watering holes and windmills that furnished water from deep underground. He liked it when he found men working on the pump jacks, keeping the liquid gold flowing. Bix liked to ask questions and learn more about the business that also pumped money into the family bank accounts.

Uma was worried about the fact that she had no offers of employment. The time was growing short. There were only a few more months until the baby was due, and she needed to get moved and settled well in advance. *It would be much more convenient to rent a place in a new location before buying a crib and all the other things that are necessary for a baby, rather than buying them while living at the ranch and then have to move them.* She hoped she could find a job somewhere in Texas, instead of some far-off spot like Seattle. *What if I don't find another job soon? I wonder if there is another cottage like Annie's or Lovie's on the Big B, and would Bix let me use it? I couldn't have a baby here in the Big House. It might disturb everyone. Maybe I should talk to Tom about that, or Bix.*

Each day she checked the mail carefully, looking for letters that were addressed to her personally, not by way of Big B Enterprises, and each day she was disappointed. Then, one day there was an envelope to her, Uma Thornton, and a thrill ran through her body. The return address was an attorney's office in Chicago. *Odd, but there are several colleges and universities in and around Chicago. Maybe this is connected with one of them. That's what I was hoping for, that word of my work on Alex's book would spread to the people who need someone like me to help them get it ready for publication.* But the excitement over a possible job was immediately diminished by the thought of leaving the Big B Ranch. *Moving again to somewhere I don't know anyone. Finding a new apartment. Making a new home.* She knew, deep inside, that nowhere could replace the Big B and her friends. That was bound to come, though. She had to move on with her future.

Using a letter opener, Uma carefully opened the envelope and unfolded the cream-colored parchment inside. As she read, her mouth dropped open, and she sucked in a breath, which quickly turned to a shuddering sob.

When Bix entered the office a few minutes later, he found her with her elbows on the desk and her face in her hands. "What's the matter?" he asked. "Is something wrong? Don't you feel well? Is it the baby?"

Silently, Uma handed him the letter and watched him as he read it.

A curse spilled from his lips. "What are they talking about? Unfit mother? Of course you aren't going to be an unfit mother, and how would anyone in Chicago of all places know that anyway?" Bix quieted and read the letter again, then slammed it onto the desk. "'Fathered by a man with an impeccable background and education'? Fathered by a man with no morals, I'd say! Not telling you he was married! I can't believe the nerve of some people!" Bix rose to his feet and started pacing back and forth in front of the desk. "It sounds like somebody wants to take the baby away from you."

"That's exactly what they want," Uma said. "His wife"—her breath caught in a sob—"his wife said he gave me what she wanted more than anything else—a baby—and that it ought to be her raising Alex's child, not me."

"Well, that's just too bad. That was something between the jerk and her and doesn't concern you in any way."

"She's going to try to take the baby away from me."

"That dog won't hunt. You're the mother."

"I may be the mother, but I don't have a job, and I don't even have a home to bring the baby to. I've got to find a place to live." Uma was ready to break into tears again, and panic was grasping at her. "I have to do something. I can't let her take my baby."

"She won't. I guarantee you—she won't." Bix pulled a wallet from his back pocket and started thumbing through the contents. He separated a business card from a small pile and reached for the phone on the desk. Quickly punching in numbers on the new business keypad, he put the receiver to his ear. "This is Bix Crandall. Is he there? Well, make sure he stays there. I'm on my way to talk to him about an urgent matter. No, I don't want to talk to him on the phone. I want to talk to him in person. I don't care where he's supposed to be. He'd better be in his office waiting when I get there." He slammed the receiver down.

"Come on, sugar. Let's go!" Bix reached for the Stetson he had placed on the rack in the corner when he entered the room.

"Where are we going?'

"We're goin' to see the best lawyer in this part of Texas." He opened the office door and held it for Uma. "Hell, he might be the best lawyer in the whole goll-durn state."

Chapter 41

The tall, lanky attorney opened the bottom drawer of his desk and, stretching out, propped his boot-clad feet on it as he leaned back in his office chair. He frowned as he read the letter Uma had handed to him right after she told him the saga of her employment in Alaska, ending with her pregnancy, Alex's death, and the appearance of his wife.

"And she knew of your pregnancy, how?" he asked after he had read the sheet of thick, creamy velum and tossed it back onto his desk.

"She was in Dallas when I gave a program for the publishing company at a bookstore up there. She saw me. It's obvious."

"I assume you didn't plan that promotion?" He looked over the top of his glasses.

"No. McDutton-Parker Publishing did that."

"Did you at any time tell her that her husband is the father of the baby you are carrying?"

"Absolutely not!"

"She's one bubble off plumb if she thinks she can just take Uma's baby," Bix said. "Why would any lawyer take on a case like that?"

"If you have enough money, you can find an attorney to sue for anything." He swung his feet to the floor and sat up straighter. "That doesn't mean you'll win."

"But I might have to go to court?" Uma said, a catch in her throat.

"Maybe." He picked up a pen and started twirling it in his fingers. "Maybe not."

"Sugar, I told you Frank Pope is the best lawyer in these parts. If we do have to go to court, you'll win. You can bet the farm on it." Bix reached over and patted Uma's hand, then curled his larger one over hers.

On the whirlwind trip to town, Bix, driving his oldest pickup as fast as he could push it, had assured her of the same thing. Frank Pope, once he got his tail in a twist for a client, would play craps with the devil and win. "That woman sounds like she's on first-name terms with the devil, trying to take your baby like that." Bix's words only calmed Uma slightly.

"I'd do anything—anything—to keep my baby, but I don't have much in savings. Probably not enough to hire an attorney like that."

"Darlin', don't worry a hair on your sweet head about that. Frank's on retainer for Big B. We pay him whether we use him or not. Let him work a little for his money. You're an employee of Big B. You're entitled."

For once, Uma didn't argue with Bix about whether she worked for the Big B or not. In her mind, what she did was simply a quid pro quo for her room and board and use of a car, but she was in no place to argue if it got her legal representation to keep her child.

"Miss Thornton?" Uma pulled her mind back to the man across the desk.

"Yes?"

"I want to check some dates with you."

"OK."

"You went to Alaska in late January?"

"Mid-January, actually."

"And you became pregnant when?"

Uma was sure her fair complexion blushed as she answered, "Late February."

"So, it's due when?" He counted on his fingers. "November?"

Uma nodded.

Pope glanced at Bix, then back at Uma. "Would you rather we talk privately? Without Bix present?" His eyes dropped to their joined hands.

She looked at Bix, then turned her attention back to the attorney. "No. That's OK. He's heard all this before." She withdrew her hand from Bix, took a tissue from her purse, and wiped her eyes. "As embarrassing as it is, I know it has to be told."

"I'm sorry if this is uncomfortable but, as you say, it has to be told." Pope leaned back in his chair, observing Uma closely. "And you didn't use any kind of . . . protection? Birth control?"

"No. I wasn't . . . that is, it was my first time. When Alex asked if I was on the pill and I said no, he went to town and got some condoms. But there were several days when we didn't use anything." Her head hung low as she told the story, and her fingers twisted a fold in her shirt.

"So . . ."—Pope looked at Uma—"this was your first time. Nobody before him that could be the father?"

Uma shook her head. "No," she whispered.

"And nobody after?"

She said nothing, only shuddered as she shook her head once more.

Pope looked at Bix, eyebrows raised, and Bix understood the question. He shook his head, frowning at the lawyer.

Pope looked away, staring at a picture on the wall. "Then the case could be made that the baby must certainly be this man"—he picked up the letter he had tossed down—"this Alex Keillor's child."

Uma could hardly speak. She cleared her throat. "Yes."

Pope frowned as he stared at a far-off spot in his mind. "And you arrived back in Texas when?"

"The first week in May. I flew from Fairbanks to Houston that same week . . ." Uma's voice broke. "The week he died." She strengthened her resolve. "The day after his wife arrived and told me to get out, that she never wanted to see me again."

"When did you get to the Big B?" He changed his focus back to Uma.

"Within . . ." Uma closed her eyes and thought about it. "Within three or four days."

"What were you doing those four days?"

"I rented a car at the airport and drove home to Freeport."

"What did you go to Freeport for?"

"To see my mother."

"Did you tell her you'd been storked?" Uma looked puzzled. "Did you tell her you were . . . ah . . . with child?" he clarified.

"No. No I didn't."

"And then you came to the Big B?"

"I spent one night in a motel to rest then went to College Station to see if they had an address for my brother, Tom."

Pope nodded his head. "And they told you he was at the Big B."

"No, my half-sister, Cindy, told me that, but I didn't know where the Big B was. I found that out at A&M, and how to get here."

"So you didn't interact with anyone else along the way?"

"Interact?"

"Talk to. Tell your story. Did you tell anyone you were . . . with child?"

"No. Nobody."

"Then there is no one, anywhere, that could say with certainty that you were pregnant when you came back from Alaska." His look was searching as he studied Uma.

"No. I didn't tell anyone."

"And you weren't showing?"

"No. Not then. But I started growing out of my clothes about that time. It wasn't any time until nothing I had fit, even a couple of new dresses I bought, ones that I thought would give me some time."

"Probably going to be a big baby," Pope mused. "My wife did that on our third one, and he was a big old boy."

"See," Bix said to Uma. "I told you it was going to be a boy."

Pope studied Bix before turning back to Uma. He folded his arms on the desk and leaned forward. "I assume you want me to answer this letter—tell this attorney that you are and will be an active and supportive mother. That you have suitable employment here in Texas and have retained me to represent your interests in this matter to the fullest of my capabilities. That you have no intention of giving up your rights to your unborn child, either now or anytime in the future. Is that right?"

"Yes," Uma said, somewhat more forcefully. "That's right."

"Ok. I'll get right on it," he said and stood up.

Bix and Uma rose and turned toward the door, when the attorney said, "Of course, there's one way you could pretty much stop this right now."

"How's that, Frank? That's what we need to do—stop this bull before it goes any further," Bix asked.

"If Uma were married, her husband would be assumed to be the father of her child, no matter when they married. Nobody could challenge that except the husband himself. His name would be on the birth certificate."

Bix broke into a wide smile. "Thanks, buddy! That's good to know!" He offered his hand to Pope. "See, darlin', I told you he was a right smart windmill fixer, and I was right."

Chapter 42

A light rain was falling when they left the attorney's office on the west side of the square and hurried to Bix's truck. As he was opening the door for her, a man approaching the vehicle parked next to them and said, "Hey there, Bix. Good to see you back on two feet again." Uma could tell he was eyeing her and her condition.

Bix slammed the door by her side as the rain came down harder. "Hey, Joe," he answered as he hurried to the driver's side. "I'm sure glad to be up and around again."

As he backed out into the street, he said, "Well, that went well. See, I told you Frank would know how to take care of things."

"I don't know how well he's going to take care of it," Uma answered. "He'll answer the letter, but that probably won't be the end of it if she's determined." She shivered and crossed her arms, chilled from the dampness of her shirt.

Bix glanced at her as he maneuvered around the square and back onto the road leading to the ranch. "But he said how we can put an end to it for good. If you are married, there wouldn't be any use in going to court. It would automatically be assumed that your husband is the father of your child."

"But I'm not married," Uma said. "Not a husband in sight."

"Huh! Look again."

Uma stared at him.

He sounded annoyed as he said, "Sitting right here next to you! I'd make a perfectly good husband!"

Uma couldn't think of anything to say to that. *Yes, you'd*

make a wonderful husband. I've even let myself dream about what a perfect life it would be married to you. Sharing kisses. Sharing a bed with you every night. Sharing life. But that wouldn't be right, bringing my problem to you in such a major way. At least I can leave now and you wouldn't be burdened with another man's child and a lawsuit and every problem that goes along with this . . . this nightmare. If I had the courage to leave, that is.

"Don't have anything to say to that?" Bix threw fleeting looks at her as he sped up on the highway.

Uma sighed. "Yes. You'd make a perfect husband—for someone you are in love with."

Bix checked the traffic in the rearview mirror before pulling off the paving onto the shoulder. Putting the transmission into park, he turned to Uma, putting one hand behind her neck and the other on her right shoulder. He pulled her toward him and kissed her, gradually moving his arms until he had gathered her into an embrace. He deepened the kiss, and somehow Uma found her own arms wrapped around his neck, and she was kissing him back. When their lips broke contact, they remained entwined, cheek to cheek.

"I've been in love with you for a long time," Bix said, "but I didn't want to push it." He sat back, releasing his hold on her, but brushing strands of her long, blond hair back from her face. "You're carrying another man's child, and you love him, and I didn't want to push . . ."

Uma was shaking her head. "No . . ." she said. "No. I'm not in love with him. I realize I made a mistake. A big one. I was attracted to Alex yes, but . . ." She sat back and looked out the steamy window. "I realize now that it wasn't love, and I should never have given in to temptation like that. Maybe if we'd been in civilization I'd have been more careful, stronger, but . . ."

"If you had been in civilization you'd probably found out he was married before it got that far," Bix commented.

"That's true. Looking back on the whole situation, I realize what a huge mistake I made." She looked down at her hands. "And now I'm in the same place my mother was when she got pregnant with Cindy. Knocked up and no husband."

"Not hardly! From what Tom has said, your stepfather is a no-good son of a bitch who married your mother for what money she had. He was a lousy father. You wouldn't be marrying me for my money, and I'd be a great father."

Uma shook her head slowly. "I couldn't do that to you." She looked at him. "I care for you too much to do such a thing."

"You wouldn't be doing anything I didn't want," Bix retorted. He eased the stick back into gear and, after checking for traffic, pulled back onto the road. The rain had stopped, and the sun was breaking through the clouds.

"We wouldn't be going into it for the right reasons," Uma said. "It just wouldn't work out."

"Who says it wouldn't?"

"Everyone says. You marry for love. You have a courtship, then you marry. You don't marry when you are pregnant with another man's baby."

"Huh. A lot you know. That's the way we do it in my family."

Uma looked over at him. "What?"

"My mother was raped. She was pregnant with another man's child—a bad, bad man who would have forced her to marry in order to get her ranch. She proposed to my father, and they ran off to Galveston to get married, so he would be the father of the child she was carrying."

Uma watched the road as she thought about what he had said. Finally, she asked, "That child was you?"

"No. That baby came too early and didn't survive. There's another story behind that. I'll tell you some day. She's buried in the church cemetery. I'll show you, if you want." He drove a couple more miles before he said, "And my parents fell in love and stayed married." He looked over at her. "We'll invite them to our wedding."

Uma had nothing to say to all that and simply watched the road and let all that information tumble around in her mind. After a minute, she asked, "What happened to the bad man?"

"He got shot dead," Bix said, satisfaction in his voice. "In a courtroom."

Suddenly he pulled to the side of the road. Throwing his right arm across the back of the seat, he looked out the back window as he backed up along the roadside.

"What are you doing?" Uma said.

"It was out here when we were driving into town, but my mind was on telling Frank about what was going on, so I didn't stop." He stopped, put the truck in park, and got out.

There on the side of a small bridge, leaning against the concrete barrier, was a puppy, appearing to be only a few months old. Wet and scared, it hunkered down as Bix approached it. He squatted down and extended his hand for the dog to sniff. After it had inhaled the scent of the stranger, it ducked its head and extended its body in supplication. Uma couldn't hear what Bix was saying, but she saw his mouth moving as he gently gathered the shivering dog into his arms.

"He's wet," Bix said. "Maybe he could sit on your feet." Uma was reaching her arms out for his load, and she took the trembling canine into her lap.

Bix pulled out onto the road and started for home once more. "I wonder if it's lost from home," Uma mused as she ran her hand over the brown and white fur, brushing it back from two sad eyes.

"There aren't any houses around here anywhere," Bix said. "But I'll keep an eye out for signs or an ad in the newspaper." He looked at the dog, who was leaning against Uma's chest, her arms wrapped around it. "All boys need a dog. We're getting prepared. Next, we'll shop for a crib and . . . what else? Diapers?"

"It's going to be a girl," Uma answered, ignoring his shopping plans.

"Girls like dogs too, don't they?" Bix asked, looking at her.

Uma's throat choked, but she managed to reply. "Yes, girls like dogs too." *At least this pup doesn't look anything like Trixie,* her beloved pet that had met its death from her stepfather's vicious kick. She had never allowed herself to become attached to another dog, lest her heart be broken once more. A white muzzle tucked itself into the fold of her arm, and she thought she was losing the battle.

"George. His name is going to be George," Bix said.

"The baby? I'm not naming my baby George," Uma protested.

"No, the dog. The dog's name is George. I always wanted a dog named George."

"OK, if that's what you want." Uma was ignoring his plans for marriage because she didn't know what to say. Yes, it would conveniently solve the problem that had been thrust into her life when the letter from the attorney in Chicago arrived, but it didn't seem right to marry Bix just to protect her from losing her baby.

Of course, marrying Bix wasn't a terrible thing to think about. Not at all. *And it isn't that he's rich and handsome. I truly like Bix. He's fun and smart. Kind, too. Considerate.* Uma realized she was trying to talk herself into accepting his plans for marriage. *I already made one mistake, a big one, by thinking with my hormones instead of my head. I can't do that again.*

All the way back to the Big B, Uma weighed the pros and cons of marrying Bix. She smoothed the fur of the sleeping puppy in her lap and tried to think of ways to work out a compromise that would be fair to them both.

Chapter 43

When Bix pulled his truck in front of the Big House, Lovie was sweeping the front porch. "Where did you two go off to?" she asked as he opened the driver's door. He walked around and opened the passenger door. Taking the puppy, he sat it on the ground and offered his hand to assist Uma as she slid out.

"We went to get a dog," he answered. Uma shook her head to signal that he was joking.

"His name is George," Bix called out as the object of everyone's attention walked a few steps, then squatted.

"Uh, Bix? Did you check? I think maybe that's a girl dog," Lovie said.

He stood watching, then said, "Well, George is a good name for a girl." He walked toward the steps. "Come on, George. Come see your new home." George obediently followed.

"We found it on the side of the road," Uma said to Lovie as she climbed the steps.

"You missed lunch," Lovie said as they passed her on the way in the front door. "There's a bowl of pasta salad in the fridge."

"OK. Good. I'm hungry," Bix said as he cut through the dining room on his way to the kitchen. "Come on, George. We'll have to find you something to eat, too."

Annie was sliding something into the oven when they walked in. "What's that, Annie?" Bix asked. "Something good?"

"Pineapple upside-down cake," she answered. "Who is

going to clean after that one?" she asked, pointing at the dog. "I do not clean after dogs. Not my job. Not Lovie's job."

"I'll do it, Annie," Bix answered, and Lovie snorted. He turned and looked at her. "I will."

"You promise?"

"Sure," he answered and opened the refrigerator door.

"You be sure," Annie said. "Uma, she not bend over to do that. It not good for baby."

"Really?" Bix turned, holding a big bowl.

"Mama bending will make baby short," Annie said. "Your mama never bend when you in her belly. That's why you so tall." She looked at Lovie. "You watch cake. Take it out when it done. Let cool before turning it onto a plate." She pulled off her apron and left by way of the back door.

When Uma looked, she saw Lovie's hand over her mouth and her eyebrows raised. She appeared to be holding in her laughter, but Uma wouldn't challenge Annie's pronouncement if it got Bix to take care of his dog's business.

"Do you think she was kidding?" Uma asked.

"I don't know, but I'm not taking any chances that my boy will turn out short," Bix said, placing the bowl on the table and going to the cabinet for a plate.

"Your boy?" Lovie asked. She looked at Uma, eyebrows raised. Uma shook her head.

There was a small whine from George, who was looking up at Bix. "You hungry, George?" Bix asked the dog, who wiggled as if understanding the question. "Let's see what we can find." He opened the refrigerator and bent over, examining the contents. "Any of that meatloaf left from last night?" he asked to the room at large. "Ah, you're in luck, George." Removing a foil-covered plate from the fridge, he took the plate he had intended to use for himself and forked a generous portion of meatloaf onto it and broke it into bits. When he set it on the floor, the pup started gobbling down the cold meat.

"He was hungry," Bix said.

"No telling how long he had been sitting out on the highway with nothing to eat," Uma said. She went to the cabinet and retrieved a cereal bowl and filled it with water. She placed it near the now-empty plate, and George immediately began to drink.

"After I eat, I'll go back to town and get some supplies for our newest family member," Bix said as he took a place at the table.

Uma ate her meal slowly as she thought about what had transpired at the attorney's office. Lovie sat with them and watched George as he explored every inch of the kitchen. After a couple of minutes, she got up and handed the roll of paper towels to Bix.

"What's this for?"

"George just puddled on the floor."

Bix frowned. He took the last bite of his pasta salad, then got up and put his plate in the sink. Taking a wad of towels, he wiped up the puddle, then said, "George, we're going to have to have a talk." He walked toward the hall door. "I'll be back for my dog."

When he was gone, Lovie said, "Can I ask what went on this morning? You surely didn't go to town to get this dog, did you?"

"No. I'll tell you about it later."

When Bix returned, he had his Stetson back on and whistled softly, then called, "George. Come on George. Let's go get you some stuff." The puppy sensed that Bix was speaking directly to it and got up and followed Bix through the house. "We'll be back later."

"You're taking George to town?" Lovie called out.

"Yes, he needs to get used to riding in the truck," he answered as man and dog went through the dining room on the way to the front door.

Chapter 44

"So, you didn't go to town for a dog, but you got one anyway? And Bix is talking about 'my boy'? What gives?" Lovie folded her arms on the table and studied Uma.

Uma laid her fork to one side. "I got a letter in today's mail," she said. "From an attorney in Chicago. Alex's widow wants my baby."

"No kidding!" Lovie sat back, eyes open wide. "How come she thinks she is entitled to *your* baby?"

"Because she assumes her late husband is the father. And because she always wanted his baby. And he wouldn't have one with her, so she wants mine."

"How does she think she has a right to it?"

"She says I couldn't raise Alexander Keillor's child in a manner suitable for such an important man, seeing as I don't have a job or home."

"You have a job and a home," Lovie said indignantly, "right here on the Big B."

"That's what Bix says," Uma answered. "He took me into town to see his attorney. Frank Pope is going to send an answer to the Chicago law firm refuting all that she says."

"So, what is Bix talking about 'my boy' for?"

Uma grimaced. "Frank Pope mentioned that the sure way to put a stop to it was for me to be married. He said with a husband's name on the baby's birth certificate no one could challenge the fact that that man was the father."

"Yeah? So? You aren't . . . oh! Bix thinks you two ought to get married. Is that it?"

"That's it."

"And you don't want to marry Bix?"

Uma sighed. "It's not that simple, Lovie. Bix is a great guy, and I'm certainly attracted to him, but it wouldn't be right to marry him just so I wouldn't lose my baby."

"Why not? Bix is in agreement, isn't he? He wants to do this?" Lovie studied Uma's expression as she asked the questions.

"Yes, Bix suggested it himself, but that doesn't make it right."

"It wouldn't be right if you were tricking him or something, or if you were trying to talk him into marriage, but if it is his idea . . ."

"It's his idea, alright, but still . . ."

"But what?"

Uma got up from the table and took her plate to the sink to rinse it off. "I care far too much for Bix to let him get into something he would regret later."

"Why would he regret it later?"

"Maybe I'm a dreamer, but I have this idea that people ought to marry for love, not just to help out a friend."

"Uma, you aren't seeing Bix the way I'm seeing him. He *is* in love."

Uma frowned at her friend.

"He's in love with you. He stays close to you, wherever you are. He's constantly touching you, putting his hand on your shoulder, playing with your hair. He talks with you, laughs with you, sits on the front porch with you every evening. He's got it bad."

"He may think he is, because he's been housebound with that broken leg and hasn't been around any other women. He'll get over it. And it would be heartbreaking for him to get over it and find he was tied to me. And a baby."

Lovie gave a snort like she usually reserved for Bix. "You have to be kidding. Bix has had his choice of women for as long as I've known him. He's rich and handsome.

He could have his pick of every single woman in several counties, plus some married ones as well. He doesn't want them. When word got out about his broken leg, they started coming around with pies and cakes and plates of cookies. Bix had me send them all away. They were nothing but a nuisance, and he wouldn't see them. It was different when you showed up. He was a changed man. Even Tom saw it."

"He did?"

"He certainly did. We've talked about it. You didn't flirt with him, and you smart-talked right back to him. He couldn't send you away at first because you're Tom's sister, but then, when he saw you weren't here to try to catch a rich husband, he was hooked, but good. Admit it. You two are good together."

Uma didn't answer, but Lovie's words stuck. *Yes, we're good together, but that doesn't change the fact that we wouldn't be marrying for love. We would be marrying for necessity.* She looked out the kitchen window. The scent of the pineapple upside-down cake reached her nose, and taking a hot pad, she opened the oven door and withdrew the golden-brown treat.

"We'll see, I guess," she said as she set the iron skillet holding the cake on the wire cooling rack, "what comes of the letter Mr. Pope sends to Chicago. All this talk about marriage might be for nothing." But she couldn't imagine Alex's widow would give up so easily.

Chapter 45

Bix returned with three dog beds, two kinds of puppy chow, dog treats (for training, he said), and tennis balls. George was sporting a red collar, and Bix had a matching red leash, just in case it was needed, he said.

"What did you get three beds for?" Lovie asked. Uma wondered the same thing.

"One is for the office, one for my bedroom, and one for Uma's bedroom. George ought to have a comfortable place to sleep wherever she decides."

"So you decided George is a she?"

"Yeah. I checked. You are right." He grinned. "But that's OK. Girl dogs are just fine. My boy will like a girl dog." Uma looked at him and frowned but didn't make any comment about the "my boy" statement. It would have only egged him on to more outrageous remarks.

They returned to their usual schedule: Uma working in the office, writing letters, and making and answering phone calls about Big B business deals. Bix checked in at the barn daily and rode out on the range every few days, checking on the cattle and chatting with oil field mechanics before he joined Uma in the office to discuss various businesses he thought Tom ought to see about buying.

Each evening after supper they adjourned to the front porch, where Bix worked to train George. When Tom was not off in some other part of the state, he and Lovie often joined Bix and Uma, watching as George improved at such commands as "sit," "lie down," "fetch," and "come."

"That's a smart dog you have there," Tom said one evening. "Have you tried her around the cattle?"

"No," Bix answered. "She's not going to be a cattle dog. For one thing, she's too short-legged. She couldn't keep up."

"She looks like she might have some Corgi in her," Lovie said.

"What is a Corgi?" Bix asked.

"You know, that's the kind of dog the Queen of England has. Short dogs. Cute. Easy to train."

"That's George," Bix said. "Cute, short, and easy to train." He looked at Tom. "Anyway, she's not going to be a cattle dog. She needs to stay around the house for the baby to play with."

Tom didn't say anything about that statement, just raised his eyebrows and asked, "Why did you name her George?"

"Because I always wanted a dog named George," Bix answered.

"Why?" Lovie questioned.

"Because when I was in the fourth grade, Kevin Sommers had a dog named George, and it was real smart. It could do tricks and all. So, I wanted a dog named George. Kevin was a little bitty thing when he got George, he said, and they had grown up together. I always wished I had a dog like that."

Bix threw a ball and said, "Fetch, George. Fetch." He leaned back and watched as George scrambled down the steps into the yard, chasing the toy. "We always had dogs here on the ranch, but none of them were mine, just mine, like George was Kevin's." He looked at Uma. "So, I decided this baby was going to have a dog right from the beginning, to grow up with."

Uma felt a hard bump at that pronouncement. "Oh!"

"What?" Bix was on alert.

"She just kicked hard," Uma said. "Oh, again over here." She moved her hand to the other side of her belly.

"A hand on one side and a foot on the other," Lovie said.

"I guess he wanted in on the conversation about George," Bix said.

"Sometimes it's like she's turning somersaults," Uma replied.

"Maybe he's going to be a football player," Bix remarked. "He's going to be a Cottonport Cougar, like I was." He turned to Uma and grinned. "I can show him all the moves."

"Or maybe she's going to be a cheerleader," Uma countered, then could have kicked herself for getting pulled into the fantasy Bix was creating.

"Were you a cheerleader?" he asked.

"Nope. I had to study and get good grades."

"I'll bet you got real good grades," he said as he reached over and tucked a strand of long blond hair behind her ear.

~ ~ ~

Days passed, and Uma wondered if she dared hope the threat of a lawsuit over the baby had faded into nothing. One morning she had worked a couple of hours at the desk and needed to stretch. Standing, she arched and put her hands on the small of her back. It was getting harder each day to spend many hours sitting in the office chair. "Come on, George. Let's go out for a while."

When they reached the front porch, George immediately headed down the steps to the yard, and Uma walked up and down the length of the shady veranda. When George finished her business and had sniffed the grass and trees, checking for any new scents, Uma called her back, and they went back toward the office. When she reached the far end of the hall, the telephone was ringing, and she hurried to catch it before the caller gave up.

When Bix entered the room a few minutes later, Uma's face was buried in her hands. "What's wrong?" he asked. "Is it the baby?"

She put her hands down and looked at him, but there were no tears in her eyes. "That was Frank Pope on the phone. He said he has received two letters I need to know about. He wants me to come in to see him."

"Did he saw who from? Or what about?"

"No, but he sounded serious."

"Well, let's go," Bix said. "I'll go get a vehicle and meet you out front."

Uma used the attached bathroom to freshen up. She didn't want to take the time to change out of the jeans she was wearing. She was hoping the attorney would tell her that Mrs. Keillor had abandoned any plans for trying to gain custody of her late husband's child, but Uma was afraid that would not be the case. He didn't have a cheerful tone in his voice. *And two letters? What can that be about?*

When she reached the front, Bix had pulled his Cadillac next to the walkway to the porch and was hollering at Peanut, who was rounding the side of the house. "Peanut, come get George. I don't want her following us." He held out the red leash that Uma had never seen him use before. "Put her on this and take her with you to the back. Keep her up real good."

"OK, Boss. Come 'ere, Georgie," the wiry man said, and got hold of the pup's collar. "We gotta stay here." George looked sad at that prospect, but when Uma looked back as they pulled away, she was following Peanut along the side of the house on the way to the backyard.

Chapter 46

"How's it going, Frank?" Bix asked as he shook hands with the attorney. "'Bout to get this business taken care of?"

"Bix, Miss Thornton," the man replied. "Have a seat." He returned to his own chair behind the big desk. "I'll tell you, Hoss," he said, "it's gettin' a bit more complicated."

"How's that?" Bix asked.

Pope slid open a drawer and withdrew two sheets of paper, appearing from the fold marks to have been letters. "To start with, I drafted a letter to the law firm that contacted you, Miss Thornton, stating that you denied any and all allegations made by them. You denied that Alexander Keillor was the father of your unborn child . . ."

"But—" Uma started.

"Don't say anything, Miss Thornton, please." He stopped her from speaking. "I questioned you thoroughly when you were here, and you did not outright tell me he was the father, nor have you told anyone, to my knowledge, that he is the father. It is only the assumption of Mrs. Keillor that he is. She does not have any direct knowledge of that fact." He looked into Uma's face. "Does she?"

Uma shook her head. "No, she doesn't. The only people I've told are . . ."

"I don't want to know who you have told anything to, nor do I want to know what you told them, at least at this point. It is going to be my job to prevent anyone you might have said anything to from being interviewed on the matter. Do you understand?"

"Yes," Uma said meekly. "I understand."

"You didn't tell any of your family you were expecting when you visited in Freeport. Is that right?"

"That's right. But I told my brother Tom when I got here."

"And Tom's on the Big B?" Pope looked toward Bix.

"When he's in town, he is," Bix replied.

"When he's in town?" Pope frowned.

"Yes. He travels for Big B Enterprises—buying properties and such."

"You need to talk to him," he looked back at Uma, "about keeping his mouth shut about you. Not a word about your condition."

"Frank, from the way you are talking, something must be stirring," Bix said.

"Yes. Yes, I'd say so," the lawyer said, rubbing his forehead. "I got a letter from the law firm Mrs. Keillor has retained. She has no intention of letting this rest. If it were just her, I'd just pass it off as a jealous wife, but . . ." He picked up the other letter from his desktop. "Now we have Keillor's parents to contend with."

"His parents?" Both Uma and Bix blurted out at the same time.

"What do they have to do with anything?" Bix asked.

"Well, seems like Alexander Keillor was the only surviving son of Judge and Mrs. Benjamin Keillor. And they want their grandchild to be raised in the full benefits and glory as befits the heir of a Keillor dynasty, whether that child is the progeny of their son's wife or not."

"Well that's just too bad," Bix said.

"What can they do about it?" Uma asked in a quiet voice.

"They can stir up a lot of trouble," Pope answered. "They can support and encourage their daughter-in-law, both with money and with influence. And don't think the influence isn't a big thing. A judge has a wide-ranging reach of friends and associates.

"I'll tell you what they can and probably have already done. They can hire a private detective to investigate you and find every little bit of mud they can to prove you would be an unfit mother. They can smear you so badly that any judge would think twice before letting you keep custody of a child. If it were only the widow, I wouldn't be worried. With a judge for a grandfather, I'm re-evaluating the situation."

"Son of a . . ." Bix muttered.

"I'm thinkin' you want to go all out to prevent this," Pope said, looking from Uma to Bix and back again.

"You betcha we do," Bix said. He reached for Uma's hand. "Spare nothin' fighting these no-good . . ."

"Have you given any thought to what I suggested last time?" Pope asked.

"I certainly did," Bix said, "but Uma thinks she would be doing me wrong to marry me." He looked into her eyes, into the depths of her. "She doesn't realize that I want to do this, and that I—" He stopped talking and swallowed. "She doesn't realize I'd be proud to be her husband and father of her child," he said, his voice low and gravelly. "She doesn't realize that I'm not grandstanding, like I do sometimes, like I was when I got on that bull. I love her. I fell in love with her the first time she sassed me back, and it's grown the more I get to know her." He stopped talking but continued staring at Uma, as if willing his thoughts into her mind.

"Well, that might not completely solve the problem," Pope said, ignoring the declaration of love that Bix was beaming toward Uma. "But it would go a long way toward heading it off. Nobody can prove that you aren't the father of her unborn child. There are no tests for that. You could have er . . . gotten together the first week in May. Nobody can judge how far along you are, when the baby is due, by how big you are. I'm thinking you haven't seen very many people around here in Cottonport since you've been here." He looked at Uma questioningly.

"No, not many," Uma replied, pulling her gaze from Bix. "Of course my doctor knows how far along I am."

Pope sat back in the office chair. "Oh yeah, the doctor. I didn't think about him." He pinched the bridge of his nose and shut his eyes. "I'll call him and caution him. Of course, he wouldn't talk to a private investigator about one of his patients anyway." He opened his eyes and looked at Uma. "It's Doctor Hastings, I take it? Since he's the only obstetrician in town?"

"Yes, that's right. Dr. Hastings."

"I'll see to it he doesn't say when the baby is due. As far as the general public is concerned, you're just showing early. Some women do, and Bix is a big man. He'd father a big baby."

"And you think a private investigator will be asking questions about me around here?" Uma asked.

"I'm sure of it," Pope said. "When you read this letter, you will be too." He shoved it toward her. "And with the grandfather being a judge, he'll have a lot of friends . . . a lot of pull. They'll try to get you back to Illinois to fight this out."

"Fight this out?" Uma froze with the letter in her hand. She looked toward Bix.

"Uma," Pope said, "you need to think hard about Bix's proposal. He says he's willing. You're going to have a rough time of it otherwise. I'm not sayin' you wouldn't win the case, but you wouldn't be the better for it after goin' through what they'll try to lay on you. They'll do their best to ruin you—ruin your reputation."

Uma looked at Bix, without a word.

"Uma, darlin', would you do me the honor of becoming my wife?" Bix asked.

"Yes, Bix. Yes, I'll marry you," Uma said in a quiet voice.

"Yippee!" Bix shouted, and pulling his hand away from

hers, he stood and danced around the room. Reaching into the pocket of his jeans, he pulled out a dark blue box, snapped it open, and removed a ring. It sported a large diamond center stone with three smaller stones on each side. "I've had this waitin' until you said yes."

"Oh, Bix!" Uma said. "It's so big!"

"Darlin', you're going to be a Crandall. The Crandall's of the Big B Ranch have a certain image to uphold. That means you have to have an engagement ring to make other women envious."

"I don't want to make other women envious," Uma said as he reached for her hand and slipped the ring on her finger. "I just want to keep my baby."

"You will, Uma. You will," Frank Pope said. "And actually, the big ring is a good move. It shows Bix is committed and serious. If you had married just any old person, they might accuse you of a set up. Marrying the richest man in this part of Texas and wearing that rock, it gives evidence of the honesty of the marriage. No one would imagine Bix would spend that much money on a sham marriage."

Uma could only stare, first at the attorney, then at the ring. It was lovely, she'd admit to that. She looked at Bix with tears in her eyes at last. Tears because he was doing so much for her.

"Couple more things," Pope said. "Bix, this needs to be done as rapidly as possible. Now, I know women like to plan things like weddings, but . . ."

"I have an idea about that, Frank. Don't worry," Bix said.

Uma looked from the ring to Bix. *I hate to think of what other ideas he might have!*

"Good. Good," Pope said. "The other thing is something I reckon you might not have thought of, but needs to be taken care of before you marry."

"What's that?" Bix asked.

"A pre-nup."

Chapter 47

Uma awoke slowly, pulling the ever-so-soft comforter up around her shoulders. The light was entirely different in the master bedroom from what it was in the room she had been occupying since she arrived at the Big B. The master bedroom faced west, and the light was soft and muted early in the morning, unlike the brighter glow of daybreak in her previous bedroom.

She stretched and wiggled her toes. Bix was still asleep, his breath coming in short bursts. Uma remained as still as she could in order not to wake him. The previous two days had been a whirlwind, and the arrangements for the trip and wedding had fallen entirely on him, and although he never complained, she could tell he was tired and his leg aching when they returned from the hurried visit to Las Vegas.

Turning away from the sleeping man beside her, she closed her eyes and thought back over the events that had spun her life in this new direction.

~ ~ ~

When Frank Pope had mentioned a pre-nup, Uma had no idea what he was talking about. Then he explained that it was an agreed-upon document that set down the terms in case she and Bix were ever divorced. That, Uma thought, was a very good idea, considering the reason they were marrying.

"OK," Bix agreed, "as long as it is simple and quick. I don't want to be sitting here arguing about stuff when all I want to do is get married as soon as we can. Isn't that the point?"

"It is, Bix, but it's my job to protect you. Both of you," Pope said, looking at Uma.

It didn't take long to come to terms that were acceptable to Uma, Bix, and Frank Pope. If they were to get a divorce for any reason, Bix would support Uma, now *their* unborn child, and any other children born of their marriage, in the style which was appropriate and suitable for a wife and member of the Crandall family. The attorney wanted to put a monetary cap on it, but Bix refused. He would pay all schooling and medical bills for any and all children born in their marriage, including the one Uma was currently carrying, until said children were twenty-one years old.

The one thing Uma insisted on, the most important thing, the one she would not sign without, was that custody of any and all children born in the marriage, including the child she was expecting, would always go to her, no matter what. No argument about it. No suing for custody. It would be their children according to the birth certificate, but hers and hers alone if custody were to be split.

The thought that other children might result from the marriage surprised her. That possibility had not entered her mind when she was considering the possibility of marrying Bix. A child with the handsome cowboy sitting next to her sent a thrill running through her body. *I have enough to tend to without thinking about yet another child. Grow up, Uma!* she told herself.

When she and Bix had agreed on the terms, and Frank Pope was satisfied, the lawyer called his secretary in and had her type it up. It only took a few minutes for them to sign the document, which was then notarized by the same secretary.

"Come on, darlin'," Bix urged her when they left the law office. "We've got to get a move on. I've got to call Steve."

"Steve?"

"The pilot, Steve. You remember him?"

"Yes, I remember Steve the pilot. Why are you going to call him?"

"See, if we go to the courthouse and get a marriage license here, everybody in town will know about it before the day is out. Then we'll have to wait three days before we get hitched. That's so either one of us can back out before we do the deed. The whole family will have to get involved, and there'll be plans and guests and a lot of hassle. It'll be a lot simpler if we fly to Vegas. No waiting." He looked at Uma to see if she understood.

She stared back at him, not believing he would decide on something as important as their marriage, no matter the reason for haste, without talking it over with her.

"Do I have a say in this?" she asked, her voice cold.

"Of course, sugar! Of course you do!" Bix was trying to drive and look at Uma at the same time. Finally, he pulled over to the shoulder of the road. "Look," he said, putting his arm around her, "I'm sorry. I didn't mean to take over. Do you want to do something different?"

"No," Uma said, her voice trembling. "It's just happening so fast."

"I know, darlin', I know." Bix pulled her close. "Tell me what you want. I'll do it."

"It's OK. You're planning it fine." She sniffed. "Tell me."

"I thought we'd take Tom and Lovie with us to be our witnesses. That OK with you?" He studied her reaction. She nodded. "And take the jet to get there. We could be there in no time. And get married and fly back." She nodded again.

When Bix was sure Uma was okay with his suggestions, he put the car in gear and started toward the ranch once more. "After all," he said, "we own that plane now. We might as well get some use out of it." The word *we* buzzed around in Uma's head for a long while.

~ ~ ~

As quietly as she could, Uma slipped out of bed and padded to the en suite bathroom. It was a luxury the master bedroom afforded that her previous room hadn't, and with the growing baby putting pressure on her bladder, the fact she didn't have to go down the hall to relieve herself was a blessing. When they returned to the Big B the night before, Uma had headed to her old sleeping arrangement, but Bix caught her.

"Uh-uh, darlin'. We share a room and a bed now. You wouldn't want Fran to tell anyone we sleep apart, now do you? If there's going to be anyone poking around town, looking for dirt on you, that's not something you'd want spread about."

So, she had shared the king-size bed with her husband. Later that day, she would move all her clothes into the closet with his. They must present for all the world to see that they were husband and wife. As she looked into the mirror that covered the entire wall behind the bathroom counter, she practiced in her head. *Uma Crandall. Mrs. Bix Crandall.* She couldn't help breaking into a smile. It was a good feeling, being married to Bix. Having a home—a real home. Whether it was forever or not, Uma didn't know, but she could be happy in the moment. The baby kicked, and she placed her hands around her ever-growing belly. *And you'll have a home, little one, and a daddy.* Bix was so excited over the baby that Uma had no doubt he would treat the child as his own. Not many men would do what he was doing, especially with such enthusiasm.

Of course the reason for this marriage is to ensure that I can keep my baby, but why can't I be happy just because I'm married to Bix? That's a bonus I might as well enjoy now, just in case the marriage falls apart later. She chided herself for thinking negatively, when all her life she had strived to think positively in whatever situation she found herself.

When Uma moved from the bathroom into the bedroom again, she paused by the dresser and ran her fingers over the bouquet of flowers she had put in a glass jar of water and brought upstairs the previous night. They were the only flowers anyone had ever given her, and she wished they would last forever. She leaned over and smelled the lingering scent from the roses and carnations. There were many different kinds of blooms in shades of pink and lavender in the bundle of blossoms wrapped in tulle and tied with white ribbon. The gaiety of the mix made her happy, and the fact that Bix had picked them out for her doubly so.

~ ~ ~

Bix had rushed back to the Big B when they left Frank Pope's office, calling out for Tom and Lovie.

"You two throw some things in a suitcase," he said as Lovie came from the kitchen and Tom from the office, "we're going to Las Vegas."

"Las Vegas?" Tom repeated.

"Why?" Lovie asked.

"Guess!" Bix said. "What do you do in Las Vegas?"

"Gamble," Lovie said.

"Get married!" Bix shouted. "Uma has agreed to marry me. I'm gonna call Steve to come pick us up." He paused at the door to the office. "I'd like you both to come along and be our witnesses." He went in and closed the door.

"There's going to be some upset people," Tom said. "A bunch of folks would want to be involved in this."

"Yeah, like his parents and sister, for example, and Annie, and . . ." Lovie started ticking off on her fingers.

"We're sort of in a hurry," Uma explained. "The . . . uh . . ." After Frank Pope's admonitions, she didn't want to say, "the baby's father's parents," so she said, "Alex Keillor's parents want to claim custody of my baby. The attorney thinks they will be investigating me, trying to prove I'll be an unfit mother."

"Along with his wife—widow?" Lovie asked.

"Then we'd better get this done," Tom said. "Let's go get packed and tell Annie."

When the four reassembled, Bix reported that Steve would be at the airfield on the ranch in two hours. True to his word, they were in the air by midafternoon and in Las Vegas by early evening.

"We need limousine service to an excellent hotel," Bix told an attendant at the cab stand in front of the airport.

"Yessir! Comin' right up, sir," he said, and waved toward a long white luxury vehicle parked down the drive. As it pulled up in front of their party, Bix asked, "What hotel would you recommend for a nice suite?"

"We got lots of nice places, sir. I'd say the Tropicana is one of the best, or maybe the Riviera or the Flamingo."

"And wedding chapels. Do you have a suggestion about that as well?"

"There's lots of them, sir. You can get any kind of wedding you wants."

"I want the best one money can buy!" Bix exclaimed.

"Probably that'd be the Chapel O' Flowers. They has any kind a person wants, I reckon," the attendant said.

Half an hour later, they were checking in at the Tropicana. Bix paid for two one-bedroom suites. It only took minutes to find themselves in luxury accommodations with Lovie and Tom right down the hall. Before they parted, Bix asked, "Y'all want to go to a show tonight?"

Lovie took one look at Uma and said, "I think your bride needs to rest, Bix, not go out."

Bix studied Uma. "You're right, Louvinia. She looks beat. You tired, darlin'?" Uma nodded her head. She was, indeed, worn out.

"You and Tom go do whatever you want," Bix said. "We'll stay in."

"If you want to go to a show, Bix, go on with them," Uma said. "Don't let me hold you back from having fun, but I am tired to the bone."

"Don't you worry 'bout me, sugar," Bix said. "Not at all."

She intended to rest a few minutes while Bix watched television. The next thing she knew, it was morning.

~ ~ ~

"Come back to bed," Bix called as Uma was admiring her wedding bouquet. He lifted the covers, and she slid back between them. Throwing an arm over her, he pulled her closer. A solid thump hit his arm. He chuckled. "Get used to it, son," he said. "Daddy's going to be putting his arm around Mama a lot from now on. You're gonna have to share."

Uma didn't make her usual reference to having a daughter instead of a son. She was enthralled with the concept of Bix as the father of her unborn child. He had wholeheartedly thrown himself into the role of the baby's father. Maybe it would work after all.

He kissed her cheek and snuggled his nose behind her ear, lying quietly. Uma could feel his breath on her neck as they stayed nestled, content in their closeness. She started to drift off, when Bix kissed her neck. Once, twice, three times, and his mouth moved down to her shoulder. "If I'm slow, if I'm careful, if I take it real easy, do you think . . .?"

Uma took a deep breath. He was her husband now. There was no reason for her to be hesitant, except for the baby in her womb . . . another man's baby. But she had chosen, for better or worse, to begin a life with Bix—a life that might be a forever kind—and love-making would be part of it. She turned toward him and accepted his kiss.

Chapter 48

"I'm going to be leaving in about an hour. I have a doctor's appointment," Uma told Bix at the breakfast table. "I can have the machine answer the phone, or else you can."

"Doctor's appointment? Is anything wrong?"

"No, nothing's wrong. It's just my regular checkup."

"Oh, good." Bix continued eating for a minute before asking, "Can I come with you?"

"Come with me?"

"Yes. I want to get a head start on being a good daddy," he answered.

"Sure, you can come, if you really want to," Uma replied.

An hour later he was ready and waiting as Uma appeared. "Let's take my truck," he said.

"The new one?" Uma asked. "The old one rides too rough, and I don't feel like being bounced around today."

"Sure thing," Bix replied. "No, George, you can't go this time," he told the dog as it followed him to the truck, wiggling excitedly. "Peanut!" he called. "Come keep George from following."

"You have George trained to go with you everywhere," Uma commented.

"Yep. Soon I'll have both a boy *and* a dog to keep me company," he said as they pulled down the driveway. He turned toward Uma. "When you and I aren't keeping company, that is," as he patted her on the knee.

Uma just smiled. She was tired of playing the boy-versus-girl game.

Later, Uma was glad Bix was with her when Doctor Hastings gave her the news.

"Hmm," the portly doctor mused. "Seems like I hear two heartbeats. Thought I did last time, but thought I'd give it another month to be sure." He pulled the stethoscope from his ears.

"Does that mean what I think it does?" Bix asked.

"It means two babies in there. You're having twins, Mrs. Crandall."

Uma lay on the examining table and let the news roll over her. *Twins! How would I ever have made it on my own with two babies to care for and work to support them?*

"Twins!" Bix exclaimed. "I'm gonna be daddy to two babies! Wait 'til I tell everybody!"

"Bix, Uma," the doctor said. "We need to talk a bit. Uma, when you get dressed, let's go to my office and visit. OK?"

"Is something wrong, doctor?" Uma asked worriedly. "Is there a problem with it being twins?"

"Is there any kind of problem at all," Bix asked. "Is Uma OK?"

"No, not a problem. I just want to speak to you privately," he said. "The both of you," he added and left the room.

The nurse helped Uma slide from the table. "You go to the next room," she said to Bix. "That's Doctor Hastings' office. Your wife will be along shortly."

When the nurse escorted Uma to the doctor's office, she said, "The doctor will be with you soon," and shut the door behind her.

"I wonder what Dr. Hastings has to say that he couldn't have told us in the examining room," Uma said as they sat in the chairs in front of the desk.

Bix took her hand in his. "Probably just about having twins. He said you are doing fine."

They waited. Bix got up and studied the framed

diplomas hung on the wall. Uma picked up a magazine from a nearby table, glanced at it, then returned it. Finally, the doctor entered the room and took a seat behind his desk. "Uma. Bix," he said, looking directly from one to the other. "Frank Pope came to see me the other day. He almost made me mad when he cautioned me about talking to people about my patients."

"Aw, Doc," Bix began. "We have an unusual situation here. He just—"

"Settle down, Bix. He let me know, without *him* betraying client confidence, that it was possible that somebody might come around asking questions about Uma's pregnancy. Most specifically about whether you, Uma, would be a fit mother, but also about when the baby is due."

"Well, you see—" Bix began again.

"Let me finish, Bix, if you please."

Bix settled back into his chair, hands folded in front of him.

"Just the other day, there was such a fellow. I wouldn't talk to him, of course. That is, I made it plain I wouldn't talk about one of my patients. I did say that you would make a fine mother, Uma," he said, looking over top of his glasses at her. "But I wouldn't say more than that. He seemed to want to find out how far along you are. He asked when you first came to see me, but I didn't answer that either." He looked over the top of his glasses, studying Uma's reaction. After a moment's pause, he said, "I also want you to know that, as your doctor, anything you tell me is strictly confidential. Am I to gather that this stranger is trying to establish who may or may not be the father of your baby?"

Uma wanted to cry. She wouldn't, though, and took a deep breath to gain composure before speaking. "Yes. You have that right." She glanced toward Bix.

"Go ahead, sugar. Doc Hastings' been a friend of the family for a long time. Tell him all of it. He won't let it slip out."

"You know, of course, when I got pregnant—I told you that—and when the baby— babies are due. And anyone who knows when I arrived at the Big B knows that Bix isn't the father."

"From this point on, I am," Bix interjected. "From the minute I said my marriage vows, I became the father."

"So, who wants to fight you about that?" the doctor asked. "The biological father?"

"No, he is dead. First it was his widow," Uma said. "She wanted a baby with him, she said, and when she saw me— saw that I am pregnant—she decided immediately that it is her husband's child, and she decided to try to take my baby. So the child could be raised in the manner appropriate . . ." Uma trailed off, tears threatening.

"And now," Bix chimed in, "she has been joined by the man's parents. Seems like this would be their only grandchild—or grandchildren, I guess I should say—and they have some political clout. The grandfather-to-be is a judge."

"I left Alaska a couple of days after the father was killed. I hadn't known he was married, you see, and then his wife showed up and told me to leave."

"But you weren't very far along at that point, were you?" Doctor Hastings asked. "You weren't showing. Did anyone know then that you were expecting?"

"No. Nobody. And I returned to Texas immediately and was at the Big B a couple of days later."

"Now the widow and her in-laws have retained an attorney to try to take Uma's baby," Bix said.

"But you blocked all that by getting married. That makes it difficult to prove Bix isn't the father," Doctor Hastings said.

He cupped his chin in his hand and appeared to study a spot on the wall. "Hmm . . ." After a few moments of silence, he turned back to the couple in front of his desk. "As far as I'm concerned, Bix is the father. I heard him say so. As a married woman, Uma, it is entirely between you and your husband—and your doctor, of course—when you became pregnant. As far as other folks are concerned, it is conceivable—if you'll pardon the pun—that you became with child as soon as you arrived at the Big B. Nobody can say yea nor nay on that subject, except you two. People will think what they want to think.

"The most common problem with having twins is that they tend to come early sometimes, especially if they are big babies. So, if you conceived in early May, when you arrived at the Big B, the due date would normally be early February. If the twins were to decide to arrive around the seventh month, which twins often do, they might possibly arrive in late November." He looked from Uma to Bix and back again to see if they understood him.

"So, if the babies are born in November, people might think they are my babies come early," Bix said, catching on quickly.

"They might," Doctor Hastings said. "On the other hand, if the babies are due in November, then we would need to start taking precautions that they don't come anytime now."

"Oh, my goodness," Uma said. "I've been getting more uncomfortable by the day, with what I thought was one baby."

"So, I'm doing my job as your physician to tell you to go home and go to bed now. Stay quiet. Spend as much time in bed as you can. Just get up to go to the bathroom and maybe for meals. The closer you get to November, the more you stay in bed. Let's see if we can keep these babies where they are for a couple more months."

As they all stood to leave the room, the doctor said, "I think the man asking the questions is still in town. I saw him walking along the sidewalk the other day. I imagine he's trying to get information from anyone he can find to talk."

"Thanks for letting me know, Doc," Bix said. "I imagine I need to do some talking of my own."

Chapter 49

"I need to refill my prescription for prenatal vitamins," Uma said when they left the doctor's office. Bix circled the town square and pulled into a parking spot in front of City Pharmacy.

"Want me to run in and get it while you sit out here?" he asked.

"No. I don't want to be sitting out here if it takes a while. Besides," she said, hands on her belly, "someone has moved over on top of my bladder. I need to go in and use the restroom."

When they entered the pharmacy, Uma made a beeline for the back of the store, while Bix took the empty pill bottle to the window for prescriptions. "Hey there, Mr. Carter," he greeted the man behind the counter. "I have this to get refilled for my wife," he said as he handed over the container.

"Your wife! Bix Crandall, I didn't know you were married," the older man said and looked at the name on the label Bix had handed him. "Uma Thornton." He looked over the top of his glasses. "When did this take place?"

"Which one? The baby or the marriage?" Bix asked.

"Either. Both."

"Well sir, I'll admit to planting the crop before I built the fence. That I did. But we're legal now. Didn't make much of a fuss about it. If you remember, I was recovering from the broken leg that old bull gave me, so we didn't have a big, fancy shebang."

"Well, Bix. That's fine. You just surprised me, is all. Have a seat. I have a couple of orders to fill before yours."

Bix sauntered over to the area with tables and chairs near the small lunch counter. He was greeted by several buddies who were seated in the lunchroom section near the soda fountain. He noticed a stranger sitting at a table by himself. The man was wearing western clothing but didn't look like a Texan. Small, skinny, no suntan, ill-fitting new western shirt. *Yep. I'll bet that's the guy who's been asking questions. I'll give him some info to take back to Chicago.*

"I got some good news to tell you fellas," Bix said, spreading his arms out to include everyone sitting there. The soda-jerk behind the counter and a clerk stocking nearby shelves stopped to listen. "You mighta already known that I'm gonna be a daddy," he said and paused to let that sink in. "But we found out today that it's gonna be twins! I'm gonna be a daddy to twins!"

"A daddy?" "Twins?" "Congratulations, Bix!" The greetings came from every direction. "Who's the mama of these twins?" one man asked.

"My wife, Uma," Bix answered. That started another round of exclamations.

"Who's that?"

"I didn't know you was married!"

"Married?"

"You're married? Since when?"

Bix took care to speak loudly enough that the stranger could hear every word. "Y'all know Tom Thornton, don't you? My general manager? Been my friend since I started at A&M." Calls to the affirmative rang out.

"Yeah, I've met him," said a portly man in a shirt and tie. "Seems like a fine fella."

"I almost think of him as another Crandall," said a woman who had been shopping and stopped to listen.

"Yeah. He's been like family since my freshman year at college. Well, Uma's his sister. She may have been like a Crandall too, but I made it plain that even if Tom is like a brother to me, I definitely didn't think of her as a sister."

"Why didn't we hear anything about a wedding, Bix?" a woman sitting with a friend at one of the tables asked.

He gave the same explanation he gave the pharmacist. "When Uma arrived at the Big B, I was laid up with a broken leg and not in any shape for a big fancy wedding for a good while, but Uma got so big so quick, bein' that she's carrying twins, we just had a simple ceremony. And since I'm up and around again, we can't keep it under wraps any longer."

The two women got up and left, chattering about who they were going to tell about the latest gossip. They were the first people in town to know about the marriage of the most eligible bachelor in the county.

"I thought you was pretty stove up after that tangle with the bull, Bix," one of the men said.

"It was my leg what got broke, Larry, not the rest of me—if you get my meaning," Bix answered in a lower voice, but still loud enough to be heard by the stranger at the next table.

Bix claimed the table where the two women had been sitting before anyone else could. He pulled out a chair and sat down as the clerk came to clear it off. Uma walked up about that time.

"Uma honey," Bix said, "it'll be a while for your vitamins. What say we have little lunch to tide us over until we get home?"

"That sounds good. I'm hungry all the time these days."

Bix stood to go to the counter to order, but he paused. "Sugar, I'd like you to meet some friends of mine." He went around the group, telling her the names of everyone. Except the stranger. Uma looked at the unknown man, then back at Bix. He nodded. They were on the same wavelength. That was the spy.

"What do you want to eat, sugar? They don't cook much here, but they have tuna salad, plain or in a sandwich, pimento cheese, grilled cheese, and . . ." He looked at the board on the wall behind the counter.

"Grilled cheese sounds good," Uma said. "With chips."

"How about a milkshake to go with that?" Bix said. "Got to feed those growin' boys."

"Yes. Chocolate, please."

"You havin' a pair of boys, Mrs. Crandall?" a man at the next table asked. She had already forgotten his name.

She smiled. "There's no way to tell whether they are boys or girls, but Bix has been saying for a while now that he's having a boy." She deliberately said "he's" instead of "I'm," aware that the unnamed man at the table on the other side of her was listening to the conversation. "I've been arguing with him about the possibility of having a girl, but I've given up."

"Yeah, when Bix Crandall sets his mind on something, you aren't going to change it," another man, she thought his name was TJ, said.

"I wish the doctor had some way of telling whether they are boys or girls or one of each. That would stop the argument," Uma said.

"Well, there is a way." A woman who had risen from a table farther away walked closer to Uma. "You can take a piece of thread with a little weight hanging from it and dangle it over your belly. Hold it real still, and it will begin to move all on its own. Vibrations or something. It will settle into a pattern. If it goes around in a circle, it's a girl. If it swings back and forth, it's a boy."

"I'll have to try that," Uma said, fascinated.

"Works every time. Told all four of mine and my sister's three. Most people use a needle as a weight, but I think it works better with your wedding ring." She looked down at

Uma's hand. "My goodness, what a gorgeous engagement ring."

"Nothing but the best, Mrs. Jones. Nothing but the best for my sweetheart." Bix smiled at Uma as he returned to the table.

"What do your folks think about all of this, Bix?" Mrs. Jones asked.

Bix's eyes widened, but he answered calmly enough. "They're thrilled for us. Just thrilled."

By the time they were through eating, Uma's pills were ready. "I was going to suggest that we shop for baby stuff," Bix said on the way to the truck, "but I think I need to hurry home and call my parents. The cat is out of the bag now."

Chapter 50

Uma and Bix entered by the back door. The ramp was still in place that had helped Bix when he was on crutches. Uma found it easier to use it than to manage the steps into the house since the weight of the babies made it exhausting to climb even the lowest of steps. Even now, Bix was there with his hand under her elbow to help her up the incline.

Annie and Lovie were in the kitchen when they arrived. Annie was sliding a cake into the oven, and Lovie was washing the bowl.

"Y'all will never guess," Bix exclaimed, arms held wide.

Annie took two steps over to Uma and patted her belly. "You having two babies," she proclaimed.

"Aww . . ." everyone said in unison.

"How did you know?" Bix asked.

"Easy to see," Annie said.

"We've got to go call my folks," he said and pulled Uma along with him.

Uma listened as Bix got the long-distance operator and placed the call to his parents in Galveston. She could guess the other side of the conversation from what Bix was saying.

"I wanted to let you know some great news. I got married." Pause. "Uma Thornton, Tom's sister. . . . Uh-huh. Very happy. . . . Well, there's more. Lots more. . . . I'd rather tell you in person. It's a complicated story. Something like yours with Dad. . . . Why don't I send the plane down to pick you up and bring you up here? That would be best."

When Bix hung up, he said, "They're going to call me

back and tell me when to have Steve fly down there. They'll come stay a while."

"Oh?" Uma was nervous over meeting her in-laws, more so because of the circumstances of the marriage and the babies on the way. *How will they feel about Bix being father to someone else's babies? How will they feel about keeping the details of the marriage a secret? Will they act as grandparents to my babies?* The situation had Uma's nerves on edge.

"Doctor Hastings said you were to take it easy . . . maybe even stay in bed. Do you need to rest a while?" Bix asked.

"Yes, I think I do," Uma replied.

Bix helped her to bed, and she slept until suppertime. When she got up, he told her that his father called and told him to have Steve pick them up the next morning.

Chapter 51

"They'll love you," Bix said, trying to reassure her.

Lovie encouraged her to think positively. "They are both great folks," she said. "They treat everyone like family."

"But it's different for me," Uma contended. "I married their son, and I was pregnant at the time. I married him to keep my baby, to scare off the predators coming after me."

"That may be so," Lovie agreed, "but I think if you were here, not pregnant, you and Bix would end up together anyway. I know he is crazy about you, and I suspect you are crazy about him as well."

Uma looked away. It was true. She was enamored with her husband. If she had come to the Big B, waited a few days to see Tom, then gone away to a new job, she probably would have continued to dream about what might have been with Bix.

"Well?" Lovie pressed. "Am I right?"

Uma paced the floor. "You're right, I am, but this is different."

"Bix loves you, and you love Bix. How much easier can it be?"

Uma turned back to Lovie. "How much easier? It would be easier without my being pregnant by . . ." She stopped herself before she said "another man." Frank Pope had warned her about acknowledging to anyone that she was pregnant when she arrived at the Big B. One could never know what they might be asked under oath in court.

"I understand that," Lovie said. "But Bix is raring to

be a daddy to those babies. You'd be depriving him of pure pleasure if it were any different."

Just then, they heard the car pull up in front of the house, followed by car doors slamming and excited voices in the yard. Uma's real test was about to begin—meeting her mother-in-law and father-in-law.

The woman who walked in the front door was nothing like Uma expected. Slim, dressed in camel-colored slacks, an off-white sweater, and a colorful scarf around her shoulders, she threw her arms open wide and welcomed Uma in. "I always wanted another daughter, and now I have one," she said. She set Uma away at arm's length but kept her close with hands on Uma's shoulders. "And look at you! Twins for goodness sakes. I'll be grandmother to twins." She released Uma and turned to the tall man behind her. "Look, Jonah, at our new daughter. Isn't she beautiful?"

"You were always more beautiful when you were pregnant, and I suspect that is true for her as well." He gathered Uma into a bear hug, but gently, due to her belly between them. "Welcome to the family, daughter." His words, spoken in a deep voice, gave Uma a serene feeling.

"Thank you, Mr. and Mrs. Crandall, for welcoming me so warmly, especially after the surprise it must have been when Bix called you with such an unexpected announcement," Uma said.

"Please, just call me Dorie." "No need to be so formal. Call me Jonah," the voices overlapped.

"Welcome home," Lovie added to the vocal sound. The moment she spoke, she was added to the group hug that was forming in the foyer.

"Tom and Lovie were our witnesses when we got married," Bix said. "In Vegas," he added.

"I want to see Annie," Dorie said, "then we will sit down and hear the whole story."

Dorie and Jonah headed toward the kitchen. Lovie said, "I'll go fix some glasses of tea for everyone, then help Aunt Annie with lunch." She followed along behind the newcomers.

"Let's go sit in the parlor," Bix said. "You look tired, especially for so early in the day."

"It seems like I get tired not long after I get up in the morning," Uma replied.

"You tossed and turned a bit last night," Bix commented.

"I did. The babies were busy turning somersaults all night, and I was nervous over meeting your parents today."

Within a few minutes, Dorie and Jonah joined them, Dorie carrying a tray of glasses. "It's only been a few months since we've been home—not a year yet—but Annie seems to have aged a lot." She was frowning.

"She only comes to the Big House a couple of times a day. Usually she starts breakfast, and sometimes lunch and supper, then goes back to her cottage. Lovie takes care of everything else. But I have a feeling we'll be losing Lovie soon."

"Oh?" Dorie and Jonah's eyebrows rose.

"She and Tom are getting pretty serious. I imagine they'll be announcing plans to marry any time now, and I reckon they'll want their own home somewhere."

"I've been trying to get Annie to retire for ages now. It doesn't do any good. I can't fire her . . . I just can't," Dorie said. "And now, with the twins on the way, she'll stay no matter how slow and frail she becomes."

"And where would she go?" Jonah asked. "She's not really close with any of her family still alive in Oklahoma. This is home to her." He looked around the group. "Enough of that. I want to hear about Bix and Uma. From the very beginning, if you please."

Uma started the tale—it was her story, after all. She

touched on her jobs in Texas, New Mexico, and Seattle—just to give an idea of what she did for a living. Then she told about Alaska and Alex. About the interesting aspect of the research and putting the tales into book form, about the remote village reached by small plane, about becoming close to the professor she shared the work with. Finally, she told about realizing she was pregnant. "I was going to tell him that night," Uma said, "but he didn't come back. An avalanche pushed his truck down an embankment into a creek, and he was killed.

"I didn't know he was married until his wife . . . his widow . . . showed up and told me to get out, that she never wanted to see me again. She indicated that it was Alex's custom to have a young coed on the side." Uma twisted a tissue in her hands. "So there I was, pregnant, no job, no home."

Dorie reached toward Uma in sympathy. "So you came here. It was the right place."

"Not at first. I went to Freeport first, to see my mother. It was as bad as it ever was. I got out without saying a thing about my condition. Then I started looking for Tom. The only clue I had was that he possibly worked at the Big B, and I came here."

"That's when I got my first look at her," Bix said. "I was laid up with that broken leg, and I was as grouchy as all get out. She didn't take any guff off me, and that's when I fell in love."

"I always knew," his mother said, "that you'd fall in love with a girl who wasn't chasing after you."

Uma looked at him. *Can I believe that? Did he really love me from the start?* She continued her story. "Tom was away on a business trip, and Bix convinced me to stay until he returned."

"No way was I letting her get away," Bix said.

"When Tom got back, I told him the whole story, and he and Bix convinced me to stay until I found another job, since I didn't have any place to go anyway."

Jonah spoke up. "So, you are in Texas, and the widow is . . . where?"

"Chicago."

"How did she find out that you were expecting?" he asked.

"A couple of months passed, and I still didn't have a job. Bix had convinced me to help with the projects he and Tom were working on."

"She straightened out the mess I had made in the office and started getting me organized. That had been her job before coming here—organization."

"Yes, but it was organization of notes and research for publication of books," Uma said.

"That was what I needed and you provided. Organization of notes and research."

"That's true. I hadn't realized the job would be so similar. Anyway, about the time I started showing and had to start wearing maternity clothes, McDutton-Parker, the publishing company, was getting ready to release the book about Alaskan folktales. They had rushed it into print. The fact that Alaska was made the forty-ninth state earlier this year coupled with Alex's death in an avalanche stirred up interest in it."

"Also, they said Uma did such good work that it was ready to print—they didn't have to change anything," Bix said proudly.

"A representative of McDutton-Parker called me— he had tracked me down from the letters I had sent to all my previous employers. The publisher was having release parties all over the country and asked me to attend the one in Dallas, give a short speech and answer questions. I would get paid and might make some connections to find a new job."

Dorie spoke up. "You would have had to move to a new town and a new job while you were pregnant. That sounds like a terrible hardship."

"It was something I had to do. I had to find a job and a place in life," Uma answered.

"I kept telling her I'd hire her and pay her to be my executive assistant," Bix said. "She was doing a terrific job in the office. We'd never been so efficient."

"I didn't want him to hire me because of Tom, or because he felt sorry for me," Uma said. "But to continue answering your question, Jonah, Mrs. Keillor was at the release party in Dallas. She saw that I was pregnant and attacked me, verbally, not physically. She said she always wanted a baby with Alex, but he refused her. Now, here I was, pregnant with his child. I said nothing to her. I didn't acknowledge that her husband was the father, but she assumed it. Correctly, of course."

"So now she is coming after the baby . . . babies," Dorie said. "Through an attorney?"

"Yes, and what is worse, she has been joined by Alex's parents. He was an only child, and these babies will be the only grandchildren they will ever have."

"Who is handling this for you, Bix?" Jonah asked.

"Frank Pope," he replied. "He told us right off that if Uma were married and her husband claimed the child as his own, no court would challenge that. But Uma still wouldn't marry me."

"Why?" Dorie asked, looking at Uma.

"I didn't want Bix to marry me out of pity. I didn't want him to feel forced into a union he would want out of."

Bix looked at her. "But I wanted to marry you because you are you," he said. "The baby, er. . . babies, are just icing on the cake."

"What made you change your mind?" Dorie asked.

"When the grandparents entered the picture," Uma said. "The grandfather's a judge and has a lot of clout. He might be able to get things done that others couldn't."

"And Frank said there would be people—private investigators—in town checking on Uma. And there are," Bix added.

"Really?" Dorie raised her eyebrows. "Talking to folks about Uma?"

"What are we doing to fight this?" Jonah asked. Uma noticed that he had used the word "we" instead of "you."

"First thing, we flew to Vegas and got married. Unless they check there, they won't know how long we've been hitched. And Doctor Hastings says we should try our best to keep the babies from coming for as long as possible."

"Bedrest," Dorie said.

"Yes, bedrest," Bix agreed. "If they come when they are actually due, in November, he can pass them as seven-month babies. He says twins often come early, especially if they are big babies. But we don't want them coming early for November."

"You were almost ten pounds when you were born," his mother said. "It would be expected for your children to be big as well." She turned to Uma. "You look tired. As soon as we eat lunch, I think you need to go to bed and rest. Let us take over some planning. Rest your worries with us."

"I think we are going to spread it all over town that we are excited about being grandparents, especially to twins," Jonah said.

"Exactly," Dorie said. "And being pregnant with twins is why you got so big so early."

Annie and Lovie had fixed a big spread for lunch, and everyone sat around the kitchen table, Dorie having proclaimed she felt more at home there than in the formal dining room.

Over lunch, Dorie asked, "Have you made any preparations yet? Cribs and all that?"

"No, I haven't," Uma answered. "Bix and I just got married, and I didn't feel that I should take over in someone else's home."

"It's your home now," Bix said as he reached over and squeezed her hand.

"We need to make one of the bedrooms a nursery," Dorie said. She turned to Uma. "Do you think the twins can share a room for a while?"

"Definitely," Uma responded. "It would be easier to take care of them in one room. I had in mind, if I was still here when my baby was born, to have a crib in my room." She paused. "I mean the room I was using."

"Which room was that?" Dorie asked.

"Sarah's room," Bix responded. "But I think the twins ought to have my old room."

"Is that alright with you, Uma?" Dorie asked.

"Yes, that's fine with me." She leaned back to give more room to breathe as she pushed her plate away, one hand on her belly.

"Time to get you to bed," Bix said as he pushed back from the table.

Chapter 52

Uma woke up two hours later with faint sounds of bumping and subdued voices in the hall. She put on her robe and opened the door to see Peanut and another hired hand going down the stairs with a dresser between them. She walked down the hall to what had once been Bix's room to find Dorie rolling up a large rug with western designs. A stack of boxes sat in the corner.

"Hi," Uma said.

"Oh, hi, Uma. I thought I'd get started on this room. I'm stripping it down to the bare bones. Peanut and Shorty are taking all the furniture out to the barn, and I put everything Bix left in the drawers into boxes. I'll have the fellows put them in the attic. When I get it all empty, you can look at it and decide what you want done."

Uma looked around. The whole project overwhelmed her. She had put off thinking about preparations, and now she stood motionless, unable to plan what to do next.

"Fran comes tomorrow," Dorie said. "We can get her to vacuum and mop." She looked around. "And clean the windows." She looked at Uma. "Any ideas what you want in here?"

Uma shook her head. "No. None. I've never done anything like this before." She backed up to a wall and leaned against it to relieve her aching back.

Dorie approached her. "Time to be back in bed. We don't want those babies coming for a while yet." She walked down the hall with Uma and helped her off with her robe. "I'll tell you what," she said as she settled Uma back in bed, "why don't I get some catalogues and paint samples, and you can stay in bed to pick what you want. I'll see to it that what you want gets done."

"That sounds like a good plan," Uma said. "I should have done things before now, but I was so unsettled . . ."

Dorie sat down in the only comfortable chair in the bedroom and looked around. "This room hasn't been redone since I did it years ago. I would have thought Bix would have put his mark on it by now. You can redo it once the twins are born and you recover . . . and you have time. You're going to have your hands full, I imagine."

"But this is your house . . . or Bix's house . . . and I've come along, and . . ." Tears filled her eyes.

"I think it is time I told you my story," Dorie said. "You are feeling bad because you think you have pressured Bix into marrying you. Your marriage isn't anything like the way mine started out. You see, I proposed to Jonah, and it wasn't out of love. It was out of necessity.

"A neighbor was determined to marry me to get his hands on the Big B Ranch . . . and the oil underneath it. When I refused, he raped me, thinking it would force me to give in. When I discovered I was pregnant, I knew I had to do something. I had noticed the handsome new cowboy, so I offered him a good deal: elope with me, stay married a year, claim the baby as his, and I'd give him a divorce."

Uma was riveted with the story. "Bix mentioned something, but he didn't explain."

"The evil man sent someone to kill Jonah and make me a widow so I'd marry him, but it was me in the truck that was pushed into the Brazos, not Jonah. The baby, a little girl, came too early to survive. I tried to turn Jonah loose, even though I loved him, to live up to the bargain, but he wouldn't go.

"And we had Sarah, as well. She was Jonah's sister's daughter. That's a whole other story. And Sarah thought of the Big B as her home. I couldn't hurt Sarah, and Jonah was determined to make it a real marriage." She stood up and started toward the door. "And it is—a real marriage, that is. With love and children and now grandchildren coming." She smiled. "I'll send Lovie up to get you anything you want. You stay in bed." Her expression turned serious. "I've had enough of babies coming too early."

Uma relaxed once she stretched out on the comfortable king-size bed. It gave the babies more room that way. But she was bored. When she heard more bumping, and it was coming her way, she perked up, placing extra pillows behind her back. A moment later, Peanut and Shorty appeared, a table between them, Dorie following close behind.

"I found this gate-leg table out in the barn when I went to cover the furniture the fellows took out there. I thought we'd put it in here so you wouldn't have to eat in bed. With the sides down, it'll snug up against the wall when not in use."

"I thought I'd be coming downstairs to eat with everybody. I'm getting stir-crazy already, and it hasn't even been a whole day yet."

Dorie looked thoughtful. "With a table up here, I don't know why several people can't eat up here with you. I'll gather up chairs from around the house. You don't need to be going up and down those stairs."

That was the start of the bedroom being a gathering place. Dorie took charge and ran everyone out if Uma began to look tired, but at least Bix or Lovie, or both, ate breakfast and lunch with her. It felt good to get out of bed and walk across the room to eat in a chair, but she was ready to stretch out again when the meal was finished. She suspected supper was going to mean a gathering of everyone, visiting and keeping her in the loop.

Bix found a radio and plugged it in next to the bed. Uma discovered that when she found a station playing the mellow music of the '40s, the twins settled down right away. "Now you've found how to put them to sleep after they are born," Dorie said. "We'll have to put a radio in their room."

Lovie asked if she could read aloud to Uma from the book she was writing. "That's a good idea," Uma said. "You catch mistakes when you read to someone else." This evolved into a daily routine, with Uma becoming intrigued with the plot of the developing story of a female Cherokee detective, often suggesting plot twists as the story progressed.

The second day Uma was confined, Dorie asked, "Do you have an idea of what color you want the twins' room painted? That blue that Bix chose when he was a teenager is a bit bright for babies, don't you think?"

"I agree it is too loud, but I have no idea what color it should be."

"I wish somebody would invent a way to tell if unborn babies are boys or girls," Dorie said. "Then we'd know if we could go pink or blue or both."

"A woman at the drugstore said to dangle my wedding ring on a thread over my belly. If it swings back and forth it's a boy, and if it goes around in a circle it's a girl," Uma said.

"I had forgotten about that old trick!" Dorie exclaimed and went in search of some thread.

Lovie came up to observe the experiment, but one time it would swing one way, and when a different person tried, it the result was opposite.

"Either this is a bunch of bunk," Lovie said, "or you're going to have one of each."

"We won't know for sure until they get here," Uma said. "And I'll be happy whichever they are."

~ ~ ~

Fall was fully in the air, with the trees outside bare of leaves and a cool breeze blowing in the open windows. Dorie was busy organizing the babies' room. First, she brought a handful of paint samples, and everyone in the family gave an opinion. Finally, Uma settled on a soft yellow, named Buttercream, which she, Dorie, and Lovie agreed would be perfect for either a boy or a girl.

Tom came home to learn he was going to be an uncle to two babies instead of one. He conferred with Bix and Jonah, then left on another trip. Big B Enterprises was growing at a rapid rate with the properties he was buying.

Dorie called department stores and baby shops in both Dallas and Houston and had them send her catalogues. From those, Uma picked matching cribs, a changing table, and two dressers. She tried to get Bix involved in the decision-making, but anything Uma liked, he did as well. It was up to the women in the family, he said.

Every day the mail brought new treasures. Dorie brought them upstairs for Uma to have the pleasure of opening. Bright sheets, blankets, curtains, and matching wall hangings soon decorated the nursery. Stripes, dots, and geometric designs in an array of matching colors bedecked a room that everyone agreed would be perfect for either a boy or a girl. Everyone except Bix.

"You need to put some horses in there," he said, "and dogs. Boys like horses and dogs." He patted George on the head as he said that. George was brought upstairs to Uma's bedside and to the nursery every day. "So she'll get used to it," Bix said. "And so the babies will get used to George." He would pat Uma on the stomach and say, "See, George? Babies. Babies to protect and play with."

"We'll get some, Bix," Uma said. "When they are born, we'll put more decorations."

"Horses," he repeated. "Horses and dogs."

Each day Uma took three walks down the hall to the nursery. Once after breakfast and once during the afternoon, she and either Dorie or Lovie visited the room. Dorie continued to order things from Dallas and Houston, and the dressers filled with diapers, blankets, and simple white clothing. She ordered nothing without Uma's approval.

"I hope you know," she said one day, "that when the twins are born and you are on your feet again, I'm going to buy whatever I want for them."

Uma laughed. "Are you going to spoil them?"

"If I don't, Bix and Jonah will. You can bet on it. They are already talking about the ponies they are going to buy when the babies are big enough."

Every evening after supper, Uma hooked her arm through Bix's, and they walked down the hall. Dorie had bought a big, comfortable rocker from the furniture store in town and had it delivered. Uma sat in it, and Bix sat down on the colorful rug as they talked about the babies, and Dorie and Jonah's story, and when Lovie and Tom would marry.

Dorie reported that she was spreading the word in town about how happy she and Jonah were that Bix had married Uma. "When people ask me, 'Did Bix marry a stranger? I've never heard of her,' I answer, 'Don't you know Tom? Tom Thornton? He was Bix's roommate starting freshman year at A&M, and now he is a manager for Big B Enterprises. Uma is Tom's sister. Of course, both he and Uma were too young back at the beginning. She was still in high school. But when she returned to Texas from her last assignment, it was time for them to get serious.' I have everyone convinced that you two have known each other forever, without lying one time."

As the months progressed and Uma's belly continued to grow, instead of Uma going into town for her doctor's appointments, Doctor Hastings came to her. "She doesn't need to be making that trip if we're going to keep those babies inside as long as we can," he said. He took her blood pressure, listened to the heartbeats, and pronounced both mother and children in fine shape. "Keep on doing what you're doing," he said.

One day, Lovie and Bix were sitting on the bed with Uma playing cards. "Have you two talked about names?" Lovie asked. "You'll need two boys' names and two girls' names to be prepared for any combination."

Uma leaned back against the pillows, easing her hand behind the small of her back. "No, I haven't," she said.

"Me either," Bix replied.

"In my family, we name babies after an ancestor," Lovie said. "That's how I got stuck with Louvinia."

"I think Louvinia's a good name," Uma said.

"I guess it could be worse."

About that time, Dorie walked in the door. "Louvinia's a beautiful name," she said. "I gave my children family names. Bix is named after my brother who died just after the Great War. Barney's full name is Daniel Barnett, after my younger brother who died in France, and my maiden name was Barnett. Then, when Daniella showed up here, we found out her mother named her after Danny as well. He died never knowing he had a child. None of us knew until she escaped the Nazis and made her way here."

"That's sad," Lovie said. "Don't you have any family you want to name a baby after?"

"Not hardly. I don't want to be reminded of my dysfunctional family."

"How about your father?" Bix asked. "Do you remember him at all?"

Uma leaned back against the pillows and closed her eyes. "Yes. A little. He was a loving father. I missed him for a long time after he died, even though I was very young."

"What was his name?" Dorie asked.

"Thomas Elijah. Tom is named after him."

"We already have another Thomas in the family," Dorie said. "Jonah's brother. We might get the names mixed up if we had yet another one. But Elijah is nice."

"Yes," Uma said, sitting up. "I like Elijah, and Eli as well." She straightened the covers over her legs. "In some of the native villages in Alaska, they give a new baby the names of all the people who have died in the past year. If a lot of people have died, the child may have a dozen names or more."

"I'd better be satisfied with just Louvinia," Lovie joked. "And nobody has died around here that I know of."

"It's time to check on supper," Dorie said. "Annie has a roast with potatoes and carrots in the oven. I'm going to go pull it out and fix a salad."

"I'll help," Lovie said then left the room with Dorie.

Chapter 53

The days grew crisp and cold. The windows were closed against approaching winter. Discussion was started about Thanksgiving dinner. It was the custom for the whole family to spend it together, but everyone agreed that it might be too much to plan with everything that was happening.

Dorie and Jonah were still staying in the suite at the hotel but had announced plans to build a new home on a hill about a mile from the big house. "I want a one-story ranch house," Dorie said. "No more steps for me, except when we visit Galveston."

"I thought you loved Galveston," Bix said.

"I do," his mother replied. "I love watching the ocean. But the house has to be so high in case of flooding, and all those steps are tiresome. Besides," she said, tucking her hand around his arm, "I want to be here to play with my grandchildren. We'll be about a mile away. Far enough we won't be a bother to you, but close enough if you need us."

"I hate to think we are taking over your home," Uma said. "This is, first of all, your home."

"Oh, Uma! You aren't! We've been talking for years about building a new house. We've even had the spot picked out. Come spring, we'll break ground. I'll have all winter to study house plans and make decisions."

~ ~ ~

They had made it to late November, and the twins were still in the womb, fully formed and ready for the outside world. But as far as the world was concerned, if they were born now, they would be seven-month babies. Uma was miserable. Unable to do more than waddle to the bathroom and back, she still tried to walk down the hall to the nursery at least once a day. She never attempted it, however, unless Bix was there supporting her.

Bix and Jonah spent time talking business but also saddled up and rode out to all parts of the ranch at least once a week. They observed the pump jacks bringing up oil. They stopped and visited with the mechanics who kept the rigs working, learning more about the industry that had made them rich, all the while checking the cattle that were the original commerce of the Big B.

Dorie declared there would be no cooking for Thanksgiving, so she ordered a bounteous meal from a restaurant in town that catered. It would be delivered Thanksgiving morning. Only those living on the ranch, including Dorie and Jonah, were participating. Barney was in the middle of filming a movie and would stay in California. All the relatives living in Waco would entertain friends there.

The day before Thanksgiving, Annie said she wished to visit with Uma. With Bix on one side and Jonah on the other, they helped her up the stairs and into the master bedroom. With a chair pulled up close to the bed, she sat with one hand on Uma's belly.

"The Great Spirit came to me last night," she said. "He tell me these babies going to be born healthy. They will grow up here on this ranch and be happy all their lives."

"That's good, Annie," Uma said. "Thanks for letting me know."

"Bix, he will be good father to them. Sometime, many years from now, they will learn of the man who sired them, but not for a long time. His family will not bother you anymore." She moved her hand over the area where one of the babies was kicking. "You want to know boy? Girl?"

"No, Annie. I've gone this long without knowing, I can wait a while longer."

"Will not be long now. They are fully made now and ready to see the world they will live in."

Uma didn't know if Annie had a direct line to God, or the Great Spirit, as she called Him, but it was reassuring, nevertheless.

"You make me feel calm, Annie, and safe, and secure. As long as they are healthy and no one takes them from me, I'm happy."

"You will be happy with Bix, too," Annie said. "You will have a long, happy marriage. Great Spirit has told me."

She stood and walked to the door. Turning, she looked back at Uma, then walked out into the hall and to the top of the stairs. Jonah and Bix were waiting at the bottom, and when they saw her, they came to help her back downstairs.

~ ~ ~

Thanksgiving morning, the caterer and his helper arrived early to deliver the turkey, a ham, stuffing, mashed potatoes, sweet potatoes, several other vegetables, cranberry sauce, and rolls, along with pumpkin and pecan pies. "How are we going to eat all this," Jonah said. "It's way too much."

"It'll keep," Dorie said. "You know it's not Thanksgiving if we don't have everything I ordered. If one thing was missing, you'd be fussing."

"I thought Aunt Annie would be here by now," Lovie said. "I think I'll go check on her."

"She's probably sleeping in," Dorie said. "I told her to take it easy today, that we'd take care of everything."

A few minutes later, Lovie came in the back door, tears streaming down her face. "She's gone," she said.

"Gone?" Dorie murmured, a stunned expression coming over her face as she realized what Lovie meant.

"She looked like she was sleeping, but when I touched her . . ." A sob escaped.

Thanksgiving wasn't the joyous occasion of the past. When the funeral home had come and gone, the food was spread out, and everyone filled their plate and took it upstairs to eat with Uma. She had been crying. "I don't know that I can eat," she said.

"Annie always loved Thanksgiving," Dorie said. "She always gave thanks to the Great Spirit for this family. She loved every one of us."

"This is the first real Thanksgiving I've ever had," Uma said.

"We were lucky to have turkey on our TV dinners growing up," Tom said.

"And I was on my own during and after college. I usually found some café open wherever I was, but I never had a traditional Thanksgiving."

"We are blessed to have you in our family now," Jonah said. "You'll have to get used to big Thanksgiving dinners with the whole family around."

"Jonah, we'll have to be sure our new house has a dining room big enough to hold everyone," Dorie said.

"We may have to celebrate in the barn," he said, "to have enough room."

"Annie came upstairs to see me yesterday," Uma said.

"I heard about that," Lovie said.

"She wanted to tell me that the Great Spirit had come to her and told her that my babies would be healthy and have good lives"—she looked at Bix—"and that Bix and I would have a long, happy marriage."

"I could have told you that," Bix said, and everyone laughed.

Chapter 54

Annie's funeral was held the following Tuesday, December first. The service was held in a small church close to town. It was the first time Dorie and Jonah had been in the church since the funeral of Dorie's baby, Dawn. Her firstborn child, born too early to survive, was laid to rest in the adjoining cemetery. Sarah, who was to become Dorie and Jonah's adopted daughter, stood up and pointed out her father, which caused an uproar that lasted months, if not years.

Annie was laid to rest in the Barnett family plot, alongside Dorie's parents, Bix's namesake, and baby Dawn.

Uma insisted on going to the service. With Bix and Jonah supporting her, she made it through the ceremonial observance in the sanctuary and stood outside for the brief prayer the pastor said over the grave, before turning to Bix and saying, "Now I need to go to the hospital. It's time!"

Bix slapped his Stetson on his head and gave a war-whoop that echoed throughout the headstones. "Make way, folks. We gotta go have us some babies!" He swung Uma into his arms as mourners cleared a path for him, smiling broadly at his exuberance.

As they reached the car, he stopped and looked into Uma's eyes. "I love you, wife, and I love our babies." He kissed her.

Uma tightened her arms around his neck. "I love you too, husband," she whispered in his ear. "Now let's get to the hospital. We don't want to have to tell them that they were born in a cemetery."

Epilogue

Elijah and Annie Crandall were born December 1, 1959. Uma had plenty of time to make it to the hospital, since it was early evening before they made an appearance.

Loved and coddled by everyone in the family, they grew up healthy and happy, only slightly spoiled by everyone around them. Their father and grandfather carried one or the other in front of them in the saddle as they rode all over the ranch. "Pay attention," they were told, "someday you'll have to manage all this." They were given ponies for their fourth birthday.

George stayed by their sides and had a hard time choosing which one to follow if the twins split up. When they stopped sharing a bedroom, George had to decide where to sleep, and usually alternated rooms. She lived to the ripe old age of seventeen.

Bix and Uma did have a long, happy marriage.

Tom and Lovie married the next summer. They moved to Houston in order for Tom to stay closer to his work. Lovie wrote a series of books set in Northeast Oklahoma featuring a Cherokee female detective. They included Cherokee folk stories that Lovie's family and Aunt Annie had told her. Several of the novels were on the bestseller list.

Big B Enterprises grew every year and provided jobs and income for family members and employees.

Barney continued making movies. He wined and dined movie starlets, moving from one beautiful woman to another—until he came back to Texas to make a movie. But that's another book!

AUTHOR'S NOTES

This book, like all my others, is pure fiction. None of the characters or plots are real.

However . . .
My grandfather, Benjamin Franklin Brannam, was an oil field mechanic all his working life. When we visited him and my grandmother in north-central Oklahoma when I was a child, they lived in a company house among the wells on the oil field, furnished by Phillips Petroleum. The creak and thump of the pump jack nearest the house kept me awake at night. The field containing the oil wells was fenced, and Granddad was allowed to run cattle on the land. I thought of that as I wrote about the Big B Ranch.

When he retired, he and my grandmother moved back "home" to northeast Oklahoma. They lived near Tahlequah, the Cherokee capital. It was fascinating to visit there, where some street signs and many store names were, and are still, written both in Cherokee and English. The college Lovie attended does exist there in Tahlequah.

I didn't use any actual people in this book, nor are any of the characters suggested by real people.

However . . .
I do like to use names of my ancestors. My paternal grandmother—my father's mother—was Isadora Barnett, but her nickname was Dora, not Dorie. Dorie's father was Bigelow, Big B, Barnett—thus, the name of the Big B Ranch and Enterprises. Bigelow is the name of the town where my son lives.

Louvinia was a family name far back in my family tree. It is so pretty I just had to use it.

Thomas Elijah was my paternal grandfather's name. He died a few months before I was born. Nobody in the family is named after him so far, although I have hopes that the great-grandson due in March might be his namesake.

Although each of my books "stands alone," the characters overlap in some of the Tales from the Brazos books. If you enjoy this one, you might want to read The Marriage Bargain, which tells the story of Dorie and Jonah. And there will be more, God willing, that let you know about other branches of this family.

Planned for the future:
The story of Daniella, who was conceived when Dorie's brother, Danny, was in France during WWI. He died there without knowing the woman he fell in love with was expecting a child. When Hitler started persecuting the Jews, Daniella's family sent her to America to find her father's family. It was a surprise when she showed up at the Big B.

Sarah's story: Annie called her Little Bird, and when she grew up, she learned to fly airplanes. With Amelia Earhart as a role model, she was active on the home front during WWII, even though she was only in her teens.

Barney Crandall was used to the Hollywood life. He had turned his back on Texas when he went to California to make movies. Then he decided to make a western—they were popular in the theaters. That brought him face to face with a spunky widow and her teenage daughter, and he decided Texas wasn't so boring after all.

Are there other characters you would like to read about? If so, leave me a message on my Facebook Author's page: https://www.facebook.com/Nancy-Smith-Gibson-Author-521194474570462/

Also from Soul Mate Publishing and Nancy Smith Gibson:

BETRAYAL ON THE BRAZOS

When Maggie Lancaster's uncle sent her to Texas to care for Cousin Annabelle's children, Maggie didn't expect Annabelle's husband to be disdainful or her cousin's murderer to show up at their ranch.

Jeb Sutton assumed his wife's cousin to be as useless and complaining as Annabelle had been, but he was surprised when Maggie adjusted to her new surroundings with ease. His children adored her and she loved them, too. Soon his attitude toward Maggie began to change.

When Maggie's former suitor shows up, it's time for Jeb to make his feelings clear and ask Maggie to stay forever.

Available now on Amazon: BETRAYAL ON THE BRAZOS

THE MEMORY OF ALL THAT

They tell her she's a cheating wife—a neglectful mother. She can't remember any of it. Her husband wants her memory to come back so she can tell them where her lover went with the plans and prototype for a secret government project. But if her memory returns, will she go back to being the selfish, narcissistic person she was in the past? She'd just as soon the past stays forgotten.

Available now on Amazon: THE MEMORY OF ALL THAT

GUSSIE AND THE CHEROKEE KID

When twenty-one-year-old Persephone Augusta Gomance is appointed to accompany a six-year-old orphan to her uncle in Texas, she is expecting to meet a wealthy ranch owner who is married to a schoolteacher and living in a fine home. When Travis Thacker, unmarried cardsharp, receives word that he is gaining custody of his niece Julia, he is expecting her chaperone to be an old battle-axe who will challenge his lifestyle. They are both in for a surprise. When Persephone and Travis first meet, sparks fly! The real trouble begins when Persephone receives a telegram with some unexpected news.

Available now on Amazon: GUSSIE AND THE CHEROKEE KID

Full of comedy and sweet romance, this turn-of-the-century tale will have you laughing and rooting for the couple to work out their differences.

THE MARRIAGE BARGAIN

Successful rancher Dorie Barnett thought if she married her hired hand it would offer protection from the man who had been relentlessly pursuing her, so she offered him a marriage of convenience.

Jonah Crandall thought if he accepted Dorie's proposal, it would put him a better position to find his sister's murderer without tipping off the enemy.

They were both wrong.

The marriage bargain put them in more danger than they could ever imagine. As they faced the challenges together, it was soon apparent that more than their lives would be at risk.

And when all threats had passed and it was time to end the marriage, it was their hearts that were at risk.

Available now on Amazon: <u>THE MARRIAGE BARGAIN</u>

MRS. MOMMY

When Grace Belding moves back to her hometown of Mineral Wells, Texas, she brings with her a young son and a secret that could potentially destroy their lives.

Grainger Davis is the local deputy sheriff. His attentions could spell disaster for Grace if he asks too many questions.

As Grace finally lets her guard down and becomes comfortable in her new life, dangers surface that threaten to unravel the well-crafted lies that keep her and her son safe.

Grace must learn to trust Grainger. With a secret of his own, Grainger must learn to trust Grace. Is their love strong enough to face the dangers together?

Available now on Amazon: <u>MRS. MOMMY</u>

CPSIA information can be obtained
at www.ICGtesting.com
Printed in the USA
FFOW01n1651240418
46356444-48020FF